PURCHASED FOR SUBMISSION

DARK BWWM GREEK MAFIA ROMANCE

GREEK MAFIA ROMANCE BROTHERHOOD
BOOK 1

JAMILA JASPER

WWW.JAMILAJASPERROMANCE.COM

ISBN: 979-8-3302-8205-0

Copyright © 2024 by Jamila Jasper

All rights reserved.

No part of this book may be reproduced in any form or by any electronic or mechanical means, including information storage and retrieval systems, without written permission from the author, except for the use of brief quotations in a book review.

Thank you to my Patreon subscribers for your support with this book. I could not have done it without you. www.patreon.com/jamilajasper

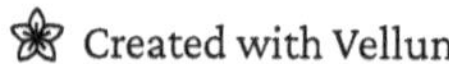 Created with Vellum

GREEK MAFIA ROMANCE BROTHERHOOD

Purchased For Submission

Purchased For Pregnancy

Purchased For Seduction

DESCRIPTION

Stavros purchases a curvy, dark-skinned African American woman from a mafia underworld auction block against his father's commands...

He never wanted to hurt her.
He meant to set her free.

Once Stavros has her close,
Desire overwhelms his morals.
Her body is *too irresistible* for him to let her go.

It's a case of love at first sight under the worst conditions.
Fallon could never love her captor...

As Stavros falls for the African American woman he purchased for
submission, he faces his darkest truth:
He can't ever let her go.

**A dark and twisted mafia romance that isn't afraid to "go there".
Sensitive readers, caution advised.**

Thank you to my patrons for your ongoing support. This new edition is only made possible because of your support.

*Here's to manifesting your **happily ever after...***

Click here to subscribe:
www.patreon.com/jamilajasper

ONE
AUCTION BLOCK

Eight auctions a year. That's how many of these papa forces me to sit through.

"It's important you understand the men we deal with," he answers gruffly when I complain.

I loathe auctions, but when you're a part of this family, you get used to doing shit you don't want to do. At least the women are always beautiful. Too beautiful. You'd think someone would notice this many beautiful fucking women missing around the world.

Khalid has a knack for what he does — luring beautiful women lusting after fame or power into his clutches. Once he has them, he brings them here to the auction. You get the location the day before. The invite arrives as a mysterious text message sent to your phone with a link. You can't trace the number. Once you click the link, the web page looks like a spam website unless you expected a text message. Unless you know how Khalid operates.

Type the PIN and the location flashes on screen for 120 seconds. You can't take a screenshot without turning your phone into a brick. Khalid can pack a room wall to wall — especially when he gets back from places like Vegas or Dubai, where he finds the prettiest girls. He holds the auctions in a private club, normally owned by a friend or someone who owes him big time. Fifteen girls a night once a month.

Papa sent me here to bring back my sister. It's the only reason I'm smiling and drinking vodka with the sick motherfuckers at my table — an oil magnate and his bastard son — instead of brooding in a corner like I normally do. The auctioneer rattles off details about the first girl like he's talking about a Ming dynasty vase.

"Meet Kim, she's Korean, loves a big dominant man but willing to work for a woman. She's been pregnant once but would make a great surrogate or breed mare for individual gentlemen. We begin the bidding at €20,000."

Kim got herself on Khalid's nasty side because she has a black eye and she's whimpering, showing visible signs of distress that Khalid hates people to see. Men here like the illusion that women give a shit about them, like any chick in her right mind would get on that auction block without coercion. They tell themselves the women want it, that Khalid only finds sex freaks.

I'm here to rescue my sister from this horrible fate. My mind wanders, as usual. She left our family, promised us she could keep herself safe. *Helen.* We've never gotten along, so when she sees I'm the one here to save her, I'm sure she'll react poorly.

Fuck, I hate this place. Our father should have Helen beaten or married off if this is what she's going to do with freedom.

The girl on the auction block cries loudly. *I need more to drink.* If Kim's trembling and now loud whimpers affect the price Khalid and his team get for her, she might make it to her new master's house with a broken bone.

My mouth is dry. There's not enough vodka in the world to desensitize you to this shit. Only time, my father tells me. I don't know if I ever want to be sick enough to enjoy these places. I hear someone call my name and look over my shoulder. But there isn't anyone there.

I've had too much vodka. Either that or I haven't had enough.

I glance over at my father and he shakes his head. We're not in the habit of buying sex slaves, although once or twice, we've purchased a girl or two — for re-sale. We mostly have Loukas to blame for that.

"We have a bidder! €20,000. Can we get €21,000?"

The bidding continues until Mr. Reichenbach buys Kim for €40,000. I wonder what happened to the girl he bought last quarter. He has a newer, younger woman with lip-fillers, cheeks caved in and a dead expression on her face hanging onto his right arm now, desperately straining on his sleeve to tear his gaze away from the woman he's purchased. *Tick Tock, gold digger.* She may be his date to this auction and think she's not like these other chicks, but women are all disposable to him — the ones he buys and the ones he keeps as pets.

A gaunt server with a black collar around her neck approaches and offers a drink. One of Khalid's personal harem. A little "K" hangs from her neck, marking her as his personal sex slave. Her voice is raspy and strained. There are purple bruises around her neck and a placated look in her eye. Dilated pupils too.

She's been beaten and she's on drugs. This place makes me sick. These people sicken me. *Helen, you idiot. How did you allow a man to drag you into this world?*

"Vodka martini, Mr. Pagonis?"

"Dry," I growl. I'm so drunk that speaking feels like it'll turn my stomach. I'm normally much better at holding my liquor. It's just the walls of this room are closing around me. Suffocating me.

"Just the way you like it," the woman says. "That'll be right up."

I grunt thanks and she seems surprised that I acknowledge her enough to say thank you.

I finish the martini in one gulp. If I have to watch female after female parading out there with horror on her face, I get sick to my stomach. Don't these women have fathers and brothers to protect them?

Yiayia is the only person who enjoys these events. Not even my father enjoys them, and he's technically the boss man. Everyone knows Yiayia really calls the shots.

A Thai girl who looks nineteen sells for €14,000 because she isn't a virgin. A Duke from England buys a blonde-haired, blue eyed American from South Carolina for €65,000. He likes Southern accents and women twenty years younger than him. My father raises two fingers and I'm the only one who notices his signal. It's simple. We bid on her, we get her out of here and our year of hell ends. We all want Helen home again. Even me.

But the night doesn't go according to plan because Khalid's man on stage announces, "Sapphire. A beautiful, fertile African American with perfect proportions. She'll need a handler with a firm hand, someone willing to engage in frequent discipline. This fresh-faced adult female has never had a baby and skilled enough for domestic labor. We recommend keeping her outside the United States."

She stares ahead, unflinching and proud. Khalid hasn't broken her yet, which means he mustn't have had her long. I can't take my eyes away from her.

Straight shoulders. A slender neck. Dark skin. Well, much darker than mine. She isn't the darkest woman I've ever seen, but she's the color of a whole walnut. And thick. She has wide hips, a pretty face with full lips and that face. She looks like she could kill a man with her bare hands.

She's fucking pretty. I run my tongue over my lips and imagine doing something very dirty with her. *Sick, this place has already made me sick in the fucking head. I need to drink more.*

She's not the girl I'm here for. I'm here for my sister. Helen. Khalid's a bastard and making us buy her back. One year searching for her and tonight we finally rescue her. My instincts draw me away from my purpose. Sapphire. She's beautiful, with a raw umber skin tone and perfect lips. She's fierce and sensual in a way that scares me. I can't take my eyes off her.

"Bidding starts at €13,000."

An eighty-year-old man with mottled skin raises his card. He looks older than the first Smith and Wesson.

"We have one bidder at €13,000. Anyone for €15,000?"

I raise my placard. Foolishly. Impulsively. Because I want her. Neither my father nor Yiayia can control what I do with my money, and from the second Sapphire steps onto the block, I want her. She must be an American girl.

I can tell from her proud expression, the disgust quivering in her lower lip and barely concealed. She doesn't have visible markings on her which means whoever she is and wherever she came from, she was wise enough not to piss Khalid or any of his men off. She has one bruise on her shoulder but it's healing. A week. She must have been with them a week. And Khalid's eager to rid himself of her so she must be trouble.

I stroke my stubble, poor Helen temporarily forgotten. *I'll win this auction. I must.*

"€15,000. Anyone for €20,000?"

That aging bastard raises his placard again. Breaking protocol, I stand and blurt out, "I'll take her for €45,000."

My hand rushes to the handle of my weapon and everyone in this room knows that you don't fuck with a Pagonis. The aging bastard might be a billionaire, but a billion dollars can't stop a bullet. I'm crazy enough to pull the trigger. Everyone in this room knows. The old man clears his throat and raises his hand.

There's one way to win a battle.

"Sold!"

Khalid sends one of his girls over with a card containing handwritten instructions on what to do next. I've been through this before. My cousin bought a sweet Syrian girl off Khalid two years ago. She stabbed him a week later. Bastard deserved it.

I glance over at my father once I sit and he's scowling. But relief floods the room because I have what I want and my hand isn't on my weapon.

I don't know why I did this, but now I owe Khalid €45,000 and he hasn't trotted my sister out yet to force my family to bid on her. It's been too long since I've seen Helen. She comes on stage after Sapphire. She's bruised and bloody. Khalid's head would end up on a platter if he was the one who did this to her. Ironically, he's the one who saved her, but the bastard refuses to give Helen back without making us pay.

"Helen Pagonis. Bidding starts at €10,000."

No one in the room is stupid enough to bid on my sister. I raise my placard. My father strokes his chin and observes the transaction silently. I've done what I came here to do. Once the auction ends, I follow Khalid's instructions to the waiting room. After a brief wait, he sends the girls in. My sister strides over to me and wraps her arms around me. I don't hug her back. I haven't seen Helen in a year and the last time I saw her, she wished me dead.

"My brother..."

Sapphire stands against the door, terrified, like she's thinking about running but smart enough to realize if she does that, she's dead meat. At a private club like this, I'm not the scariest or most powerful guy in the room. Helen pulls away from me and I think she's going to say something deeply sentimental.

I have the words balancing on the tip of my tongue. *I forgive you, Helen.*

Then, my sister slaps me across the cheek. Hard.

I save her life and this is how she repays me? I glance over at Sapphire. She's the most beautiful thing I've ever seen. Still catching me off guard, Helen slaps me again.

Fuck...

TWO
THE GIRL I BOUGHT

"What the hell was that for?" I growl.

After a year sold around Southern Europe, you'd think these men would have tamed Helen by now. She's like Yiayia — unchanging.

"Bastard," she hisses, "Why did you take her?"

She gesticulates madly at the girl I bought, cowering against the door, terror in her eyes as she considers her options. Typical loud-mouthed Greek woman involving herself in my business. I remember why I don't get along with my older sister...

"I wanted her," I answer, eyeing my sister for her reaction as she gazes at me in disgust.

"Fool."

"Careful, sister. I might find you another buyer. Did the ones who had you ruin you entirely?"

"You've always been a filthy chauvinist, but buying a woman..."

I push past Helen, who doesn't want to let me go. She slaps me again.

"Helen, what is your fucking problem?"

"Don't touch her," Helen says, her voice shaking. "I swear, Stavros... You touch her and—

"Can you shut up, Helen?" I snap. "It's bad enough Papa had me in that fucking room all night. I just need you quiet."

My sister scowls and I look my new purchase in the eyes for the first time.

"Sapphire. Come," I command her, trying to keep my voice soft and gentle to avoid another attack from Helen, or worse, an attack from the girl herself.

She glances at Helen, who nods approvingly, and then she follows me. How well do they know each other, I wonder? I don't need to drag her down the hall or look to see if she's following me. By now, she knows well that escape isn't an option. And I'm far scarier than a bastard like Khalid — without a weapon.

"Where are we going after this?" Helen inquires, nearly tripping over herself to catch up to me. She's thinner than I remember, and weaker.

"We're going to the boats," I say to Helen. I still can't take my eyes off the girl. *Sapphire.* That doesn't sound like her real name, but it suits her. She's a rare beauty.

"The boats?" Helen's shrill voice interrupts my focus on the new girl.

"Yiayia wants to see you," I reply disinterested. She's just as curious as I am about how Helen ended up in this predicament.

"I don't want to see her," Helen complains.

Nobody does, I want to tell her. But I don't want to encourage Helen's dissent. Yiayia will be furious enough considering I explicitly disobeyed my father by bidding on someone else. We have business to attend to and when I'm working, they want me focused. I put Helen into her car. Papa sent a driver. I turn around and take a full look at the girl standing behind me. She's younger than me. And pretty.

The girl I *bought.*

"Sapphire. I will not hurt you. I'm taking you to my family boat. Do you speak English?"

I thump the door to Helen's car and her driver pulls away, leaving me on the curb with my new ward. Maybe my family is right to question my decision making lately. I'm in no position to drive. I'm drunk and I think this girl can tell.

"Yes. I speak English," she says, glaring at me. I don't know why her loathing expression surprises her. I'll have to be gentle. Or at least I'll give gentle my best shot since it doesn't come easily to me.

"Do you know where you are?"

"No."

I ask her, "How do you know Khalid?"

Most of the women he finds go with him voluntarily — at first. He buys some of them like he bought my sister. But Helen's trouble differs from my beloved's trouble. The Italians got their hands on my sister after an incident in Bosnia. Loukas and I had to kill Demetrius, Helen's previous ex-boyfriend, a complete troll.

That was a fun night.

When we find Nikola, the second ex responsible for this, we'll kill him. *I'll* kill him because it's always my job. I have the better stomach for it and unlike Loukas, I don't have any children.

Sapphire doesn't answer. She glances over her shoulder once and I clear my throat.

"What are you —

She runs. Fuck. I should have known she'd try. She doesn't get far, even if she makes a solid break away from me to run. I wrap my arms around her and pull her close to me as she screams and thrashes.

"No, you don't," I growl, subduing her flailing limbs and clamping my hand over her mouth.

No one who witnesses a Pagonis putting a girl in a car would dare say a word. It's pointless to scream and most people here don't speak English.

My car isn't far, and she's easy to carry. I thrust the door open as she bites down on my hand. Hard. I'm screaming as I shove her into the back seat and lock the car doors.

I hurry into the front seat while she screams and thrashes in the back. I start the car and she lunges forward, screeching and trying to climb into the front.

I take a sharp turn, throwing her off balance. She yells and I step on the gas.

"SETTLE DOWN! NOW!"

She screams and pulls on the door handles, but she doesn't lunge forward again. She gasps and shudders and appears to reconsider, settling into a silent sobbing in the backseat. I am in so much fucking trouble with this one. I don't have a plan for what to do with her.

I'm at the docks in ten minutes. Loukas and Gal already left on Loukas's boat. I assume my younger sister's with them. Helen and Yiayia stand on the dock in front of Papa's boat. Yiayia's blue eyes flame with rage. I park the car and look over my shoulder at Sapphire. If I was a younger man, Yiayia would never let me keep her. She'd make me throw her overboard, or worse.

"I need you to behave yourself," I tell her gruffly.

"You're a sick fuck," Sapphire hisses, "Is your dick so small that you need to kidnap women to get laid?"

I raise an eyebrow. Khalid would have broken her jaw for speaking to him like that. I wet my lips and realize I'm too drunk to come up with a clever retort. I need to get her out of the way so I can meet my grandmother.

"I'm taking you onto my boat. You'll be safe there."

She doesn't answer.

"Sapphire, I need you to answer me."

"My name isn't Sapphire," she hisses, "That's a cruel, racist joke your sicko friend played on me. My name is Fallon."

Fallon. Her name sounds regal and beautiful, much like she is. My heart quickens. I need to get control of myself. I can't show this woman what her every movement does to me.

"It doesn't matter what your fucking name is," I growl.

But it matters. And now I know, I want to call her Fallon out loud and say her name until she gives a shit about me. *This is why everyone thinks I'm insane.* She quiets down.

"If you want to make it out of here alive, you'll be respectful. I show mercy, but no one in my family does. I swear, I don't want to hurt you."

She whimpers and nods.

"Come."

I lead Fallon onto the boat and lock her in my spare bedroom before I hop back off onto the dock. Yiayia sneers at me, "Is there a good reason you've purchased an African?"

I correct her calmly and tell her that Sapphire is American. The less my grandmother knows about her, the better. For now, that includes her name.

Yiayia folds her arms as a breeze blows her shoulder length grey hair off her face. She's a beautiful woman, especially for her age, but she looks as mean as she is. You would think it would make her less beautiful, but she only looks cruel.

"If you want women for sex, you can have any Greek woman you want. There isn't a woman alive who would turn down a Pagonis."

She smiles and fixes the collar on my linen shirt, smoothing it with a perfectionist's hand. She's proud of all of us — especially her grandsons, known for their success with women.

"Yes, Yiayia," I reply politely.

"You're looking frail, Stavros. You need to eat."

"I'll feed myself on the boat."

Yiayia. She's not like other grandmothers, but she still keeps us fed.

"Good. I need you to work tonight once we get back to Thessaloniki."

"Eh? What work?" I don't like the sound of this.

She dismisses Helen and pulls me aside. When Yiayia says I have a job, she means that she wants me to kill someone and I always do what my grandmother asks.

She's too old to be in charge of anything, and she's a woman. Women don't lead mafia families. Not in Greece. Helen retreats and Yiayia touches my shoulder gently, when she knows she's going to ask something I don't want to do.

"Who is it?" I ask gruffly, stroking my facial hair. Judging by the expression on her face, it's definitely a murder.

Yiayia sighs.

"Your father will not be happy with me. He doesn't understand what I do for this family. Especially for the *future* of this family."

"Tell me, Yiayia. I will do whatever you ask."

Her soft expression turns harsh as I take her hand. Perhaps that was a touch too far. I've been disobedient (the Fallon thing) and attempting to weasel into Yiayia's good graces never works the way you want it to.

"Manipulative bastard," she hisses, "I don't need you to kiss my ass."

"I wasn't..." I begin to defend myself and then change my mind. "All I need is a name."

She touches my forearm again and smiles. My grandfather would always tell us that her smile made men weak.

"Arturo Castillo. He's coming to Thessaloniki for the week and I expect him in the water before tomorrow morning."

"Yes, Yiayia."

She presents her signet ring for me to kiss. I kiss her ring.

"Good boy," she whispers.

I strut onto my boat and lean over to untie it from the dock. I don't bother saying goodbye to my grandmother.

Yiayia knows I went to university with Arturo. She could ask Loukas to do this — and it would be nice if my idiot younger brother Gal did something for this family for a change.

When there's dirty work and bodies to put in the water, they always call me. Stavros Pagonis — the Executioner of Thess.

THREE
FOUL-MOUTHED WOMAN

The trip to Thessaloniki would have been nice, but Fallon's screaming ruins the mood. She bangs on the door the entire time. Her gusto for escape picks up when she realizes we're moving to yet another country and I'm bringing her there with no passport, no identity, just the brand Khalid put on her nape and the chip millimeters beneath her skin on her neck.

We paid to have Khalid deactivate Helen's chip once we get home, but he won't remove Fallon's. *She's different.*

I hear my brother Gal calling from below deck.

"Gal!" I call back to him. "Gal!" I scream his name a couple more times.

I remember that he isn't on the ship. I didn't hear his voice. Fuck. It's happening again. I imagined my brother's voice. I hear him calling clearly when he's nowhere around. And I believe it's real at first. Voices. Music too. But mostly voices. I ease the boat into my spot at the dock.

The girl must be hungry, but all her damn yelling pisses me off. I'll feed her later. And what was that lip back there? Doesn't she realize what a worse man would have done to her by now? I get my weapon ready on the deck, whistling as I work.

Unlike my brothers, I don't have a fetish for guns. To kill someone, you don't need a machine gun or anything fancy. I work with a Glock 22. I love how fucking powerful this thing is. Galanos prefers rifles, but I love the absolute control that comes with a pistol, especially one as powerful as this police issue.

I bought it off a drunk American cop and sold him enough crystal meth that he scrubbed the serial number off the gun himself.

It's a standard weapon, not traceable, and I could kill Arturo in front of a crowd of fifty and not a single person would witness it. I don't want to do that. Unlike my brothers, I don't enjoy the way people look at us. I don't want to be a Demi-god. I do this work because it's the only thing I know how to do.

I put my family first, even if they're fucking crazy because that's who they raised me to be.

Arturo walks out of the bar with a Slavic looking woman with fake breasts on his arm. A tight black corset pushes her enormous breasts together, and she's hanging onto his arm like she plans to milk him for every dollar he's worth — approximately $25 million, which everyone knows since he brags about it all the time.

Yiayia wants him dead so he dies. That's the law of Greece. *Her law.*

I wait for them to turn around the corner. I cock the gun.

Arturo stops walking and the girl shrieks.

"Get out of here and shut your mouth, or I will kill your entire family."

She runs. She doesn't even attempt to get Arturo out of it. Ouch. He should be grateful I've revealed the tramp for her shallow interest in him.

"Fuck."

"Yes. Fuck. That's what you did to my sister."

"I never touched Helen," he stammers, "I swear. I never knew where she was."

"I'm not talking about Helen."

He turns pale. I take a step closer.

"I don't want to do this. But... you know the rules. You don't lay a finger on a Pagonis girl. Cassia's beautiful. I understand that. But she's my sister."

"Let me go and you'll never hear from me again. Tell them I fought back."

"Pray," I tell him, "I'll give you time to pray."

He whimpers and starts, "Dear God —

I shoot him in the head. We're close enough to the water that I drag him down the docks and get him on the boat. It's close to three in the morning. No one else is here and that girl won't say a word to anyone important — not if she wants to survive to see Christmas. I load Arturo onto the boat and put a blanket over him on the deck. I'll take him far out to sea where he can sink in peace. He was always good at cards.

"You were a human once," a gruff voice comes across the deck, like it's coming from a creature crouching on Arturo's body.

The voices will never stop, no matter how many people I kill. I walk below deck. I'm not in a hurry to leave and I want to make sure Fallon hasn't found a way out of here. I knock on the door.

"Who is it? Who are you?"

"It's me. Stavros."

"Stavros," she repeats.

I never told her my name before. And she's not from around here so she probably has never heard of me. It's possible she's heard of Gal, but not me.

"We're going for a little ride and then I'll open that door... and we can talk."

"Talk? Is that what you call it?"

"Call what?"

She doesn't answer. I rap my fingers across the door again.

"You're going to rape me," she says through the door.

I stop tapping. She thinks I'm a monster. I hate that.

"I'm going to take this boat for a ride. And then we'll talk."

I walk away before she can respond. I take the boat out for an hour and drop Arturo's body in our spot. I hose the deck down with vinegar and say a prayer after I haul his heavy ass overboard.

"He was a good man," I whisper, taking the ring I peeled off his finger and dropping it in the water after him, an offering to the old gods. Or something. Maybe all my superstitions are what drove me mad.

I go downstairs. Fallon won't run away from me here. She can't.

There's nowhere for her to go but the sea. I don't want her to leave, anyway. I want to have a conversation with her. How the fuck did an American girl end up in this predicament?

She's beautiful, but she loathes me, which I wish she didn't. I can't expect better but...

I open the door and she screeches, crawling across the bed to the corner of her room and squeezing her legs together tightly.

"I'll shit all over your dick if you try to do it," she yells, "You like that? Sick pervert? I swear, I will *shit all over your dick* if you try to rape me."

I ignore her emotional outburst. Her cursing at me doesn't bother me, although she's foul mouthed for a woman.

"Fallon. No last name?" I ask her, gazing at her beyond my lashes. It still makes my chest do a funny thing when she looks at me. Even angry, she's gorgeous.

"I have a last name," she says, her voice dripping with contempt. Despite her hatred, I have to remain calm.

"Does Khalid have your documents?"

"No."

"Where are they?" I ask her, circling her like a hawk. Like a hyena. I sense her nerves rising. *Good.* It's wrong of me, but I want to punish her for glaring at me like I'm a monster.

"Burned," she says, her voice dropping.

"You're fucked," I say plainly. "Without documents, I can't just set you free. I can't get that chip out of you."

"Thanks," she snaps. I bite my lower lip and try to stop myself from saying my next words.

It doesn't work. I'm too much of a bone-headed idiot to stop myself from commanding her, "Take your clothes off."

"W-what?" The ferocious fury falls away from her face. I terrify her.

I fold my arms and lean against the wall. My impulses lead the way again. I'm testing her obedience more out of instinct than any proper reason.

"Do as I say. Take your clothes off."

"No!"

"I want to see what I purchased," I snarl at her, hoping to scare her even more.

"I will never let you use me like a whore," she snaps.

"If I wanted to rape you, I could have done that easily. You are mine and we are in the middle of the sea on my boat. Every inch of your body belongs to me already. I don't want to rape you. I want to see you."

"Let me go," she begs, "If you have any ounce of humanity, you'll let me go."

Her lower lip trembles and I want to kiss it and comfort her. She'd probably try to kill me if I dared. Which makes me want to kiss her more.

"Beloved, I would enjoy setting you free, but without any identification but the brand on your nape, Khalid would have you back within a week. He has people everywhere. But... I can help you."

"I don't believe you," she says, strength returning to her voice. No matter what happens, this woman will not break. I admire that, but I also have a perverse desire to dominate that spirit. To claim her.

"I don't care. Now take your clothes off."

She takes off the clothes Khalid gave her and shivers before me entirely naked. My cock stiffens instantly. I don't know why I thought I had the strength to do this — to observe her naked body and not erupt with unimaginable lust that nearly pushes me to commit the very vile act I promised myself I wouldn't do.

"You shouldn't wear slave's clothing," I tell her, "I must keep you confined… but you are not a slave, Fallon. I won't have you dressing like one."

I reveal a surprise I brought for her. It was in my other spare room — a dress that belonged to Helen that my ex-girlfriend never returned to her. I kept the dress because I never thought Helen would come home. And it still smelled like Ana-Maria. At the time I enjoyed returning to the smell but it made me nauseous now. Fallon sniffs.

"I love this perfume," she says.

"If you like it, you'll have it," I respond. "At least until I get rid of you."

FOUR
I EXPECT COMPLIANCE

She holds the dress up, covering her body with the fresh linen. The dress smells like the borrowed perfume. Cassia wears the same perfume now since she moved into Helen's room. Teenagers. The first thing Cass asked when she found out we were getting Helen was whether she'd have to move to a different bedroom.

"You want me to wear this?"

I nod and she struggles through making conversation with me. She wants information. A sense that if she escapes, she'd find justice. But with that thing in her neck, there's no true escape from me.

"Your name is Stavros, right?"

She faces away from me, nervous goose bumps spreading down her spine as she slips the fabric over her naked body. I shouldn't ogle her. But I can't help myself. She must notice I'm hard by now. Hence the goose bumps.

"Yes."

"You kept me locked in here for hours."

"You screamed the entire boat ride over here," I remind her. "I couldn't let you out."

She keeps scowling at me. "I hate boats."

"Ah."

Disappointing. Pagonis men love boats. My father's the worst out of all of us.

"And you kidnapped me," she reminds me. She insists on seeing me as the villain here.

"I bought you."

The correction is only an exercise in semantics. But it's a worthy one.

"That's better, is it?"

This is the part where I need to be romantic. I see a man standing behind her. I know a man can't possibly be there. But she's real. Fallon is real. She tilts her head cautiously to the side. I must be getting pale.

"I wanted to save you from Khalid, I know what he's like."

She scoffs.

"If you're anything like what Helen told me, you're as big a monster as he is."

I lunge forward and grab her forearm. She shrieks and starts shaking but never breaks my gaze. Even in the face of danger and death, she's unflinchingly strong.

"I am nothing like Khalid. Men protect their women. They don't sell them or hurt them. I sat there to buy back my sister and protect her chastity for her husband. I will do my best to honor yours."

Her voice drips with sarcasm, "What a hero. Now you'll take some other man's daughter. Does that make you feel powerful?"

I release my grasp on her forearm and swallow. She doesn't believe me when I tell her I will not hurt her. Why should she believe me? I'm a liar, clearly. I wet my lips and answer with what's honest on my mind.

"You look beautiful in that dress."

She steps back.

"Don't," she whispers, "Don't start flirting and think that will change things. No matter what, if you touch me, it'll be rape."

"I know that."

"Then get out of this room."

"You're in no position to make demands."

"Please..."

Everything about her makes me stiff. Fuck. I never wanted a woman this much. And I own her. Her entire purpose in life now is to submit to my will.

I want to act like I'm better than Khalid and every other mafia asshole that I know, but the truth is when I'm alone on my boat in the middle of the sea with a beautiful woman, I want to have her. I want to take her. No one would know. No one here would talk.

I can't allow myself to act on my darker impulses. I'm already a murderer. If I want God's forgiveness, I can't show up at the gates of heaven as a rapist.

"I'm taking us back to the family villa. You won't talk to anyone there. Especially none of my brothers."

She nods. I leave the room and don't shut the door. She walks into the entryway.

"You forgot to lock me in!"

I forgot nothing. She has no upper hand and I have no reason to deny her moderate freedom.

"You aren't a prisoner. Where would you go, eh? Come above deck."

She doesn't want to, I know that. But given the option of staying below deck in her prison, I'm sure she'll follow me. Fallon climbs the stairs behind me. She's quiet, but I can tell she's thinking. She's looking for an escape. The next time she tries, I'll let her succeed. But she'll regret having to deal with Khalid's men instead of me. Above deck, she wrinkles her nose.

"It smells like blood up here."

"I was working."

"What are you, a butcher?"

She teases. But I don't laugh, and her expression sobers up. She approaches gingerly, like she hasn't decided how scared she is of my bite.

"It's cold up here."

"Blankets over there," I point and answer gruffly.

She finds one and wraps it around her shoulders.

"What are you going to do with me?"

"Keep you. Sell you. I haven't decided yet."

She purses her lips. The idea of someone selling her again doesn't appeal to her. I know men who would buy her and wouldn't hurt her. Decent men, except for their relationship to Khalid.

"You'd sell me again?"

"Yes. To someone who could take good care of you."

"I can't believe this is happening to me," she mutters.

"How long has Khalid had you?"

"Two months. He hasn't raped me yet, which is more than your sister can say."

Is that what happened to Helen? It would explain why she's even angrier with me than normal. I love my sister and even if she wants to put out her cigarettes on my arm, she doesn't deserve that sort of pain.

Khalid must have had Fallon for as long as a week. How did she weasel her way out of this with barely any bruising? I grip the handle of my handgun instinctively. I won't shoot Fallon, but if I ever find out who raped my sister, I'll kill them.

"Do you know who hurt my sister?"

She shakes her head and mutters an apology. She's not the one who has to apologize.

"Was it one of Khalid's men?"

She nods.

"They paid."

"Bastard..."

I utter more choice phrases in Greek and realize I look insane, muttering to myself in a strange language. I rake my fingers through my hair coolly, letting dark brown strands fall loosely in front of my face, dusting my jawline before a gust of wind pushes it all back. Fallon's hair whips around in the wind too — long black hair, well-coiffed by Khalid, no doubt to make her presentable for sale.

"You must be hungry," I grumble.

"Yes."

"I will feed you. And provide for you. I know what you think of me. And I'm worse than whatever you think. But I'm no rapist, and whoever you end up with, I'll do my best to make sure he's a good man."

"I won't thank you."

"I don't expect gratitude."

I expect compliance. And so far, she hasn't tried another escape. We approach the shoreline. The Thessaloniki shore brings a familiar jolt to my heart. Home. Greece. The most beautiful country on this earth, and the most beautiful city within it. We have the charm Athens lacks, the convenient port for our family business and old school values alongside it all.

"Have you ever been to Greece?" I ask Fallon, as her dark brown eyes widen with awe. It's like she's seen nothing this beautiful. It's so beautiful, she can forget for a moment I'm a monster and she steps even closer to me, peering over at the skyline.

"Where is this?"

"Thessaloniki. Your new home. See that giant house? With the blue roof?"

She nods.

"That's my family villa. I own two apartment buildings downtown. They do little profit, but they're very nice."

My bragging doesn't impress her. There's not a woman I know in Thessaloniki who wouldn't have swooned at the mention of my property ownership.

She wets her lips and murmurs, "It's breathtaking."

She's more taken with the landscape than with my wealth. Or with me. Hm. I've never met a woman like that before. She fascinates me. I gaze at her, enjoying her tawny brown skin and how it glows beneath the sun.

She gazes over at the shore and I feel a moment of connection between us. I tell myself it's real connection, bonding that happens because of the beauty of the landscape. *I will always love my home.*

"Fallon" I enjoy saying her name more than I let on, even if she flinches when I say it. I move closer to her. I want to touch her hand.

"Where did Khalid grab you from?" I ask her in a voice that I hope sounds gentle.

FIVE
YIAYIA'S ATTACK DOG

leave her in my suite with a bodyguard and a locked door. She has two windows but there are bars on them, so she's safe and has no chance at escape. She wouldn't make it off the villa compound if she tried.

It's nearly five in the morning when I walk onto the porch of our family villa. It's loud, because it's always loud with our family.

Loukas sits at the table, telling a loud story about his first wife and a fat Arab gun runner who offered to buy her for his harem in Medina. He always exaggerates and I'm tired of hearing Loukas. He's just another annoying fucking voice.

"Shut the fuck up, liar," I interrupt him.

"Finally, Yiayia's attack dog returns," Helen taunts, tapping her cigarette in a ash tray. "I was *really* enjoying Loukas' horrible, boring story filled with lies."

Loukas glares at me, and Helen laughs. It's nice to feel like she's on my side, even if it only lasts a moment.

Gal rests a new handgun on the table. It's nothing like the Glock 22, but the gun looks sturdy. *Where does he get this shit?*

"Helen, look at my new baby. Stole it off Pablo in Milan last week."

"You're never going to get a girlfriend if all you care about is guns," Helen chides our younger brother.

He scoffs.

"You know nothing. I have 3 million Instagram followers. Dozens of chicks begging to fuck me in the direct messages. Look."

Helen wrinkles her nose with disgust.

"That's sick. Did she offer to eat your... I go away for one year and you people are licking each other's buttholes!?"

Helen won't look at me.

"I was telling a story," Loukas interrupts gruffly.

"No one cares," I point out, "I'm here now."

"I heard you bought a sex slave today," Gal says, smirking. "How is she? Tight?"

"Cigarette," I command Gal.

He hands me a cigarette. My brother needed more time with decent people. What the hell happened to his nannies?

"Where's Cassia?" I ask once I have a cigarette in my hand. Smoking always helps me to feel much better.

"Who cares? Probably getting fucked," Gal snaps, "I want to ask about the girl you bought."

I take the cigarette and slap him across the face. Hard.

"You never talk about your sister like that. Ever. Stupid cunt."

Gal takes his gun off the table and I put my hand on the handle of mine. Gal wisely sets his gun on his duffel bag instead of making the stupid fucking moves I expect of him. None of my siblings flinch. It isn't a Pagonis get together if guns don't make an appearance. We're hot-headed Greeks with more money than we know what to do with, more guns than anyone should have, and most of the people sitting at this table have killed someone or witnessed a murder.

Cassia flits into the room, wearing red lipstick. I grab her by the forearm and growl, "Where the hell were you?"

"Helen, tell him to leave me alone!"

I snarl at her, "Where were you!?"

"Out!"

"Stavros, stop it!" Helen interjects, "I know Pagonis men never understand, but your sister isn't your possession."

Helen's scowl reminds me of Yiayia. She has Yiayia's extraordinarily beautiful face. A face that turns men's heads. I let go of my younger sister.

"When papa finds out who it is, I'm the one who will have to kill him."

Cassia's lower lip trembles.

"Is that where you were tonight? With Arturo?"

She'll find out about Arturo when rumors spread around Thessaloniki or when his body washes up from the Aegean.

"No," Gal interrupts, "He took the slave girl out to sea to rape her in peace."

Loukas snickers and puts on a mocking female voice, "Oh, don't put your cock in me, Stavros. I don't like tiny cocks."

Even Helen laughs. I light the cigarette and put my feet up with a groan.

"I need rest and I need to get away from you sickos"

"I need a fuck. Can I borrow your girl?" Gal asks.

I ignore him.

"Seriously," my idiot younger brother goads me, "I've always wondered what it was like. To take a black girl. I had a friend who fucked a Sudanese model, and he said she was the loudest fuck he ever had with a pussy like a giraffe it was so deep — OW!"

Helen has a good hold on Gal's ear and he shrieks as she hovers a cigarette over his forearm tattoo.

"HELEN!"

Cassia snickers.

"Do it! That tattoo is stupid," she laughs as she watches Helen threaten him with fire. Pagonis women are as fierce and unhinged as Pagonis men.

Loukas finishes his drink.

"Leave Galanos alone. I'm off to bed."

"Five in the morning. This is early for you."

Loukas grunts and storms off.

"Why the fuck is he so moody?" Helen asks once he's out of earshot, hand-rolling another cigarette mindlessly.

Cassia leans forward and whispers, "Molly died while you were gone."

"Who?"

"One of his women. Carlotta's new stepmom," Cassia explains. But Carlotta has a lot of new stepmoms. It's hard to keep track.

Loukas has a way of losing his fiancees. They all die eventually, and we're all certain he's the one killing them off. But he gets more upset with each one gone. The last time I pointed out that he could stop killing them if he wanted, he stabbed me.

"Yiayia wants you to talk to the Israeli tomorrow," Helen casually switches over to business talk, which means she's told everything about the past year to Yiayia and Papa. That explains why she's cranky enough to burn Galanos' forearm over a crude comment.

"The Israeli's a shithead. He wants to undercut us by €3,000,000. Cheap bastard."

"The Israeli is good business. He's bringing in a new client from Ethiopia. Some war lord type."

Gal's bored because the conversation hasn't been about him for over a minute.

"Will you let me fuck the girl, Stavros? I'll only take her arse if you want her intact."

Helen burns his arm. He screams and then lunges for her. Helen dodges and then artfully blows a cloud of cigarette smoke into Galanos' face. Cassia laughs. I polish off his drink. If Yiayia wants me to talk to the Israeli tomorrow, I'd better get a few minutes of sleep.

But I leave my little brother with a final warning.

"Talk about the girl again and I'll chop one of your balls off. Nobody in this house is going to rape her. Understand?"

Gal is the only one of my brothers who hasn't killed before. And he knows my body count because I wear it on my body, a tattooed fresco of dots to represent my kills. He turns ghostly pale, his eyes glittering aquamarine in the early morning light.

I walk away without another word, hearing my siblings whispering as I walk out of earshot. I turn around and they aren't saying a word to each other.

SIX

YOU... DISMEMBERED SOMEONE?

The door to my suite slams against the wall. Fallon makes a squeaking sound and jumps away from the window. We're three floors up here and my windows have bars on them — for good reason, it turns out.

"If you try to escape, I'll be the least of your worries," I remind her.

"I wasn't trying to escape."

I know she's lying. She glowers at me with fierce wickedness behind her stare. I don't have time for another problem right now. I dropped a body in the harbor and whenever I kill, the voices come back. Tonight, they're bad and if I can't keep it together, I'm screwed. I can feel my face's pallor increasing by the second.

"Get into bed," I tell her.

I want a warm body next to mine. I won't touch her. I just want to feel warmth. Is that such a bad thing?

I can't allow myself to be a worse man than Khalid by fucking a girl I purchased. She's making me weak.

I only need the myth of companionship so I can get the voices in my head to *fuck off right now*.

"Are you going to do it now?" She whispers under her breath.

My cock stiffens in my pants. Rape doesn't excite me. But she does. Every inch of her quivers in foreign beauty. Her skin is darker than the darkest girl from the coast. And I can smell coconut and pineapple scent lingering on her hair. Her American accent flattens every vowel into smooth perfection. My voice comes out on the wings of hot breath.

"I will not rape you."

I sound like I'm trying to convince myself.

"Fine. Prove it."

"How can I prove it?" I respond gruffly, trying to make the adjustment in my pants subtle and failing.

Her eyes snap open wider. She's conceiving of every way she can get out of this. Her gaze darts to my holster and I watch her calculate that she could never reach my weapon in time. It's not loaded anyway, so I consider letting her have it. I want to understand my new purchase. Why did Khalid call her Sapphire? How did an ordinary girl like Fallon end up in my sick world?

"Be honest about something."

Honesty will be easier than lying next to her without spreading her legs. I have no reason to lie to Fallon or hide anything from her. Her body belongs to me. She has a microchip in her arm marking her as one of Khalid's girls, and if she comes across any sicko in Khalid's line of work, he'll have her back to me within the week.

"What do you want to know?" I ask her. Is this another moment between us, or am I imagining things again?

"Who are you?" She asks.

"Stavros."

"That's not what I mean," she says. "I need more than your name."

Her voice trembles. She's putting on her bravest face, and her gaze on my gun becomes more nervous.

"What are you?" She asks.

"A man."

I adjust my pants again. She glances down nervously and swallows.

"That's not what I mean."

"Explain, then," I ask her.

I've closed the distance between us. Fallon's lower lip trembles visibly now, and I know she can feel my warmth because I can feel hers. She's small compared to me. With curves. But still short. I tower over most men and women I meet — easily. I want to reach out and touch her cheek, but I've scared her enough for the night.

I reassure her when I notice she's too scared to continue.

"What do you want to ask?"

"Are you... a serial killer?"

"Serial killer?"

I don't know what I expected her to ask, but not that.

"Eh? A what?"

"Tell me what you are," she whispers, "Do you kill black women? Is that what this is about? Toying with your pet before you kill me?"

I bite down on my lower lip hard to keep from laughing. I sense Fallon won't find my sense of humor amusing.

"No. I am not a serial killer."

It's honest. I kill people, but I'm not a serial killer. I don't take pleasure in it.

"I heard you," she whispers, her voice coming out in a gasp, "When I was below deck. I heard you."

"Hm."

"You... *dismembered someone.*"

"You don't have to whisper. It isn't a secret."

I can't help but smile and her face contorts in disgust. She pushes me away. *Hard.*

"Stay away from me," she hisses.

I scowl back at her, but I don't reach for my weapon or clench my hands into fists. Fallon is entirely unthreatening to me, and I want to make sure she knows that. She can push me, hit me, and punch me if she wants, but that won't change the fact that her body belongs to me.

"You wanted honesty," I point out.

"A human trafficker and a rapist," she sneers, "just my fucking luck."

"Your luck seems to have run out a long time ago."

"Fuck you."

"Clubbing in Vegas, eh? And no one bothered to make sure the sicko in the VIP room slung you over his shoulder."

"My friends looked for me," she snaps, "I saw it on the news."

"What about your boyfriend, eh?"

"Shut up."

"I did my research. Two months after you go missing, he's fucking your best friend."

"Shut up!"

"You have no one," I remind her, "And I'm not a trafficker. I'm… a Pagonis."

"That doesn't mean dick to me," Fallon snaps. She's beautiful. It hurts how beautiful she is, but acknowledging her beauty isn't the point right now.

"Mafia," I explain to her, surprised that she could be so ignorant. "The most dangerous mafia family in Greece."

"Greece doesn't have a mafia," she says. I can't help but laugh at her comment. Could she really disbelieve anything I say given where she's come from?

"Everywhere has a mafia if you hang around with the wrong crowd long enough. I don't buy fuck pets. I get plenty of women on my own."

Her face flushes a darker shade of bronze as I approach her again, daring her to push me away again. I put my finger beneath her chin and whisper, "I will sell you to a proper villain. I might be a killer, but I only kill people who wrong my family. Make no mistake, when some sick billionaire bastard is fucking you senseless with a shriveled cock, you'll wish you were back here with me."

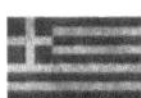

SEVEN

FALLON IVERSON

She's looking at me with so much rage, I expect to burst into flames.

"Fuck you."

"Is that what you'd prefer?" I snarl, intimidating her so she steps back and keeps going until I have her backed against the wall, cornered and terrified. My forearm lands against the wall with a thud and I wet my lips as I enjoy the inches between us. I can't fuck her. But I can play with her. Tease her.

"I'm not a serial killer," I tell her, running my thumb over her lower lip, "And I don't want to hurt you."

"Then don't. Help me."

"I will. I'll find someone who will take good care of you. An old man... who can't get it up."

I smirk and her shoulders relax.

"That isn't funny."

"I wasn't joking."

Her expression darkens.

"Why can't you set me free?"

"It doesn't work that way. Khalid only takes girls who meet a profile. Let me guess, you live alone, made around $45,000 a year, never travel fifty miles outside of your home city and have no passcode on your phone."

"I have a passcode," she protests, but averts my gaze.

"Let me guess, it's your birthday."

"No!"

"So it isn't June 16th?"

"No. It isn't."

"Liar," I whisper.

"Fine. But how the hell do you know my birthday."

I lean forward, pressing her body against the wall and brushing my nose against her neck, inhaling her scent and letting the tip of my aquiline Greek nose brush her sensitive skin.

"I bought you," I whisper, "I know everything about you. I know that you're 5'6" and 170 pounds. Fallon Iverson graduated from the University of Nevada Las Vegas with a Bachelor's degree in nursing in 2010. You wanted to move to Los Angeles, but you could never work up the courage to leave your mother behind. I know your birthday. I know about the mole under your left ass cheek. You belong to me, Fallon."

She whimpers and pushes my body away from her.

"Get off me."

"Angry?"

"Angry!? You bought me like a *slave*. Is that what you people do? You kill people and then go around trading black slaves? You sicken me."

"I was there to save my sister. Purchasing you was only a coincidence."

She scoffs.

"The sickest thing about you is that you expect me to be grateful."

"You should be. Another week with Khalid... and someone would have had your cunt."

She tenses up again.

"Don't say that word," she says, her face contorting like I've called her a slur. I love getting her to react to me. I love getting to know the different ways her face changes with her emotional state.

So I don't listen. "Cunt?"

I smirk.

"YES! That one."

"I like it. Cunt. It sounds deep. And warm. And inviting."

She keeps her palms outstretched and planted firmly against my chest. I tense my muscles purposefully and pretend that I don't notice her reaction to them. I don't need to rape Fallon to have her.

Fallon growls at me through gritted teeth, "You're too close to me."

"I enjoy getting close. And talking to you. About cunts."

I'm getting harder and less capable of controlling myself. *Calm yourself, Stavros.*

"Stop it," she says.

"Why? It's only a conversation."

I take a step back, and she visibly relaxes.

"Stop it."

"Stop what? Be explicit, beloved."

"I'm *not* your beloved."

"You can be my beloved... or you can be my cunt," I say to her teasingly. She doesn't like my joke.

Fallon pushes me hard. And then kicks me, mercifully missing my nuts but hitting me hard enough that I groan and double over, turning red in the face.

"I was joking," I wheeze.

"Has anyone told you that you aren't funny?"

"The voices in my head."

She thinks I'm joking and cracks a smile. When she catches me noticing her, that nasty little frown returns. I've earned that frown.

"If you plan on keeping me here, I can't sit around waiting for you with nothing to do."

"You're free to enjoy the villa, but... I'd avoid my brothers if I were you. And Yiayia."

"Yiayia? What kind of name is that?"

"Grandmother. She's my grandmother."

"Why should I avoid your grandmother?"

I want to tell her that Yiayia would eat her alive and chew on her bones, but I smirk and give her a wry response instead, "Trust me."

"I'd rather die than trust you."

She pauses a beat and I can almost see the thought crossing her mind. She might die anyway. I'm a crazy motherfucker. Fallon has proof of that. And she knows that I've killed before.

"What do you want from me?" She asks.

"Obedience. We're leaving Greece in a few days and you're coming with me."

"You don't expect me to wear this weird dress for *days*."

"You know my sister?"

"Yes. Helen."

"She'll help you find clothes."

"It's all too tight tight. If this is hers, she's *tiny*."

Cassia is larger than Helen, built more like a boy. Cocaine and a disturbing diet of cigarettes and caffeine keep Helen slim. Fallon would fit better in Cassia's clothing, but my younger sister wears dresses short enough to deserve a good beating from papa. Even Loukas keeps his daughter under tight control.

I don't want Fallon dressing like that. Cassia gets away with it because most men aren't stupid enough to lay their hands on Pagonis' youngest daughter. I don't want a single bastard laying their eyes on Fallon. *She's mine...*

"Tight dresses look good on you."

The dress is tight, but at least it's modest. A flowing white gown with tiny red and orange flowers hugs Fallon's curves. Her breasts lunge forward, begging me to notice them. I don't stop myself from staring. Fallon scowls when she notices me and covers her chest with her forearms.

"Pervert," she snarls.

I can't stop staring at her.

"They're nice breasts. I like them. Large. Sext,"

"Bastard," she calls me, testing out another boundary. I don't care what she calls me.

"You can call me any name you want if you show them to me. I've seen them once, but some nipples never get old."

"Sick freak."

Her arms tighten around her chest. I'm too tired to toy with her any longer. If I keep teasing her, I'll only want to fuck her more than I already do. My cock can't stand anymore aching.

"Listen. If you get into that bed, I promise I won't touch you. My head hurts and I need to rest."

"I don't want to rest. I'm not getting into your stupid king-sized bed so you can have your way with me."

"I am too tired to fuck you tonight," I snap, "now get into bed before I give you to my brother. He's a much younger man and has twice my energy."

She sits woefully at the edge of the bed.

"Get under the sheets."

She silently slips under the sheets and sighs as her head hits the pillow. I get on top of the sheets. There's no need to break my word. I sigh and lay my head on the pillow. The visions get more intense. I only know they aren't real because of Fallon. She can't see what I'm seeing. And if she could, that doesn't change the facts. I killed Arturo. So he isn't in this room and he isn't pacing back and forth, stroking his chin and muttering my name under his breath.

I hear her whisper, "Stavros", once I've turned off the lights.

"What?"

"I hate you, stupid motherfucker," Fallon hisses, genuine hatred in her voice. *Shit.*

She puts a pillow over my face and presses down. There's no light. No air. Just her weight on the pillow, smothering me.

EIGHT
TRUST NO BITCH

oly fuck. This chick is strong. She's far stronger than I would have guessed, and if I don't get her off me, she'll smother me to death in my bedroom. Stupid fucking idiot, my father would tell me, *trust no bitch.*

I flail and grab her forearms, hoping foolishly at first that physical contact with her arms might convince her to have a moment of mercy. I'd use her moment of mercy to free myself and restrain her, but... fuck. My nails dig into her forearms and I realize she isn't the merciful sort.

She throws another punch my way, breaking free. I have to use my full weight to pin her down, but Fallon doesn't stop fighting me. And scratching. *Ouch.*

I can't blame her. I'm the idiot who impulse bought a human female from Khalid — one with thoughts and emotions, one who wouldn't let Khalid's men break her. I force my knee up and she pushes down on the pillow harder.

But I can get the upper hand, even if she has the element of surprise. I've handled bigger dangers than Fallon Iverson. She grunts as I push her off me and throw the pillow across the room. Air floods my lungs and I gasp for breath as she screams and rolls across my king-sized bed, nearly falling off the other side.

She lunges for me, screaming like a wildcat. I open my side drawer and pull out the pistol. It's a vintage weapon papa gave me and unloaded, but I don't expect her to know that. I draw the gun and she stops dead in her tracks, contorted on all-fours in the bed, but still.

Yiayia taught me one thing when I was five years old, never point a gun at someone unless you're willing to pull the trigger. Then she pointed the gun at our family dog and shot him dead.

I learned several valuable lessons that day. We're both panting, coming down from the rush of hot adrenaline coursing through our veins, the adrenaline still pumping potently as we teeter on the edge of action. She speaks first in a low voice that isn't quite a whisper, "Go ahead. Shoot me. I don't care."

"I don't want to shoot you," I answer honestly.

She's beautiful. Even like this. And I want her. With all the hot blood coursing through me, some of it had to end up between my legs. My cock stiffens as she takes it in her grasp and bends her head forward slightly.

"Go ahead," goads Fallon, "I'll close my eyes."

Her throat trembles and her eyes flutter shut. The gun isn't loaded. I toss it behind me and she flinches as the metal clatters to the ground.

"It isn't loaded."

She exhales and sits back on her calves.

"You weren't going to kill me," she says, sounding surprised.

"No," I growl. "Of course not."

"I tried to kill you."

I smirk and play it cool, "Yes. I remember."

"I don't understand," she whispers, struggling to hold her voice steady.

"What don't you understand?"

"What do you want from me?" Her stern confidence returns, but for the first time since I brought her to my room, she hasn't used every chance to search for a weapon.

I could answer her question. But I want nothing good from her. I want to fuck her. I want to own her. Fallon doesn't want those answers. She wants answers that make her feel safe and reassured.

"I want... to keep you safe."

"WHY?! This would be much easier if you did something. UGH!"

She takes the other pillow and lobs it at my head. This time, she doesn't have enough of an advantage and I catch the pillow, tossing it to the ground.

"I don't want to hurt you."

"Right. You're one of those freaks who pays hookers to talk about feelings instead of going to therapy like a normal person."

"Are all American girls this... rude?" I ask her, wanting to tease her more. To draw the wildcat out of her.

"Are all Greek men such pigs?" She shoots back.

Fair point. Although I can assure her that yes, we're total pigs. All of us. I change the subject.

"My siblings will hear all this noise and assume I'm fucking you."

She freezes because I'm talking about fucking again. And every time I talk about fucking or cunts, she assumes the worst. She inches away from me.

"I should have let you go to sleep," she whispers.

"Probably."

"What are you going to do to me?"

"I'd tie you up so I could get some sleep. But you'd scream all night. How about we make a deal?"

"What?"

"You let me sleep one night without trying to kill me. Because if you try to kill me, I will overpower you."

She knows what I mean by overpower. Fallon wets her lips.

"You wouldn't," she breathes. But she knows I would. She's witnessed enough to know that Pagonis men don't make idle threats.

"You need sleep as much as I do. And I won't touch you. I just... want sleep."

"Fine. But I don't get much out of this deal."

"You get a good night's sleep," I respond gruffly, "Now shut up before I change my mind."

She slips under the covers, dejected. My heart skips. I'm an idiot. I bought this girl and now I'm angry that she doesn't have feelings for me, that she hasn't given me every inch of her body on a silver platter. Knowing I could take what I want mercilessly doesn't make it easier because I don't only want to fuck her. I want to know her. My victim.

My stomach lurches as I rest on top of the covers. I'll sleep with one eye open now that I know how she thinks. But why didn't she find my gun? If she'd been looking for a way out, she would have found it. She could have tried to kill me that way. I tell myself that I'll ask her in the morning.

I tune out the whispering in the back of my head long enough to fall asleep. I hear her snoring before I let myself sleep properly. It's like Ethiopia all over again. Shitty sleep. Uncertainty. The threat of death. At least this threat is easy to disable. She forgets herself in a blissful slumber and rolls onto my side of the bed. I could push her away but I'm on the covers and she's under them so I curl my body around hers slowly so she doesn't wake up.

My back curves around hers, and she wriggles until her bottom nestles against my crotch. I won't get any sleep now. Her ass makes me instantly hard.

"Fallon," I murmur, pushing her away from me gently and hoping momentum will take her body off my genitals. Holy fuck, she won't budge. And now she has my arm around her and her head pins it to the bed so I'm stuck cradling her with a raging hard-on growing between my legs. She makes a low whining sound and I murmur her name again.

"Fallon, wake up."

She rolls over, so she's facing me, but she doesn't release my arm any further. Fallon strokes my cheek with her palm and I hold my breath. She's still asleep.

Fallon has no idea what she's doing, and if I breathe, I could wake her up and ruin all of this. But her lips are centimeters away from mine and my hands yearn to explore every inch of her body, but especially the apex of her thighs.

I force my eyes shut and fall asleep with temptation in my bed. The sun barely peeks over the horizon when I wake up to her whispering, "Stavros... let go of me... please..."

My heart thuds again and I remember I'm a monster and in my sleep, my monstrous arms pulled her little body next to mine. I cough and my eyes flutter open as I try to play it cool. I push her off and Fallon rolls across the bed, pulling the covers tight around her neck without taking her gaze off me.

"You were holding me."

"I'm sorry. You... looked cold."

It's a stupid lie and we both know it's a lie, which makes both the lie and the stupidity somehow worse.

"I see how you look at me," she whispers.

"Does it scare you?"

A dribble of sunlight filters through the room and she nods.

"Sorry."

"A guy like you must have plenty of *interested* women."

I clear my throat because while I have plenty of interested women, none of these interested women look like Fallon. The African girls in Thessaloniki know better than to mess with a Pagonis.

"I stay away from women while I'm working."

That's a simpler answer.

"When's the last time... you... you know?"

"Had sex?"

She nods. I wet my lips. It's been a long time. And just thinking about Fallon and sex in the same hemisphere of my brain makes my cock stiffen.

"Why do you want to know?" I growl.

My stern scowl doesn't scare her anymore. I tell myself she's coming to trust me, even if the experienced part of my brain tells me that can't be true.

"I want to know how long I've got before you... do it," she whispers, "I can tell you're going to. And if you don't get it somewhere else —

I interrupt her before she can accuse me of anything worse.

"The last time I had sex was two months ago. A hooker in Amsterdam. Nice breasts. Too skinny."

She wrinkles her nose in disgust. I'm lying. It's been a very long time since I've slept with another woman. Now that I've seen Fallon, I can't even remember the last woman I've seen who turned my head.

"So you pay for it? I thought guys who looked like —

"What?"

"Never mind," she grumbles, not wanting to test me.

"Say it."

She can't resist my commanding voice. Mostly because she's fucking terrified of me, which comes with its own drawbacks.

"Guys who looked like models don't need to pay for it."

She may be right, but guys who spent 15 years in prison for murder might. Also, a model? Flattery won't get her anywhere.

"I'm the most dangerous of my brothers. Women prefer Loukas. Or Galanos."

"I doubt that."

A curious response.

"And anyway," I correct her, "I didn't pay for it. She was a hooker, yes, but she's a delightful girl. With hobbies. She quilts in her free time."

Fallon giggles and then whispers weakly, "Shut up."

"I'm not lying," I answer, winking despite myself.

"So you don't make it a habit of buying women?"

"No," I answer. That's the truth.

She sighs.

"I have an idea then," she whispers.

"What?"

"Have sex with me."

I sit up and rapidly shove the pillow over the growing hardness between my legs.

"What?"

I swear, I'll never understand women.

"I'll have sex with you. Willingly."

"No," I growl. Blood rushes to my head. I want to be rational and Fallon just made that very fucking difficult for me.

"It's 100% voluntary. It's a win-win situation."

I snarl at her, "I won't fuck a woman who only wants to fuck me out of pity."

"It's not out of pity. It's helping us. Both of us."

"How would it help you?"

"You know when you're going skydiving how you're so scared of jumping out of the plane but then when you jump and it's all over, you're like oh, that wasn't so bad."

"I've never gone skydiving."

"Neither have I. But imagine."

I clear my throat and puff my chest out like the responsible one. I'm ten years older than her, so it's technically my job to be responsible.

"I will not have pity sex or skydiving sex with you."

"What about normal sex? Right here."

She sits up and lets the dress fall over her shoulders. The nipples I want to see so desperately before swing into view and my desire for her pushes the pillow off my lap. I breathe her name and try to think straight. She doesn't want me. She can't. This is a trick.

"Put your clothes on."

She takes my hand and puts it on her breast. I nearly burst. I close my eyes and wet my lips, savoring the soft flesh. My cursed fingers betray me and brush her nipples. She inhales with a sexy, high-pitched gasp that ruins me.

"Fallon," I growl, "If I fuck you..."

"When," she whispers, "When you fuck me."

That snaps me out of it for a moment.

"No!" I snatch my hand away from her, "I won't fuck a woman who looks at me like I'm a monster!"

She scowls but doesn't hide her breasts. My eyes find her exposed chest again and I can't make myself look away.

"You're going to," she says, her voice getting softer, "And I'm doing us both a favor by fucking you willingly. Or do I have you wrong? Do you look forward to me struggling while you try?"

"Damn it..."

I have to be a better man than this. I have to scare her off.

"I don't fuck like the small cock American boys you're used to," I growl.

She tries not to look scared. I lean forward, dark brown hair falling over my sharp jaw as I meet her gaze.

"When I fuck, I fuck hard. Do you understand?"

She nods.

"When I take a cunt, it belongs to me. It becomes mine to pleasure."

She whispers, "I understand."

"Then take your clothes off. Now."

NINE

WILLING WOMEN

f she's bluffing, now is her chance to back out. I'm calm when I command her. She gazes up at me with those gorgeous brown eyes, gazing at me the picture of perfect innocence. I tell myself it's an act. This woman tried to smother me.

"I need a woman to want it," I growl, "I don't take unwilling women to my bed."

Her dress slides off the edge of her bed. She doesn't answer me, but I suppose I didn't ask her a question. She positions her body on all fours, facing away from me. I kneel on the bed behind her. She flinches when I touch her bare ass. Temptation. This is what it looks like — a black girl bent over for me in bed, her cunt bare and inviting. I can't imagine how tight she must be.

It hurts how badly I want her. My cock stretches my pants forward in an awkward protrusion. I bend forward onto the bed and grab onto her thighs. She squeals and I slide my tongue between her legs and groan. There's no point in denying it with her. I love cunt. And from the second my tongue slides between her lips, I've found the perfect cunt to lick and suck on until she cums. She cries out and wriggles out of my grasp, a few inches forward but just enough that she's removed the sopping fruit from my lips.

"What's wrong?"

"I thought you were going to fuck me!" She squeals.

"I told you, I don't take unwilling women to bed. Now come."

I grab her by the hips and pull her toward me, bending my head between her legs again and running my tongue along the length of her slit. She cries out and my fingers clamp down on her thighs. She moans as my tongue presses deep into her. Holy fuck. My tongue can barely get inside her, she's that tight. I pull my lips away from her cunt and growl, "How many men?"

She's confused and doesn't answer. I lean over her, bending my muscled body over hers, and I growl directly into her ear, "How many men have had your cunt?"

"How many?" I growl after she's silent for too long.

"Five," she squeaks out.

"Twenty-six years old and you've only had five men?"

"Yes. I'm not... I don't... I don't have casual sex."

I stroke her shoulder with a bare palm, and a flicker of sympathy arises in my heart. She doesn't have casual sex. What I'm about to do with her is anything but casual. But there's no relationship between me and Fallon. She's a girl I purchased. She submits to me. She averts her gaze. I kiss her shoulder after I stroke it and she shivers.

"I don't have casual sex either," I murmur, "Sex is a serious matter."

I rest my hand on her cunt and she's dripping. Soaking wet and ready for me before my tongue has properly pleasured her. She can't help her body's response to me and I can't control my response to her, no matter how much I wish I could be a better man and leave her alone, untouched and unbothered by my cock or my tongue. I need her.

I inhale her neck and she whimpers again.

"Are you afraid?" I murmur.

"Yes."

"I want..." I growl, wanting to choke out words that sound nearly sentimental, "I want you to feel good."

"Sex doesn't feel good," she says with assurance. I'm forced to pull away from her in confusion. She's still on all fours, presenting her fleshy entrance to me obediently.

"What do you mean?"

"I've never... I... I don't want to talk to you about this," she snaps, like she's remembered I'm her enemy and she's only offering her cunt to me because she's scared I'll rape her. But I won't. I couldn't. I need a willing woman to enjoy sex. And here she is, admitting that she's never enjoyed it.

"You don't have a choice," I growl, "Tell me. Now."

"I've never had an orgasm. Most of my boyfriends were... quick."

"Do you want an orgasm?"

She bites on her lower lip until it turns red before she answers.

"Yes."

I kiss her shoulder again and kiss my way down her back before my tongue arrives at her exposed entrance once more. She grips my bedsheets as my tongue finds her entrance again. She makes a soft moan as I run my tongue between her lips and find her clit. Holy fuck, she is delicious. I run my tongue around her clit. She gasps. I grip her thighs and press my tongue between her legs again. Juices drip from her cunt and her clit stiffens as my tongue rubs in repetitive circles. Her thighs tense and she moans... loud.

"W-was that an orgasm?"

I chuckle.

"You've never touched yourself?"

I run my tongue over her outer lips and she moans before she can answer.

"No! The first time I had sex... it was... disappointing. I didn't think touching myself would make it any better."

"I can't," I groan.

"What?"

She scrambles away from me.

"I can't be the first to give you an orgasm."

"That's arrogant."

"No. It isn't. I know I will. But you're going to be the first. Touch yourself."

Fallon protests, "I can't touch myself!"

"Yes, you can. Now do it."

TEN
I WILL BE THE FIRST

"I don't want to touch myself in front of you."

I grunt and grab her hips, pulling her toward me and leaning over her.

"Are you scared?" I whisper into her ear, running one hand over her ass and over her mound, "I won't think less of you. I won't think you're a whore if you touch yourself."

She freezes, but her body won't let her lean away from me. She leans into my touch so my hand softly cups her mound.

"That's what you're worried about, isn't it?" I murmur, "You think it makes you cheap. Or slutty."

"I'm long past that, aren't I?"

"Shhh," I murmur, kissing her earlobe, "You, my darling, were anything but cheap. But hopefully soon, you'll be quite slutty."

She elbows me. Hard. Thankfully, I work out hard enough that she elbows a bulging abdominal muscle.

"Watch it, bastard," she hisses, "I still have some fight left in me."

"I'm counting on it," I murmur, moving her hair over her ear and kissing it again, "Now touch yourself."

"This is stupid."

I take her hand and help her support her weight as I place her hand over her mound, guiding it firmly to her sensitive soaking center.

"Let instinct guide you."

She parts her lips with one finger and gasps as I push her hand further.

"Touch yourself. Feel how slick you are. How perfect your cunt is. Did those men ever tell you that you have a beautiful cunt?"

"No."

I kiss her shoulder.

"Then I will be the first. Now move your hand."

She gasps again and then moves her hand, weakly stroking her clit.

"Don't be afraid," I whisper.

She scoffs.

"That's hard. There's a strange man I don't know leaning over me and kissing me."

"Am I not attractive enough for you?"

"I never said that."

"Ah. So I am attractive."

"In that conventional old-world way," she jabs.

I chuckle and kiss her shoulder again.

"Enough distractions. Massage your clit for me."

She winces.

"Don't say that word."

"Massage your beautiful pink pearl…"

She moves her fingers, and then she finds it. The spot. Every woman has that spot. One way they like to touch themselves, one part of the bundle of nerve endings that explodes with pleasure the second she lays a finger on it. Fallon finds that spot and her eyes roll into the back of her head as she moans and her hands snap away from her body like Pandora, snapping the box shut after she's opened it.

For Fallon, like Pandora… it's far too late.

"Don't stop," I encourage her gruffly.

She massages her nub slowly and then speeds up. She's teases her lips and slides her finger down the length of it and she moans.

"Put them inside you now," I murmur, "I want to watch you fuck yourself."

"I can't do that."

"You can take a cock. You can take a tampon. You can take two slim fingers."

She keeps massaging her clit, and she gasps between breaths, "Tampon? What do you know about tampons?"

"I have sisters. Very unhygienic sisters. Fingers. In your cunt. Now."

She gingerly parts her lips and then moans as she slides them into her wetness. Her body jerks forward, and she nearly falls on her face as she experiences the wonder of stroking herself to pleasure with her own hands.

"Fuck yourself," I murmur into her ear as I clutch her against my body, "Fuck yourself until you cum."

She plunges her fingers into her cunt faster and deeper. Juices spill out of her tightness and down her thighs. She makes a funny whimpering noise which morphs into loud screams and then she explodes. A sound of pleasure escapes her lips, and she's too late to bite down on them and suppress the sound. Fallon cries out again and cums hard as she thrusts her fingers deep between her legs. She clenches her thighs together and doubles over against my chest, heaving and gasping for breath.

Her hands claw their way up my chest again as she recovers. I kiss her forehead.

"Your first orgasm. Congratulations."

"I... I can't... I never thought..."

I'm not here to have a conversation. She made herself cum, and now I have animal urges in desperate need of release. I grab her cheeks and bring her face to mine.

"Shh," I whisper, "I'm going to eat your cunt, and then I'm going to fuck you, yes?"

She nods.

"You want my cock?"

She nods. I have what I need from her. I tell myself she feels desire and not fear because I need to believe Fallon Iverson wants me. I position her in front me again. Her cunt and thighs drip with juices. Khalid must have had her waxed because there isn't an inch of hair on her cunt or asshole. Now that she isn't facing me, I can ask what I want to ask. I press my firm palm on the small of her back, holding her still.

"Did Khalid rape you?"

I drag my knees across the bed, sinking into the fabric as I position my mostly clothed body behind Fallon's.

"No."

"But they must have... checked you. For a hymen."

The skin beneath my palm grows warm. She's flushed with nerves. I reach for the buckle on my belt with my spare hand.

"I didn't let them."

I chuckle but make it clear I'm serious about my demands.

"Tell the truth."

"I gave three men a black eye. He made me go four days without food. But... I didn't let them."

"They drugged you. Someone could have raped you then."

"Well, they didn't," she answers.

I kiss her lower back and she exhales in a gust. She fears that every moment passing between us will become the moment I take her. Her cunt drips as juices from her climax leak into a wet spot on my bed.

"Good," I murmur, "Because if any man touches you like that, I'll kill him."

I kiss her soft ass cheek and then kiss my way down her thighs, licking drops of juices as my tongue crosses them. She moans.

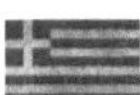

ELEVEN
STUCK IN THE PAST

Her cunt is exactly as delicious as I knew it would be. I push my tongue inside her again and Fallon cries out. She doesn't believe I can make her cum with my tongue. It's not a question of whether or not I'll make her cum, but how fast I can make it happen.

She's sensitive, and she's never experienced a man who cares about her pleasure. I massage her clit with slow purposeful movements and my tongue laps up her juices as I please her cunt.

Her body tightens as she approaches release. I flatten my tongue and lick her outer lips with broad purposeful strokes and then slide my tongue between them, massaging her clit until her moans get louder. Fallon cries out as my tongue slides over her clit and I can't stop myself from losing total control.

I grab onto her thighs and lick her pussy until she climaxes hard. She trembles and shakes and tries to free her body from my clamped fingers, but it won't work because I have her right where I need her and I'm not done making her cum.

I spread her thighs apart and force my tongue between them. The more juices that spill from her cunt, the louder she moans. I can't stop myself. My one goal is getting more of Fallon's cum on my tongue. My cock nearly bursts through my pants as she climaxes again. I pull away from her cunt once she's soaked every part of her body below the waist in her own cum.

I end with one long lick, stopping at her tight puckered ass. I'm saving that ass for later. She arched her back to present her body to me, and now she uncoils and sits up. She's soaked my bed and her nipples are stiff dark brown nubs, begging for my tongue.

Her eyes rove over my face. I can see ten million questions written across her face and I don't intend to answer any of them. She's mine. That's all that matters. I own her body. Her cunt belongs to me. I wipe my lips.

"Delicious."

She averts her gaze nervously.

"Come," I growl before either of us get post-orgasmic sense knocked into us.

She positions herself on all fours, and I ready myself for her tightness. She's seen the bulge in my pants, so she must have some idea of what I plan to fuck her with. My trousers slouch below my ass and my tight boxer briefs hug the protruding mass of my erection, so desperate to plunge into Fallon's beautiful cunt.

I have to remind myself that she's doing her duty. She doesn't want me the way I want her. A part of me wants to reassure her. Another part of me doesn't care. I'm not here to make a good impression, I'm here to fuck her... hard.

She whimpers as she senses my body moving close to her.

"Please... use a condom."

My cheeks turn red and I'm grateful she can't see how embarrassed her request makes me. Because she's reminded me of what I am. An animal. I'm a fucking animal and no matter how badly she wants it, if I fuck Fallon Iverson right now... I'll be the worst kind of man.

"DAMN IT."

I yell. She flinches and scrambles away from me. Naked.

Exposed. Covered in her own cum. She makes eye contact, like any good prey animal. Her shoulders slump when she sees the loathing on my face. I can tell she thinks I bear this loathing for her. But I'm the monster.

"Get your fucking clothes on," I snarl at her, "But you're sleeping on the floor tonight."

"What?"

"CLOTHES. ON. NOW," I roar.

She scrambles for the dress and puts it on. Fuck's sake. I'll have to take her to get better clothing. I can't have her dressing in Helen's rags — or worse, Cassia's.

"Get on the fucking floor," I snarl. I pull my pants up. Not like this. I won't have her like this.

She rolls off the bed and crawls around to the foot of it.

"You stay here until I come back," I snarl.

I put my clothes on and leave, locking the door behind me. Cassia leans on the door to her suite across from mine. She smirks at me as her tan cheeks darken to a deep plum color.

"I heard you."

"Get into the kitchen, Cassia. I'm hungry."

She kisses her teeth.

"You need a woman to make you breakfast? You're just like papa... stuck in the past."

"If you're going to give me lip, at least give me a cigarette first."

She giggles and hands me a cigarette from her purse. Fox. She shouldn't smoke.

"Is this what it takes to quiet the voices these days?"

She flicks her lighter and I take a deep inhale.

"Shut up."

Cassia is the only one of my siblings who knows about the voices. How they're everywhere. Except...

"You need medical attention, Stavros," she pleads.

"I need nothing."

"Whatever. Tonight, I'm going out with Arturo."

I freeze and tap my cigarette on the villa railing, watching the ash float to the ground.

"Hm."

"You don't approve of him?"

It doesn't matter if I approve of him or not. I separated his body into twelve pieces and dumped him in the Aegean Sea. I grunt.

"Fuck."

Her voice grows soft and her irises widen so they nearly block out the whites of her eyes.

"You killed him, didn't you?"

Her disappointment hits me hard. She sees me as a monster too. I want to reach out to her, but what the hell can I say? I have to try...

"Cass..."

"BASTARD."

She pushes me... hard. I drop the cigarette over the railing as she pushes past me. Fuck. It would have been ten times better if she'd found out about him when they reported his body missing. I chase after her.

"Cass! I did my job. You know how this family works."

She turns around, curly black hair whipping around her face like Medusa, or other mad Greek women. She's like mama. Brown hair. Brown eyes and deeply tanned skin. I hate seeing my sister cry.

"I hate you. I hate this family."

"Take that back, Cass."

Great. She's taking Arturo's death worse than she took Giorgio's.

"I mean it! And if papa thinks killing every man I love will keep my maiden head safe, he's wrong. I'm eighteen years old and it's none of his business who I fuck."

I stride over to her and grab her forearm so she can't run.

"Listen to me, Cass. You watch your mouth."

"Let go of me!"

Our conflict attracts attention. Galanos comes out of his suite, yawning with his cellphone in hand for his morning livestream. He turns the camera and narrates.

"My siblings fight every morning... They're fucking idiots. Cass, show your tits!"

Cass grabs his phone and tosses it over the railing into the pool. I have one of her forearms and Gal grabs the other.

"Fucking bitch," he snarls, "I have three million fucking followers who watched a little bitch embarrass me."

"Tone it down, Gal."

"What? You have her by the arm too. We can take her downstairs and throw her in the pool."

"Let go of her Gal."

Cassia's eyes plead with me. I might be a bastard, but Gal's a sadist. At least he follows Yiayia's biggest rule for the family. Respect your elders. He shrugs and ambles off — probably to fish his phone out of the pool. We've all thrown it in so many times he has a fancy waterproof case now.

"Cass," I growl once he's gone, "I'm sorry. Okay? Yes, I killed him. Yes, you loved him. But you need to learn your lesson. Papa has a man for you. A good, rich man. And once he... consummates your marriage, you can do whatever you want."

She sniffles and her eyes and cheeks are still red.

"Men. You think women are objects for men to buy and sell. Like we're your stupid guns. But we have a mind of our own. That girl in there? The one you raped. She'll give you what you deserve one day."

Cassia wrests her arm free and storms off. Great. I hear a splash as Gal dives into the pool downstairs, retrieving his phone from the bottom and resurfacing with a great cheer.

"Woo! It still works!"

I smell breakfast... Helen must be cooking downstairs. I wander after Gal into the enormous kitchen as Helen stands in front of the stove with my niece, Carlotta.

"Good morning, Uncle Stavros," Carlotta sings. Helen ignores me. I suppose everyone in the family heard about me and Fallon, and they think I raped the girl.

"Coffee, my niece."

"Already poured. Double shot of espresso, uncle."

I take the coffee from Carlotta. Helen mutters something unpleasant under her breath.

"I need food for the girl."

"She should come down and eat with the family," Helen responds stiffly.

"She's in no condition to do that."

"Bastard," Helen snarls. Her nose gets red when she's angry.

"Do you have a problem with me, Helen?"

I take another gulp to finish my mug of espresso. My seventeen-year-old nephew Antonio wanders into the kitchen wearing a mesh tank top and dragging along a girl dressed in a tiny tube top and hot pants. Her ass cheeks bulge out of the pants. Is this how teenagers dress these days?

Helen takes her espresso from the counter next to the stove and throws it at my face as she hisses, "Dirty rapist."

TWELVE
YOUR PET WASN'T QUIET

Helen's words sting. I wipe espresso out of my eyes as she glowers at me with wide blue eyes. Cassia might fear her brothers, but Helen understands we're all weak with women. It's the curse of having a Yiayia like the one we have. A sadistic grandmother more likely to give you tea laced with arsenic than milk and cookies on Sunday afternoon.

"I have raped no one," I growl.

Helen's cheeks darken.

"We all heard the sounds. Your *pet* wasn't quiet."

"I need your help with her, Helen. The girl needs clothing."

Helen turns her nose up and continues pushing onions around her skillet, only dignifying me with the corner of her eye. Antonio squeezes his girl's hand and interrupts us.

"Aunty, Uncle... this is my... friend. Angelica."

"It's Maria."

We all wince. Helen purses her lips together and mutters something in Greek under her breath. Antonio sidles up to her and tries to sweet talk her. He's just like his father, Loukas: convinced that he's several times more of a charmer than he really is.

"Aunt Helen, may I have some for Maria."

"Sit at the counter. Wine or coffee?" Helen barks at the girl in Greek. Maria glances at Antonio, bewildered.

"She's a tourist. She doesn't speak the language."

Helen snorts and presses the espresso machine, sliding the girl a shot of espresso without making eye contact. Antonio repays her kindness by handing Helen a cigarette. She puffs peacefully as she fills our plates with food. When Helen hands me the plate for Fallon, she shoots her signature death glare in my direction, her heavy Greek brows giving her face a truly terrifying appearance for such a small woman.

"Rape the girl and I'll cut your cock off myself. She doesn't belong in our world. You should send her somewhere else."

My stomach knots.

"I plan to resell her."

Helen raises an eyebrow.

"To whom?"

"Someone old who can't get his cock up."

Helen clicks her teeth and lets go of the plate.

"Get out of my kitchen before I throw more espresso on your shirt," Helen snaps.

I leave the kitchen as Loukas drags his feet in, hungover from the night before and grumbling to himself. My forty-year-old brother barely acknowledges my greeting. I trot upstairs and balance plates on my forearm as I unlock the door to my suite. My first thought is that Fallon has escaped.

Where the bloody hell is she?

Then I hear her on the other side of the bed. I set the plates down on my side table and murmur, "Fallon?"

She doesn't respond. Damn it... What the hell is she doing back there?

I round the corner of the four-poster bed and she's lying on my rug, whimpering. Fuck. Why does she have this effect on me? I hear my mother's voice behind me clear as if she were really there. *She's there because you want her, Stavros. You like her.*

I saved her because once in a while, you have to save someone. I crouch next to her and she lifts her head gently. Fallon stares straight through me and rests her head on my floor again.

"Get up."

In my imagination, my voice sounds harsh. In reality, I sound apologetic. She sniffles and sits up.

"What do you want?"

"My sister made us breakfast. I thought we could sit on the balcony and enjoy it. There's a view of the Aegean."

"I'm not hungry."

"I don't care if you're hungry," I growl, "I won't have you starving to death."

She stands up and averts her gaze.

"Yes, Stavros."

I'm suspicious of her sudden submissiveness. This is the same woman who wanted to smother me in my sleep. I convince myself that it's all an act — and a clever one. I toss her the key. She parts the curtains and unlocks the sliding doors.

"Were you on the floor the entire time?" I growl, sudden guilt wracking through me.

"Why don't you check your cameras?" She snipes, floating onto the balcony. She leans over the railing, her long hair whipping behind her as a strong breeze blows salty sea air over both of us.

"I have no cameras."

"Khalid had cameras."

"I'm not Khalid."

"Right."

She sits down at the table as I set our dishes down. Her lips moisten. She might claim she's not hungry, but the light behind her eyes tells me she's plenty grateful for something to eat right now.

"Eat," I command.

She gingerly dips the tip of her fork into breakfast and brings it to her mouth. I don't touch my food because I'm watching her. Mesmerized. Enchanted. I've never seen a woman with such beautiful lips. Her skin glows in the early morning sun. My first night with her and I nearly gave in to my darker urges. I nearly fucked her. Helen would have been right if she lobbed her accusation at me. *Dirty rapist. That's what I'll be if I lay hands on her.*

But I don't know how many more nights I can spend next to Fallon's body and not want her. Once I'm satisfied she has enough in her, I take some to my lips. Fuck, I missed Helen's cooking.

"So. You were a nurse."

"Yup. I was training to become a psychiatric nurse. I worked on a psych ward."

I give her a look.

"There's nothing scary about a psych ward," Fallon snickers, misinterpreting my reaction.

"I never said there was."

"Most men freak out. They think I have... you know... mental problems."

Like hearing voices. And knowing killing makes it worse, but not being able to stop.

"Do you?" I ask, struggling to remain casual.

"Have mental problems?"

"Do you?" She snaps back.

"Hm. By your account, I must. I purchase women."

"By my count, only two. And one was your sister," she says, "And you've kept me fed, which is more than Khalid can say."

"Eh? He didn't feed you?"

"He drugged the food and thought I would be too dumb to notice."

Fuck. I feel like such a fucking bastard half the time we talk to each other. But I don't want to stop talking. I don't care if she hates me, I have to know everything about Fallon. I need to know about her.

"My sister will take you into town this afternoon. For dresses."

"I don't have any money."

I wave her off.

"Money? What do you need money for?"

She tries to hide that whatever I've said is making her smile. I put my finger beneath her chin and ask, "What?"

"It's ironic," she mumbles, "The first guy to get me clothing, and it's my kidnapper."

"Not kidnapper," I remind her.

She rolls her eyes and jerks her chin away from my forefinger.

"You know what I mean," says Fallon, staring out over the ocean. A piercing woman's shriek comes from downstairs. My first instinct is ignoring it. Greek families are loud. Always. There's another shriek. Damn it. I rise from the table and run to the door.

THIRTEEN
SEW HER SHUT

I grab my gun before I kick my door open. Bright sunlight rushes in, nearly blinding me. Fallon rushes to the door behind me and peers around my body. I hear the scream again, coming from the kitchen. Fuck's sake. I leave these people alone for five minutes and this happens. I run downstairs and because I didn't tell her to stay put, Fallon follows. I nearly slip on the pool deck as I race into the kitchen.

Gal has Antonio's girlfriend Maria bent over the counter and he's forcing her underwear off as she screams. Everyone else must be eating in their suite.

"Damn it, Gal, get your hands off her."

"I didn't do anything! She's lying!" He protests, leaping off her and putting his hands up like there's a chance in hell he's innocent.

The girl scrambles to get her knickers back up as Gal reddens. I don't care about the girl. I care about what the hell is going through my little brother's mind to have him holding a girl down in his family kitchen so he can rape her.

"Don't lie to me."

"I swear! It was a misunderstanding."

I draw my gun.

"Where should I shoot you, eh? Your feet? Your cock?"

Gal shrieks like a baby left out in the sun.

"Leave me alone! I didn't hurt her!"

My gun isn't loaded, which Fallon knows, but Galanos, thankfully, doesn't.

"What would possess you to rape your nephew's girlfriend, eh?"

"I wasn't going to rape her," Galanos snipes, "And you're one to talk with a slave standing behind you."

Gal storms out of the kitchen. Fuck. There is something seriously lacking in the moral fiber of this family... I hear Yiayia greeting him outside.

"Good morning, Yiayia."

I hear him kiss both her cheeks. Great. The last person I need to see right now is Yiayia. She wanders into the kitchen, grey hair pinned back in a brown clip so the sun can hit her face directly. Yiayia never smiles.

"Stavros."

She doesn't acknowledge Fallon. I greet Yiayia and kiss both her cheeks.

"Helen's breakfast tasted like shit. Hand me a cigarette."

I give my grandmother a cigarette and light it for her.

"What was all this commotion about?"

"Gal had a girl. She wasn't exactly... willing."

YiaYia chuckles.

"He's a scamp. The poor girl was probably asking for it. I've seen how these young women dress nowadays. Fix your collar, Stavros. You look homeless."

I adjust my collar. I don't know how Papa survived a mother like her. I suppose it makes sense, how he ended up with a mother like mine...

"Are we leaving tomorrow?" I ask Yiayia, changing the subject.

"Yes. We have a shipment of 200 rifles to deliver to the Israeli on this trip. We have to go together to establish the deal and... deliver your sister."

"Father has a suitor for her, then?"

"Yes. And he's willing to pay handsomely for her virginity. We need the alliance and we need your sister to remain a virgin for a little while longer."

I scoff. Yiayia rubs my shoulder.

"You're a good man, Stavros. If you hadn't killed Arturo, she would have spread herself like a slut for him. Unacceptable behavior for a Pagonis."

I guide Fallon to a stool at the kitchen counter — a few stools down from Yiayia. She sits and Yiayia still doesn't acknowledge her.

"Have you heard?" says Yiayia casually as she moves onto her second cigarette, "Matilda found out that Loukas' latest fiancé went missing too. She doesn't have long for this world, poor lamb."

"Fucking hell. He normally waits before he kills them."

"Yes," Yiayia mutters, "just like a Pagonis to be jealous. He still claims he's not the one doing it, but who else has motivation? He's in his forties and he can't settle down. He isn't a good father."

"Loukas loves those children."

I have no wish to disrespect Yiayia, but the only person she hates more than society in general, is Loukas.

Yiayia scoffs.

"Love has nothing to do with the fact that Carlotta is a buffoon and her brother Antonio. Well, he's effeminate, but at least his girl-friends don't end up dead."

"Carlotta liked the one before Matilda."

"Still no replacement for her mother," Yiayia says, "Loukas made a mistake ending her life."

"No."

"Yes. It's a pity her father is a monster. Speaking of monsters. Is it true you're hearing voices again?"

Fallon's back straightens, and I lie to Yiayia.

"No. It only happened once. Many years ago. We have nothing to worry about."

"Good. I need you tonight before we leave. Cassia has another distraction. This one she thinks is a secret."

Yiayia's eyes light up at the idea of discovering one of her grandchildren's secrets.

"Already?"

Yiayia smiles, "She's a Pagonis woman."

I pour my grandmother some espresso and drag a stool across from her. Fallon sits quietly with her hands in her lap, pretending she isn't listening. She's smart to stay quiet around Yiayia. She's probably smarter than I think.

My grandmother continues, "It's easy to attract multiple suitors, and the poor girl has a broken heart over the unfortunate incident with Arturo."

"All I need is a name, Yiayia."

"€50,000 to your account for the job. Fair enough?"

"Yes."

"Good. Bring me his driver's license at the docks tomorrow. Sandros Demopoulos."

"The baker's son? He's only twenty."

"Yes. Old enough to know better than to look at a Pagonis girl."

"Yiayia—

She takes my hand and stabs her lit cigarette into the top of it. I wince, but I don't dare make a sound. She has dotted my hand and forearm with scars from her cigarettes. I know better than to question my grandmother. At least I ought to, according to the scars on my hand. She pulls the cigarette away.

"I will do it."

"Good. And take your negro girl with you. I don't like the sight of black skin in the morning."

Fallon rises from her stool and as she walks past Yiayia to rejoin me, she makes a simple mistake. I can't blame her for the mistake entirely, but she doesn't realize that my grandmother isn't a frail old woman. She's been in the mafia longer than any of us. Helen told me one night when Yiayia got drunk, she confessed her story. Raped and married off at thirteen, she killed her first husband before old man Pagonis rescued and married her. She breathes savagery.

Fallon mutters "bitch" under her breath as she passes my grandmother. Yiayia grabs her forearm and Fallon learns that my grandmother's strong when she can't wrest her arm away from her.

"What did you call me, girl?"

"I called you a bitch," Fallon snaps, but she still can't pull herself away from my grandmother.

Yiayia's brow darkens, "Why haven't you raped this one into submission yet?"

"Yiayia," I answer through gritted teeth, "She's traumatized. Let her go."

My hand continues to pulse painfully from where she put out her cigarette. I don't know how my grandmother expects me to aim at a twenty-year-old man with a pistol if I can barely hold it up.

"Traumatized," Yiayia scoffs with disapproval dripping from her voice "She's a slave. A woman. If she's in this predicament, the men in her life failed her. Now, girl. I need you to understand your place in this house."

"Let go of me," Fallon grunts, trying to pull her hand away unsuccessfully. I put my hand on Fallon's shoulder, hoping she gets my hint and apologizes. Family respects family. I will not defy my grandmother. Without her, none of us would be here. She reminds us all daily.

My grandmother takes the espresso I made for her and throws it onto the tiles.

"Lick it up."

"W-what?" Fallon protests, "I'm not doing that!"

Yiayia slaps her. Hard. Fallon screams. Yiayia uses the moment of distraction to grab her hair and slam her head against the counter.

Fallon screams again. I yell at Yiayia and tell her to drop Fallon because I can't worry about a cigarette burn on my arm.

"Lick. It. Up," Yiayia growls, "Now. Or you won't have a useless teddy bear like Stavros between your legs. I'll send my son. And believe me, he'll breed your useless cunt until you're bruised."

She lets go of Fallon's hair, satisfied that she can have the compliance she craves. Fallon's shaking, but she falls to the floor and presses her tongue to the tiles. Satisfied, Yiayia turns her attention to me.

"Stavros," she snarls, "Raise your voice in my direction again and I will sew her shut. Don't think I've forgotten the way you defied me and your father. I only forgive you because we need your talents. But without obedience, this family will fall into chaos."

Fallon cries as she licks the espresso up, but she stands and looks Yiayia in the eye, unflinching despite her humiliation. Yiayia smiles at her with a soft expression that belies her psychopathic nature. My grandmother presents her hand for a kiss and Fallon kisses it.

"Good girl," Yiayia says, "we will have no hard feelings between us. Now get out."

I put my arm around Fallon and lead her out of the kitchen and back upstairs. Once we're in my suite and I shut the door, Fallon turns around and pushes me against the door. Hard.

"WHY DON'T YOU JUST KILL ME," she yells.

She pulls my unloaded gun out of the holster and yells, "Load the gun and kill me! Just fucking do it!"

I'm ashamed about what happened, but she doesn't know how fucking close she came to death. I won't ever hurt Fallon, but I can't speak for everyone in my family.

She doesn't understand how dangerous these people are.

"Do it," she hisses. "Be a man and kill me instead of subjecting me to this humiliation."

FOURTEEN
SANDROS

"Stop it, Fallon," I growl.

She takes the gun and hurls it at my glass sliding door. It bounces right off. We sell guns. Our glass is bulletproof.

"I hate you!" She screams.

"I don't care. You're coming with me, anyway. I have work to do."

I stride over to her and she positions her arms like she's doing some Cartoon Network version of kung-fu.

"Is it true?" Asks Fallon, while bouncing around like a professional boxer, "you hear voices?"

"Right now, I only hear one voice..." I grumble.

I'm trying to stop her from asking questions, but the statement is true. Whenever Fallon's around, I never hear other voices. Only hers. She calms me in a way no one in my family ever has. Fallon makes me quiet.

"Don't come near me," she hisses.

"We're leaving."

"Not until you answer my questions."

I lunge for her and she screams.

"AHHHHHHH! Put me down you behemoth!"

I don't know what the word means, but it doesn't matter. I duck as I carry her out the door and toward the white Jeep Wrangler parked on the pavement below. Cassia laughs from the balcony as she gazes at me, dragging Fallon into my car in the courtyard, screaming the entire way. She calls me an idiot in Greek.

"HELP ME! IF ANY OF YOU HAVE A HEART, YOU'LL HELP ME!"

Unfortunately for Fallon, no Pagonis gets born with a heart. The ones born with a heart have the heart crushed out of them early. Once she's buckled into the passenger seat and realizes someone shot out the lock and door handle from inside the passenger's side of the Jeep, she quiets down. I get into the driver's side and she stares coolly ahead, not deigning me with acknowledgment.

"I need to find Sandros. You'll stay in the car."

She scowls and acts like she can continue ignoring me. It won't work.

"You will answer me."

"Eat shit and die, asshole."

Half the time Fallon speaks, I think she's talking another language.

"I apologize for my grandmother."

"She's a bitch," Fallon snaps and gazes at me expectantly like she thinks I'll disagree with her.

"Bitch is a pleasant word to describe my grandmother."

"She's a stupid bitch."

I click my teeth.

"Unfortunately for all of us, Yiayia isn't stupid."

I pull into the alleyway behind the bakery. I won't kill the kid here behind his family's place of business. I don't want them coming here years from now, every time they take out the trash, and thinking of Sandros' body. Yiayia would say I'm soft. But I've learned that I don't have to listen to her as long as I'm willing to get a nice round burn. Fallon reaches for my hand and surprises me so much, I jerk away.

"She burned you."

"Yes."

I park the car and lean back. I only need to lure the kid. This part should be easy. I'm a Pagonis and we own these streets. People here cower in fear and respect. Without us, justice in Thessaloniki would be a matter for the police. For three generations, it's become a matter for the Pagonis. We keep the streets free from crime but power comes with a price and in this town, the people pay by kissing the ring of every Pagonis they come across. We're feared and beloved.

"Are you really going to go... you know... whack someone?"

"Whack? No. I'm going to shoot him."

She rolls her eyes.

"You know what I mean. Like in mafia movies... when they kill someone."

"I don't know about these movies."

"Don't look at me like that. You're the weirdo who shoots people," she grumbles.

I sigh and tell her she's a very strange girl before I push hair away from my brow. It's hot out and I'm sweating.

"You're not killing him here, are you?"

"No. I'm bringing him to the Jeep. He'll come willingly. Don't say a word to him. I'm serious. One word, and I'll have to kill you too."

Fallon bites down on her lower lip.

"Nod if you understand," I tell her. She nods. Good. All I have to do now is trust that she won't break her word. My hopes are not high.

I leave Fallon with the keys to the Jeep. She's too scared to run away. I expect her to make another failed escape attempt eventually, but something about my line of work has piqued her curiosity. I don't know what it says about her that she's attracted to the darker things.

When I push the door open to the bakery, the boy's mother and father regard me with terror at first. I approach the counter and greet them politely. They exchange glances and greet me in exchange. The father, a fat old man with a handlebar mustache, approaches the counter.

"Mister Pagonis, is there anything I can do to help? A little something extra for your Yiayia."

Thessaloniki's worst kept secret is that while my father heads the family as the official patriarch, my grandmother calls the shots.

"I want to speak to Sandros. I have a job for him to do."

The mother takes the prayer beads around her neck to her lips, so smoothly that I nearly don't notice.

"Sandros is not here right now," the father tells me.

We both fall silent as boots fall against the hardwood upstairs. I smirk. We both know the old man was lying.

"I know your son is a good lad with a big heart. I will not involve him in dirty work."

"I will get him."

The father lowers his head demurely. It feels good to have people submit to you. Power doesn't corrupt, it intoxicates. Power turns you into an addict and the high is just good enough that you can ignore the shame. I'm a liar. A murderer. A criminal. Sandros bounds downstairs behind his father with reddened cheeks. His father puts his hand on his son's shoulders, but Sandros brushes him off. He wouldn't treat his father like this if he knew... this is the last time he's going to see the old man alive.

"Please bring our son home safe," his mother pleads. Sandros turns to her and snaps at her for being embarrassing and sentimental. Men always think of their mothers as embarrassing and sentimental. But mother's instincts possess more wisdom than we realize, and what his mother really is? Correct. She senses what's happening to him. She smells his pending death.

Sandros has hair the color of sand and deeply tanned skin.

"My father says you have a job for me? Anything will be better than kneading bread all day like a peasant."

"Yes," I tell him, "I have some fishing nets I need help with. I go onto the sea with my boat and I get myself in such trouble. You and your father fish together, yes?"

"Yes."

He suspects nothing.

"Come with me, then."

He hesitates in the bakery door. This is it, his one chance to turn tail and save his own skin. I let him linger because I don't want to kill this boy. I don't want to kill him before his life begins.

"Your brother Loukas doesn't fish? He's always on his boat."

"Loukas is with his daughter. You know Carlotta?"

Sandros stammers that he doesn't know her well, and he ignores his instincts, marching confidently behind me toward his death. I don't know how I'll do it yet. I don't like shooting young men. His mother will see the wound and she'll know. If he drowns, at least he'll be presentable for the funeral unless they find him after the fish eat his eyes.

His shoulders relax once he sees Fallon in the front seat.

"The black girl... is she yours?"

I open the backseat for my unsuspecting prey.

"Yes," I tell him, "She's mine."

FIFTEEN
MY CONSCIENCE

Fallon flashes me a look that says you should feel guilty for this. Fallon's judgments are the least of my worries. I can hear them. Sometimes I'm muttering what they're saying to me out loud, but with Fallon and the kid in the car, my best bet of getting this job done and managing Fallon is staying fucking quiet. I'm bringing her — and the kid — to the docks.

Sandros leans forward between our seats and grins at Fallon, speaking about her as if she's invisible.

"Galanos bragged at school about you. He said nobody got more pussy than Stavros. I didn't know you had jungle fever."

He laughs at his awkward, racist joke. Maybe this will make Fallon less sympathetic to him.

Fallon's cheeks grow red and I press my finger to my lips. She squirms uncomfortably. I don't know why I'm bringing her along. I ought to lock her in my bedroom. But she's attracted Yiayia's attention, and I still remember my childhood puppy. I park at the docks and the kid rushes out of the car. Everyone in the city knows which boat belongs to me. He laughs.

"Stavros! Such a fucking bad ass! If you ever need me to help you with the nets again, call me!"

He runs onto the ship, leaving Fallon alone with me for a moment. Great. I know what to expect from Fallon. She'll use her womanly wiles to convince me not to kill this boy. It won't work.

"He's just a kid," she hisses.

"He's trying to fuck my sister."

"So? No offense, Stavros. Your sister doesn't seem like a virgin."

I growl at her, "Watch your mouth, Fallon."

"I don't care if you threaten me," she hisses, "I want you to kill me. The quicker the better."

I can't tell if it's reverse psychology or if Yiayia's abuse made her legitimately suicidal. Fallon won't be the first Yiayia pushed over the edge. Helen's convinced Yiayia gave her an eating disorder during high school. I'm surprised Helen remembers high school since she was drunk most of the time.

Galanos and Loukas have their own litany of complaints about her. What's the point? She'll be with us until the end of her life and there's no point fighting that.

"I will put you in my quarters below deck. You stay down there until I come get you."

"Are you going to shoot him?"

There's real panic in her voice and that twinge of guilt returns. Fuck, why does she make me feel guilty for my life and the things I've always done? Why do I care what she thinks?

I can hear Sandros' boots clomping on the deck. He doesn't care that we're lingering suspiciously long because he'll get to brag to all the boys back home about helping Stavros Pagonis untangle his nets. He's probably already planning the ways he'll embellish the story.

"I won't shoot him and it's none of your business. You aren't an accomplice."

"Right. I'm your sex slave. Sorry, I should know my place," she snaps.

"Sarcasm won't get you anywhere," I snarl, "Now move."

She stomps up the stairs like a toddler having a tantrum. I don't care if she gets snippy with me. Everyone in this town knows not to mess with a Pagonis. It doesn't matter if Fallon thinks Sandros is innocent. The moment he flirted with my sister, he gave up his right to life.

Fallon gets to the deck and I hear her say to Sandros, "Hey kid!"

He looks at her and makes mocking kissing sounds. Fallon rolls her eyes. I put my hand on my weapon. I swear if she warns him...

Instead of warning him, she only tells him, "If you help him catch a big fish, there might be a kiss in it for you. You ever kissed a girl before?"

He's twenty. Of course he's kissed a girl. Sandros turns red and looks away from her. My voice booms across the water.

"Come on, Sandros. Surely you've kissed a girl before?"

He shakes his head, clearly humiliated. Fallon bounds over to him and grabs his cheeks. Kissing him. Hard. Is she trying to piss me the fuck off? I want to pull her off him. How dare Fallon kiss this scrawny little loser? She's mine. Mine. Damn it. She pulls away and winks at me before turning to face Sandros again, his face in her hands, her gaze meeting his.

"There. Now you've kissed a girl."

She storms past me and stomps downstairs, closing herself into my quarters. My stomach turns. If this boy presented such a threat to Cassia's virginity, how could he have never kissed a girl before? This isn't right. Fallon knows it isn't right, and from the moment this blond boy got into my car, I knew it wasn't right too. The voices tell me everything I would be if I killed him. Baby killer. Murderer. Psychopath. You deserve death, Stavros. It's all you deserve.

The voices are getting louder. Probably because it's been several hours since I've had a drink. Drinking helps. But drinking hurts as much as it helps. I hate the sluggish movement in my abdomen when I drink, my spinning head, the way I want to fuck and hurt every woman I'm attracted to. If I wasn't drunk, I wouldn't have bought Fallon.

Sandros starts the boat and I steer her away from the dock and into the vast Aegean. Sandros comes over to the steering and asks, "Mister Pagonis, where do you have those nets?"

I'm ten years older than Fallon and sixteen years older than the boy standing to my left. Fallon was his first kiss. She'll be his only kiss if I kill him. I have to kill him. She doesn't understand.

But... he's an innocent, isn't he? Somehow, Cassia might have herself a boy who truly loves her. A boy who waits until kissing her. A boy who thinks my little sister is special. My stomach sinks.

"The nets are below deck. What's the rush, eh? Let's enjoy a drink."

"I can steer, Mister Pagonis. Thank you for taking me out. It would mean a lot to my parents if I could bring home extra money."

I purse my lips and turn away from him. From the moment I postponed working on the nets, he became suspicious. He sensed something wrong from the very beginning and now that survival instinct crystallizes in his gut and he's realizing that there's no way he can run from this if I mean to kill him. Which I do.

I head over to the bar. It's not well stocked. A few half-finished bottles of hard liquor and a freezer with ice and soda water. I pour the boy a glass of whiskey with 3.5 mg of Klonopin and 5.5 mg of Tramadol. He'll fall into a deep sleep and I'll strangle him without the struggle or the guilt. Who am I kidding, I'll still feel guilty. I give Sandros the drink and hold mine up.

"A toast, to the beauty of Thessaloniki and to my sister, Cassia."

We drink. Once he finishes a few sips, Sandros sighs with satisfaction before repeating.

"Cassia?"

"Yes. You are acquainted with my sister?"

"Not closely."

I hear Fallon's footsteps on the stairs. Fuck. She's armed.

"Put the gun down, Stavros."

"I'm not armed," I snarl at her. But I put my hands up. Sandros, like a good but completely idiotic Greek man, finishes his drink before raising his hands and the glass over his head. He's already feeling the effects of the drugs.

Sandros stumbles over, leaning on the chair. He falls onto the ground — unconscious. Fallon's distracted long enough that I can lunge for the gun. Unfortunately for me, this gun is armed. But I can't figure out how this fucking weasel found it because it wasn't in my quarters. Damn it... I should have known her stupid heart was too sensitive.

Unlike the boy, I haven't had nearly enough to drink and along with Fallon's voice, I hear others. What is she saying? She's yelling. She wants me to do something.

"STAVROS. Focus on me. Focus on my voice."

"Shoot me, you stupid woman! You'll die out here!"

"STOP YELLING."

"Put the gun down!" I yell.

"No," she yells back, "Not until you tell me if he's dead yet."

"No, he isn't dead. But we need to make him vomit if we want him to live," I yell at her. *We don't have time to argue.*

"You were really going to do it," she gasps.

"Yes! I am a fucking assassin. Now can you put the fucking gun down or shoot me and get it over with."

She snickers, "It doesn't feel so good to be on the other end of it."

"No. It fucking doesn't. But I've handled worse demons than you, Fallon."

"Like who?" She says, sneering at me. This damned woman...

"Give me the gun."

"I don't even know how to use it," she sighs. "Fine. You win."

She hands the weapon to me and I accept it gingerly, grateful that the fucking thing doesn't misfire. I mutter a thousand curses under my breath.

She puts her hand on my shoulder, and I flinch. It isn't a good time for closeness.

"You were hearing voices," She whispers.

I nod.

"Don't you think it might be your conscience, Stavros?"

I snort and throw her hand off my shoulder.

"I don't have a fucking conscience, sweetheart."

She kneels next to Sandros and takes his pulse.

"What did you give him? His heart rate is slow."

"Tramadol and Klonopin."

She struggles to hide her disgust at me. Fallon opens the boy's mouth and sighs.

"What's going to happen when he wakes up? Will you shoot him anyway?"

SIXTEEN
MERCY

She sticks her finger down his throat before waiting for a response from me. She turns him over as he vomits, grunting as she struggles to shift the relatively large Greek man.

"Don't worry," she mutters sarcastically, "I don't need your help..."

Sandros coughs and more puke flies from his mouth. Fallon takes a towel off the deck and wipes his cheeks, checking his mouth before laying him on his back. She smells like sick, but given the compassion she shows Sandros, I can't help staring. She wipes her hands on the towel and throws it back onto the deck.

"We need to get him to a hospital. Now."

I might not shoot the boy in the head, but I don't dare bring him back to Thessaloniki. Fallon can't possibly understand what she's asking me to do.

"I'm not taking him back to shore."

"You drugged him!"

"You made him puke. If he wakes up in a couple hours... I'll figure out what to do with him then."

Fuck. It's easy to have a heart when you don't have to report to a Pagonis elder. If anyone in my family knows what I'm about to do, impressing some stupid American girl will be the least of my concerns.

"You're going to take him back to his parents."

"You aren't in a position to make demands."

"Fine. But I have a couple hours to change your mind."

"Get back below deck," I snarl.

"No way. I don't trust you not to throw him overboard."

Damn. I would have at least liked the option to throw the boy overboard. Sparing Sandros' life might cost his family more than his life. Fallon doesn't understand how ruthless my family is. I loathe her innocence. I want to crush it.

"Smart," I snarl, "But if I don't throw him overboard, I ought to throw you."

"You wouldn't dare," she hisses.

This woman tests my patience.

"I would enjoy throwing you overboard."

Fallon folds her arms and pops her hip out.

"You'd enjoy wasting €45,000?"

"It wouldn't be a waste," I snarl, "I'd enjoy watching you struggle."

I look down at the boy on the deck and feel the afternoon heat beating on my brow. I need a drink and time to think. I don't need Fallon chittering on in the background. I want her quiet. But now she isn't only quiet. She's properly scared.

"You're a monster," she hisses, crouching over Sandros' body, "And if you want to throw him overboard, you'll have to throw me too."

"Fine," I snarl, "But I'll start with you."

She darts away from me the moment I lunge and grab for her. She slips away just out of reach, but the deck is finite. Fallon screams as I wrap my arms around her waist. Then she elbows me. Hard. I groan as I double over and let go of her. She sprints away from me, climbs over the railing before I can say anything and plunges into the sea.

"FALLON!" I scream, rushing over to the railing and staring at the smooth blue sea below.

She can't just leap into the Aegean Sea. What on earth is going through that woman's mind!? Fuck. She hasn't breached the surface yet. I don't even know if she can swim. I yell her name again.

"FALLON!"

If I can see where she landed, I'll jump in after her. Next time I leave her in a room alone, I'll remember to lock the goddamned door. Her head pierces the surface and she gasps. She's treading water, but the sea is far too cold for her to last like this for long.

"Have you lost your goddamned mind, woman!?"

She gasps for breath and sinks under again. Holy fuck. She might be an okay swimmer, but if I don't get her out of there, she's going to drown. I throw her a rubber ring and tell her to grab on. She chokes out one word, "NO!"

"Are you crazy?! GRAB ONTO IT!"

"NO!"

Fuck. I have to go in after her. This insufferable woman will be the end of me. I take my shirt off. Then my pants. I dive in. She struggles as I wrap my arms around her waist, but she's weakened from the cold and like every Greek man on the coast, I'm a powerful swimmer. I pull her body against mine and squeeze her arms to her sides so she stops wriggling. I drag her to the stern where I have a few steps leading into the water for swimming close to the boat.

I toss her up the stairs and push her up. She coughs up a little water and gasps for breath on her back. I climb up the stairs and gasp for air, mostly because I'm cold and didn't intend to go for a swim. Thankfully, Sandros lies on the deck unperturbed. We would have been in deep shit if the little twerp woke up from his nap and found any of the seventeen loaded weapons stashed on my boat.

Fallon sits up and I snarl at her, "Are you fucking insane, woman?"

"I wouldn't be the first of my ancestors to escape slavery by jumping into the ocean."

She expects me to have some snappy remark, but I'm freezing my tits off and I want to dry off, not argue with Fallon over slavery. Plus, she's right. I'm morally bankrupt. When I don't respond, she adds nothing else. She doesn't stop staring at me. I lean back and shake the salt water out of my hair. The heat on my skin feels incredible.

"Enjoying the view, sweetheart?"

I shouldn't taunt her, but I can't help it.

"Shut up," she breathes, so softly I can barely hear her.

When I open my eyes again, she's standing — and trembling.

"I need to take this dress off. Please tell me you have towels."

"Below deck. Come, I'll show you."

"I can find them on my own."

"Yes. You could. Or you'd find another gun and ruin my afternoon more than you already have."

She walks downstairs, and I follow her. Her nipples stick out of the wet fabric and her hair sticks to her neck. I open the closet as I squeeze past her in the narrow hallway. This isn't one of the most luxurious Pagonis vessels since it's the one I use for... business.

I open the cupboard and hand her a magenta towel with pink hibiscus flowers on it. My niece, Carlotta, forgot the towel on the ship a few summers ago. Fallon wraps it around her body and peels the dress off her shoulders.

"Did you really think I'd let you drown in the fucking sea?"

"I had to know for sure where you stood," she says.

A test? This woman could have died just to test me. *Hmph.*

I grunt as she slides the dress off beneath the towel and it drops to the floor.

"You don't have to stare," she grumbles.

"Neither do you."

Our eyes meet. Fallon's are such a deep brown that I could get lost in them. I want to get lost in them and sink into a stupor that I never recover from. She bites her lower lip and my cock stiffens. Instantly.

"What are you going to do to Sandros?" She whispers.

"I don't know."

"Will you kill him?"

I want to do something to make her like me. Since saving her life did no good...

"No."

And like that, I've decided. It isn't my job to decide. It's my job to act. Killing is my job. Not listening to Fallon's whims or disobeying Yiayia's direct orders. We all need Cassia protected because if Cassia doesn't marry, we'll lose a client worth over £50,000,000.

An untamed Pagonis sex drive can't fuck up our family business. Yiayia enjoys reminding us we're necessary here.

"You've showed him mercy, then?"

"For now. But I can't take him back. He might wish himself dead when he wakes up."

She closes the distance between us, and her body is close enough to touch now.

"If you can show mercy, maybe you aren't as much of a monster as you think."

She tiptoes and kisses my cheek with soft and warm lips. As she sinks back to her heels, my throat tightens. I must have her. Now.

I don't care if she wants it anymore. I saved her life. I pulled her dripping body against mine. She pulled the heart out of me and... I can't stand it. I need to feel her softness. Her body. Her everything.

I need to hold Fallon. I can't stop myself this time...

SEVENTEEN

I WON'T TELL IF YOU WON'T

"You're playing a dangerous game, beloved."

My voice comes out like a growl. I know what's going to happen now. I have her trapped in this tight space, naked and utterly at my mercy. She's still soaking wet and now she can't get past me.

"Stavros," she whispers, "Please..."

"I've tried to hold myself back with you," I murmur, "I keep telling myself not to want you."

"You bought me for a reason, didn't you?"

"I didn't buy you to fuck you."

My cheeks darken. She makes me feel like a beast. I have animal urges I can hardly control around her. She sees my lust for her exposed and she loathes me and my filthy lust.

"Then why did you?"

"I can't help myself. I've always been the soft one."

"I doubt that."

I shrug, but I don't move to let her past.

"You gave yourself freely to me before."

She nods and steps back, pressing herself against a wall of the ship. She's terrified, even if I haven't moved and haven't touched her.

"I don't understand you," she says, which doesn't sound like a response to anything I've said. She's working out her own thoughts out loud and gazing up at me with the most troubling expression on her face.

"What don't you understand?"

"You're not like any rapist I've ever met."

"I'm not a rapist."

"No," she snaps, "I've thought about it. I can't be the first woman you've bought. You were too comfortable there. So there must have been others. I know you're a murderer. So, what happened to them?"

"I have never bought a woman before," I snarl, "And I'm no liar. I took you away from Khalid because... you were the most beautiful creature I'd ever seen. A creature too beautiful to cage. If I could let you go, I would. But you're marked. For life. I can't let you out there on the streets for Khalid's men to find. Because when they find you, your worst fears will come true, princess. Some grotesque Greek man a decade older than you will spread your legs and fuck you senseless."

"Is that how you see yourself?"

"What?"

My chest pulses with rage. She's convinced herself I'm a monster moments after I saved her bloody life. I could have let her drown. Now that she's standing here, naked and tempting me, exposing my monstrous urges and ogling the worst parts of me like I'm a curious fucking zoo animal, I want to slap her. Or kiss her. Or strangle her. Or make love to her. I'm only certain about one thing: Fallon fucks with my mind in ways no woman has.

"You aren't grotesque," she breathes.

I snort in response. She rolls her eyes, like she already finds my grumpiness banal.

Fallon continues, "I'm serious. It's... freaking me out. You expect a guy who bought you as a sex slave to be a total fucking nut job. But you're… fuck, I'm going to hell for saying this. You're hot."

"Hot?"

"Your body. Not your attitude."

A smirk tugs at the corners of my mouth.

"Luckily for you, you don't have to fuck my attitude."

"Shut up."

"Okay."

I close my mouth, but I can't stop staring at her. And I can't move out of the way. Fallon surprises me by leaping on me. She wraps her arms around my neck and she kisses me on the lips. At first, I think she's fucking crazy and then I realize what's happening. She presses her body against mine and her fingers run through my hair and she kisses me like she means it.

She pulls away from me, but I don't let her move too far away. I nestle her waist in my palm's firm grasp and growl, "No. You can't."

"I want to," she whispers, "I know it's crazy. And wrong. But I won't tell if you won't."

"There's a boy sleeping upstairs who could wake up any minute."

"Then you'll have to be quick."

Fuck. She's suggesting exactly what I want. And we're both nearly naked. My hands at her waist are the only things keeping her towel up. I have exactly what I want in my palms. I would be insane to say no to Fallon now. I want her. And she either wants me or she's letting me have her for her own selfish ends. I shouldn't care. Wanting Fallon isn't about my feelings for her.

"I'm not renowned for being quick," I tell her.

"Right," Fallon murmurs back, "You're known for giving orgasms to unsuspecting women and rejecting them once you're done."

"I didn't reject you. I stopped myself from hurting you."

"Why do you care if you hurt me?" She whispers, "You're a monster."

She grabs my cheeks and kisses me again, like she's trying to heal me with each one. I rub my nose in her neck and run my tongue along her collarbone. She gasps.

"Stavros," she murmurs, "Please... don't give me time to change my mind."

"I still don't want to hurt you," I growl.

My hands tighten around her towel. I'm ready to pull it away from her. I want her naked and impaled on my member. Urgently.

"You won't," she whispers, "I'm a big girl. I can handle myself."

I rip the towel away from Fallon's body. I can't resist her. Not when she's throwing herself at me like this. I'm only a man and not a strong one. Her towel falls to the ground and Fallon averts her gaze. No. I don't want her like this anymore. I don't want her body turned away from mine like I'm a monster fucking her like an object. That's not who I want to be with her.

"Fallon, look at me," I murmur.

She makes eye contact with me, and I pull her body closer to mine, firmly.

"Are you scared?"

I don't know if I'm ready to hear her answer, but it's an answer I need before I proceed. I don't want to hurt her. To rape her. To ruin her. I want her desire more than I could ever want her body.

EIGHTEEN

DAMSEL IN DISTRESS

Her voice is soft. And shy.

"Duh. Why wouldn't I fear you?"

"Because… I saved your life."

"Don't expect me to thank you," she snaps, "I'd prefer if you'd left me to drown."

I press her up against the wall, taking in every inch of her.

"That's not what I meant."

She cannot wriggle free.

"You didn't save me. You bought me."

"Yes. And you were expensive."

Her hands find resistance in my chest as she struggles to push me off. We've started something that neither of us knows how to stop, and Fallon is the only one with enough sense left to make a weak attempt to stop this assured train wreck from proceeding.

"You didn't save me," she hisses, "If I get out of this alive, I'll be the one to save myself. I'm not your damsel in distress."

I chuckle and tuck some of her dark hair behind her ear.

"You might be in distress, but you're anything but a damsel. I watched you touch yourself, remember?"

Her cheeks burn as I run my nose along her jawline and kiss her neck. She whimpers my name, pleading with me to pull back.

"Stavros..."

"I want you. And I don't want to hurt you. We both know I could have by now."

She wriggles hard, her stiff nipples grazing my chest and making self-control even more impossible.

"If you take too long, I'll come to my senses," she says, "Now hurry."

"I'm not forcing you."

"You aren't. You're... hot. I want you, Stavros."

Fuck. Hearing those words from her mouth makes me stiffen. I want her to wrap her lips around my cock. But Fallon is tender. And she's mine. For the first time since I took her off that auction block, she's submitting herself to me.

I rip the towel off and hoist her against the wall of the ship. I'm several inches taller than her and my body slams into the cabinet as I grunt like an animal and spread her legs.

Fallon squeals and digs her nails into my back, holding on for dear life as I fumble for room. I bend my head to her exposed nipples and let my tongue touch the hardened dark nub that has been screaming for my attention.

She cries out as my tongue touches her nipple. Loud. I've barely touched her, and she's already responsive. The men who have had Fallon before must have used her body like an object to masturbate into. They didn't treat her like a woman ought to be treated. My teeth sink around her nipple, but I don't bite down hard enough to hurt her, just hard enough to hold the tip between my teeth and rub my tongue along the hardened nub. Her breasts are so... textured. And firm. Fuck.

I make it a point not to fuck on the job, but thanks to her, there's no job anymore. It's too late. I listened to my conscience for far too long, and now I've passed the point of no return. I move my tongue to her other breast. Fallon whimpers and throws her head back. My arm wraps around her waist and her legs wrap around my torso, firmly intertwining us in a closeness I haven't known in years.

I could remind myself that she's only here because I bought her like chattel and she wouldn't choose to lie with me under any other circumstances, but I'm too hard to care. I spread her legs further apart, using my hand to touch the exposed apex of her thighs.

"You weren't wearing underwear with that dress?" I murmur.

"I will not wear the same thong three days in a row."

I chuckle.

"I'd like the smell of that. Three days of you…" I groan, "Fuck, that sounds perfect."

"Stop," she whispers.

"What is it, beloved? You changed your mind about my cock."

She flinches as I say the word cock. Fallon is no blushing virgin, so I assume it's my cock in particular she has a problem with. I'm a filthy hairy-chested Greek rapist, according to her. But hot enough to fuck at least once.

"It's not that," she whispers, "I just… I've only been with men who hate the smell."

"What kind of man hates the smell of cunt? We have a word for men like that here…"

"It's a word you probably shouldn't repeat," Fallon snaps.

I grab her cheeks and force her to look at me. Enough of her lip. I'm realizing it's what she does. She uses that smart ass mouth to deflect from anything emotional. Anything real. And it doesn't matter what she thinks of me, her body tells a different story. And what's happening between us is 100% real. I'm about to fuck her. To own her. To claim her.

"Look at me, beloved," I murmur, "Your cunt smells delicious and I bet it tastes even better. Come."

I pull her close to me — the come is rhetorical — and kiss her on the lips. Then, using all the maneuvering I can manage below deck, I sink to my knees and balance her legs over my shoulders so my face sits right between her thighs. I can smell it now, her damp cunt freshly coated with salt water from the Aegean. Thick, clear juices escape from her lower lips and coat both of them in fine evidence of her arousal. I want to punish her with my tongue. And please her.

Her hands grasp at tufts of my hair, forcefully. Women. They think men are impervious to pain sometimes. I wince as she tugs at my hair, but force her legs open wider. She gasps and nearly falls off my shoulders before I catch her ass in my palms and cup the thick cheeks that seem to spill out of her slender frame.

My tongue darts between her lips, and she makes a peculiar screeching noise. Fallon's had her chance to run and push me off. She knows how I've yearned after her cunt and I won't let her go with my tongue only sliding between her soft protruding lips. I slide my tongue over and between them again, clutching her ass firmly and driving the pink muscle over her clit. Fallon screams. This time, it's definitely a scream of pleasure. I can tell because she's nearly ripped off every fucking strand of hair on my head balancing herself. Her thighs tremble already.

My tongue dives between her pussy lips again and this time, I leave no part of her cunt untouched. Darting madly over her clit in smooth circles and then flattening over her outer lips, my tongue tastes every inch of Fallon's cunt. I was right. She's fucking delicious. I've never had a sweeter woman. Her grasp on my hair tightens as I focus my attention on her hardened nub and her moans increase in volume until she's nearly there. I run my tongue over the length of her pussy and dart over her asshole, making her cum. Hard.

Juices explode from her tight center and dribble down her thighs. She gasps and scrambles off me. I pull my face away from her and let her free. I'm not worried. She won't be headed far...

I run my tongue over my lips, licking her juices away and she wrinkles her nose.

"Seriously? You're going to lick me off..."

"Delicious."

"That... was incredible."

"Better than touching yourself?"

"Shut up, Stavros."

"It's a simple question."

"You are so damn stubborn," she grumbles. "I can see why you're single."

"I've been waiting for a desirable girl to walk onto an auction block."

"That isn't as funny as you think it is," she snaps.

She thinks I'm stubborn. I like that. Maybe she'll try to tame me. *Hm.* That would be nice.

NINETEEN
I FIRE MY GUN

"Spread your legs, beloved. I'm ready to have your cunt."

Fallon smirks at me.

"No."

"I'm hard. I need your cunt."

I hear footsteps upstairs. *There can only be one person.* No, Stavros. Focus on the moment at hand. She's here. Ready. The boy will stumble around for a few more minutes before you need to leave her here.

I'm unbuckling my pants and Fallon laughs. She pushes her hand against her chest and... she laughs at me. My cheeks don't darken because I find her rejection humiliating, but because I'm not in on the joke.

"You already had my 'cunt' as you so crudely put it. Now get dressed. I only wanted to buy time to make sure Sandros woke up. And... he's awake."

I scowl. I want to turn her over my lap and spank her silly. I don't. I'm not that much of a caveman, but I hate that she's won.

My cheeks burn. But I can't take my eyes off her beautiful naked body, and I can't make myself loathe her as much as I wish I could.

My thick Greek eyebrows furrow into a bushy unibrow as I scowl at her.

"You tricked me."

"No... I bought time..."

She has her towel wrapped around her body again, obscuring her beautiful physical frame from view.

She continues with a repulsed sneer on her face, "You underestimated me and this is what you get for underestimating me."

I grab her forearm and her other hand darts up to her towel.

"What?" She snarls as I raise her arm, holding her in place until I decide what to do to her and how I'm going to punish her. I need to decide whether it's worth my honor as a man to have her, if my cock is hard enough to eat away at what little morality I have left.

"Are you finally going to do it?" She snaps, "Is that all it took to break you? Bruising your pathetic fucking ego?"

She pushes me off. And I let her go. Because I'm embarrassed. I made myself think she liked me. I made myself think I had a chance with her. A real chance. Where she wanted me. Fallon will always see me as a monster. Sparing that kid's life won't make her want me anymore. I unlock the safe behind the stack of towels and grab a spare loaded pistol. Fallon has Sandros awake in her arms. He's still weak, and he doesn't understand what happened. He assumes that he's had too much to drink.

I point the gun at him when I hear Barbara's voice. One voice is an old Italian woman. I tell myself she's my subconscious mind's version of my mother. Barbara has a smooth voice and a Northern accent — too rough and Balkan for my grandmother's company. You only want to kill him because he kissed her. And she wanted it. The muttering priest returns. He asks me for forgiveness. Or am I asking him? Fuck. When did pointing a gun at a fucking kid get so fucking hard?

"Get the fuck away from him!" I roar.

Fallon might be bold, but she's not stupid. I'm pointing a gun and this time, she knows it's loaded. She stumbles back toward the railing and glances over her shoulder. She won't be so willing to jump in again now that she knows how cold the water is.

"Mister Pagonis!" the boy stutters and cries. He's quickly understanding what's about to happen, "Mister Pagonis, forgiveness. Please... Mr. Pagonis. Think about my parents... They need help."

"STAND UP!" I tell him, "TAKE YOUR FUCKING BULLETS LIKE A MAN."

He soils himself as he weakly rises to his feet. Fuck. This is exactly what I wanted to drug the lad, to give him a dignified death where he isn't covered in piss and shit. He would have had a better death than most of us. Whether it's cancer, old age, or the wrong end of some crazy motherfucker's pistol, death takes everything, especially our dignity.

Sandros clasps his hands together like he's praying.

"Don't do this, Stavros!" Fallon yells, "Please!"

"You think you can play with my heart, woman? Eh?"

"I was not playing with your heart, you egotistical bastard."

"I don't have a fucking heart."

"So you're going to shoot a fucking kid to prove a point?"

"Yes."

I fire. Fallon screams. But I'm a better shot than she gives me credit for. The boy, unfortunately, has now shit himself too. But he's alive. Fallon screams again. This time, she's running for me.

"YOU BASTARD. YOU FUCKING BASTARD."

She wallops me. And then punches me. With punches like that, she'll hurt herself before she hurts me. I grab her wrists and stop her.

"Fallon. Stop."

She spits. On me. Jesus fucking Christ, this woman is testing me.

"BASTARD."

Sandros drops to his knees and prays in Greek. Fallon isn't finished with me.

"I HATE YOU," She screams, "I FUCKING HATE YOU."

I let go of her. My eyes bore into hers, but she reflects my anger with pure loathing. Loathing. It's not love, but she feels something for me. And I'm desperate enough to accept it.

"Then go below deck," I snarl, "And don't come out unless you want me to kill him."

"What are you going to do?"

"Give him a chance to survive."

It's stupid. Defying my grandmother's wishes won't end well. It never has for anyone. Sandros glances up at me with wet eyes, dragging his knees across the deck until he clutches my trousers.

"Mr. Pagonis... Mr. Pagonis, take me home. Whatever I have done to offend your family. Please... forgive me."

"Get up, boy. I can't take you home to your parents. My family wants you dead."

He stands weakly, again. He reeks of piss and shit. Unlike Fallon, he's used to the Aegean. I growl at him, "Now take your clothes off."

"Are you going to bugger me? For my freedom?"

"No, you idiot. You smell like piss. And your shit's all over the boat. Take a swim and throw the clothes into the sea. I want them washing up."

Sandros dutifully dives into the sea. I let him swim around for a bit and steer the boat in a circle around him as he cries out, "Don't leave me, Mr. Pagonis! Don't leave me to drown!"

I take the boat back to him and he climbs up, naked as the day he was born. He'll be reborn where I'm taking him. I toss him a towel which he wraps around his shoulders — to my dismay — and Sandros follows me to the wheel.

"You can't take me home," Sandros realizes aloud, glumly.

"No. I can't. My family wants you dead and nowhere on the coast is safe."

"Then where can I go? I have no money, no identification."

"Chorefto. You can spend the night and leave in the morning. I'll give you money. Take the bus to Athens and then leave. I don't care where you go. It will be better if you don't tell me."

"Yes, Mr. Pagonis."

"And cover your cock."

"Sorry, Mr. Pagonis."

We stand in silence for a while. I'm crafting an excuse for why this job is taking an extra four hours. Five if I'm not lucky.

"May I ask a question, Mr. Pagonis?"

"Go ahead, boy."

"Why?"

"Cassia. You touched my sister."

"But sir, I never touched her. I only have feelings for Cassia but she doesn't return them," he turns red, "She says I'm too inexperienced for her."

My throat tightens. Inexperienced? If my idiotic sister has allowed some man past her maidenhead, she'll have worse than an angry bunch of murderous older brothers to worry about.

"She said that, eh?"

"She wants her first time with a real man. But I never touched her."

"Sit down, boy."

He's making me weary. And worse, guilty.

❖

TWENTY
A LOST CAUSE

I know the woman at the guesthouse well. Angeliki Baros. Only a little older than me. She and my father had a... relationship. After our mother. She takes Sandros in and promises not to tell my father.

Angeliki asks, "How is that bitch of a grandmother of yours?"

Fallon hangs behind me, listening to my every word. I had to fight to get her to walk off the boat with me. She's furious at me. And scared about what I'll do next.

"Careful, Angie."

She scoffs.

"Believe me, I spent enough time around that bitch to walk around with a gun."

She lifts her skirt and exposes a gun strapped to a leather holster on her thigh. It's strange, seeing a woman with wrinkled skin and a firearm. Old women are not meant to fight their own wars. Yiayia always told me that.

"My grandmother speaks well of you."

It's a lie and we both know it. Angeliki scoffs.

"You were always the charmer, Stavros. Is this a girlfriend? Canadian?"

Fallon says nothing. I commanded her not to say a word, but by now Angeliki probably finds her rude or standoffish.

"She doesn't speak Greek," I tell Angeliki. She shrugs and responds in English, "Come on, she could at least try to say hello."

"She's only a friend."

Fallon waves and mutters hello. Sandros comes back downstairs with a cup of tea for Angeliki. She eyes him with scorn.

"This one ran afoul of your family? How big of a troublemaker is he?"

"It's my sister. They had a... relationship."

Sandros doesn't bother correcting me. Fighting for your life is usually enough to stop you wanting more unnecessary fighting. Angeliki takes the tea and sends Sandros to grab her mop bucket upstairs. I can't imagine what filthy guest house chores she has for him tonight. I give her money and give Sandros €500 to get the job done. He thanks me profusely. I doubt he's had more money at once. Too bad five-hundred Euros isn't enough to get him far.

Fallon says goodbye to him, giving him a big warm hug. My cheeks darken. I don't know if she's trying to make me jealous or if that's who I am now: a man who becomes pathetically jealous that the woman he's pining after thinks he's a monster. I know what Yiayia would tell me. I am the man. I should take what I want from her. She'll get used to it. My grandmother has strange ideas about life. Ideas that could get a normal person sent to prison.

We return to the boat and I pay the man at the dock €50 for watching the boat. It's a lot of money in a place like this. We set sail into the sunset. I'll be late to the family event. Fallon doesn't disappear beneath deck right away this time. I don't bother looking at her. She humiliated me. She used me. The worst part is I let her use me. I let myself believe Fallon Iverson could want me.

She leans over the railing next to me. I stare at the horizon and try to ignore her. But ignoring her means paying attention to other voices, and the voices aren't kind tonight. They want me dead. They want Sandros dead. The voices remind I'm a sick killer with a sicker mind. I want to shout at them and tell them to leave me alone. The only thing that stops me yelling at them is Fallon. They aren't real, I remind myself. If the voices were real, Fallon would hear them too. But she doesn't.

"You're quiet."

"Yes."

"I worked in a psych ward."

I don't answer her.

"You're hearing voices, Stavros. And it's getting worse. It took me a while to figure out, but it's true, isn't it?"

Her voice is so beautiful, which only makes her words hurt more. She knows I'm a freak. Dangerous.

"If I bother you, go downstairs. I'll find a man for you soon. One who won't try sleeping with you."

She moves closer to me. I keep staring out over the horizon. I don't want to run the ship manually on the way home. I'm not in a hurry.

"It doesn't bother me. But it bothers you. There's this funny twitch you do. And then..."

I never realized she was observing me this closely. Or that she cared. She probably doesn't. She's a nurse, right? This is just instinctive for her.

"I don't need you telling me I look mad."

"Have you talked to anyone about this?"

"I don't need to talk to anyone."

She folds her arms and pops her hip out.

"You're hearing voices. That's like textbook crazy person."

"I am not crazy," I snarl as I white knuckle grip my boat's railing. Tightly. She's like everyone else. She thinks that because I hear voices, I'm not in touch with reality. She wants an explanation for why I kill, and she wants that explanation to be my madness. I choose to kill. I don't choose these voices. They've been a part of me for over two decades now.

"I know," she snaps, "But you wouldn't listen to me otherwise."

"Is that what they taught you as a nurse?" I snarl, "Perhaps life as a whore will suit you better."

She slaps me across the face. Hard. I hold my cheek and glower at her, considering whether it's worth it to throw her overboard. It's dark outside, so this time if she goes overboard, she probably won't come back.

"Have you lost your mind?"

"No," she says, "But you've lost yours. Somewhere along the way. Have you ever considered that there might be a connection. Between the voices and you killing people?"

"I didn't kill that child, in case you forgot. You spared him. And if we aren't lucky, we'll get every one of his family members killed for your act of mercy."

She brushes off my comment and snaps back, "He's not the only person they've made you kill. What about the voices? What do they say to you?"

"It's none of your business. I'm not the type of man who seeks therapy from whores."

Fallon tries slapping me in the face again, but I'm ready for her this time and I grab her forearm and push her up against the railing, pinning her there with my torso.

"Scared, beloved? If I'm such a crazy fuck, what's stopping me from throwing you over the edge of this ship?"

"I'm not scared of you," she hisses.

I lean in, close enough to kiss her and close enough to take what I want from her.

"You should be," I sneer.

"I'm not. And you need help. Hearing voices is serious. You don't have to suffer."

I keep her pinned against the railing because I can and because despite her insistence that I don't scare her, I can feel her heart thumping like a giddy rabbit against the arm I have pressed to her chest. She doesn't want me to toss her overboard, and she senses that the thought has crossed my mind at least once.

"I deserve to suffer," I snarl, "Consider that."

"No one deserves to suffer," Fallon whispers, "Not even you."

I release her. She slips away from me, a few inches away from me, but close enough that I could grab her again if the need occurs to me. I wet my lips and my eyes snap to hers. No one deserves to suffer? Where the hell does she come up with this bullshit?

"Some people deserve to suffer," I assure her, "I'm one of them. Your humanitarian bullshit won't get you far now that Khalid's branded you."

"I can handle myself fine, thank you. And what you call humanitarian bullshit saved a teenager's life."

A dismissive grunt emerges from my lips, but it's not enough to get Fallon off my back. She takes my hand in hers and the action surprises me enough that I stumble backward.

What is she doing?

"You spared a life too," she whispers, "You're not a lost cause."

My phone rings before I can answer Fallon. I pick up the phone call because it's my grandmother. And she sounds impatient.

TWENTY-ONE
I AM NOT RACIST BELOVED

lock the door to my suite behind us. I bolt it and take my soaked shirt off, peeling apart one button at a time as Fallon sits on the foot of the bed and watches me. I know she's attracted to me. Now that's out in the open, she doesn't mind watching me undress. Closely. I toss my shirt into a pile of laundry.

Fallon's play at revenge might have won her a short-term victory, but I won't go to sleep with Fallon's insubordination hanging over me. With my shirt off and her gaze firmly fixed on me, I'm ready for her.

"Today was a tough day, yes?"

Fallon responds, "You did something good."

I snicker.

"You think that's your mission. Force me to have a conscience and then hope I'll let you go?"

"Yes."

"I spent time with my family tonight and stirred up a buyer for you. After tonight, you won't have to worry about warming my bed."

I smirk as her face falls. It's about time Fallon recognizes how good she has it here. I stalk over to the balcony doors and swing them open, letting the sea breeze into my villa.

"You're serious," she whispers.

"Oh, yes. I did not buy you to have extra trouble. I wanted to help you. If you don't wish to stay with me, I'll let you go. But you're marked. I have no choice but to send you to another man."

"Is he old?" She asks.

She wants to know if this older man will have a higher sex drive than mine.

"You'll find out in two days," I tell her plainly, "We're going to Ethiopia to meet clients. Your buyer will take you from there."

"Ethiopia!?"

"He's not black, if that's what you worried about."

"No, you racist ass. That's not what I'm worried about," she snaps.

I scoff.

"Racist? I am not racist, beloved."

"Don't call me that," she snaps.

"I'll call you whatever I want until I get rid of you. We'll both end up happier that way."

"Good."

My chest tightens. Hurting her doesn't feel as good as I thought it would. Humph. That softness won't get me anywhere. I've been soft with her. And she still thinks I'm a monster. A monster. Fuck, I hate that word. There's no word so immediately Hearing voices doesn't make me less than anyone else.

"Take your clothes off," I snarl.

I got her a dress when we returned. I needed to convince my family she'd helped me when killing Sandros became too bloody. They were all too drunk by the time we arrived to question my lies. Fallon wraps her arms around her body.

"No."

"Take them off. I'll have you now. I'm done with the games."

"Stop it, Stavros. You don't need to prove that you're a monster to me."

She stands up and her arms fall to her sides. Her breasts jut forward through the dress. She looks perfect. And I don't want to hurt her.

"Don't I? I'm not a man who shows mercy to others. I take what I want. And I keep denying myself with you, but no more. If I'm going to give you to another man, I'm testing the merchandise."

She grimaces, and her body tightens nervously as I draw closer to her. The word doesn't help her nerves.

"You have feelings," she insists, "Or you wouldn't let me get under your skin."

She smirks, like she's discovered something about me, and I touch her shoulders, my fingers sliding beneath the thin straps on her evening dress.

It's taking everything in my power not to bend her over and put my dick inside her. She's fucking gorgeous and yes, she gets under my skin. I've never met a woman who saw right through me before.

That's a type of magic that only she possesses. I can't indulge in this. I look away from her, even if it feels as foolish as gazing away from a once in a lifetime lunar eclipse.

"In two days, you'll have another man to fight off. Hm. I'll leave you to him," I murmur. "I won't ruin you for him."

Push her away, Stavros. Don't let this get out of control.

"You can try to rattle me, but you won't. I don't care what you do with me because by the time I stood on that podium, I was already dead."

"How did you end up there? There must have been warning signs. Red flags."

She bites her lip and looks away from me.

"It's stupid."

"Tell me."

"I answered an ad. I had this... social media profile. My friend got me into it. You go on dates with rich guys, spend the night, and they give you money. I had a $24,000 student loan and $3,000 in credit card debt. I missed my rent payment by $25. It should have been a trip to Las Vegas. She promised the website was legit. One long weekend with two of my homegirls who were meeting other guys. I didn't make it past the first night."

She gathers her strength to look straight at me as she finishes her story. "The last thing I remember was tequila and a blackjack table. That's it. Completely humiliating."

"You traveled to the city of sin to meet a strange man for money? Were you going to fuck him?"

I feel oddly possessive. I could kill this motherfucker, and I don't even know what he looks like.

Maybe it's a mistake to sell her. Maybe I like her too much.

Her story only makes me like her more. She's naive. She needs saving. And for what? Just money.

Yiayia likes to remind us that no Pagonis has ever known a want of money for the past 100 years. She intends to keep it that way. Every bastard child and every legitimate one gets money. We never let family suffer.

"I would have done anything to get debt collectors off my back," she says.

I try not to sound horrified. "You would sell your body?"

She's too good for that. Far too good for that.

"It's not my choice anymore, is it?"

I scowl at her.

"It's not my fault you are here. I've done what I can for you. If you won't stay with me, and if you find me too repulsive, I'll have to make you another man's ward. Where I'm going, I need a woman at my side who wants to be there."

"Tell me what he's like."

I dry swallow. Fallon doesn't want to know what he's like. In a drunken moment of frustration with her, I agreed to sell her to one of the most ruthless Sicilians I know. My first cousin on my mother's side. He's bought girls before. I don't know what happens to them in the end, but I know that most don't make it a year. Last year, he showed me a bite mark on his hand from a girl he bought at auction in Croatia.

"Don't worry," I lie to her, "If you don't want to go with him, you can always ask me to stay. You'll meet him soon enough."

"Fine."

"Since you have no plans to fuck me, I suggest you get into bed. I'm drunk and hard... and tomorrow we'll be on the boats all day. I need sleep."

"Good night, Stavros."

I grunt and flick the lights off. We settle into bed next to each other. She always sleeps with her arms at her sides beneath the covers. Sometimes, I don't think she's sleeping. Her breathing is shallow, like she's lying in wait, expecting me to press her into the bed in the middle of the night. She's ready to fight me off if she has to. I fall asleep for a few minutes and wake up to feel a little head jutting into my bicep.

"Fallon..." I groan, hoping she'll stop her wriggling once she hears my voice grumbling a fair warning.

I put my arm around her instead. She nuzzles close to me, resting her head on my chest. She mutters something in her sleep and then throws her leg over me, pinning me to the bed. What the fuck have I done. I've agreed to let her go, but I don't want to send Fallon away. I'm a better person when she's around.

For the first time in years, I don't think of myself as a monster.

TWENTY-TWO
PERVERTED DREAMS

awaken in the mid-morning to muffled sounds. I groan in response. Too early. And I'm nursing a hangover.

Mmppffjkddsahhh!!

The noise gets louder. The sounds are coming from beneath me.

"You're crushing me, you big idiot!"

Shit. There's a person underneath me. I'm so used to sleeping alone, I forgot about Fallon. Now I have her in my bed and she's stuck underneath me with blankets tangled between us. She makes a muffled squeaking noise again followed by, "Get off, you oaf!"

So much for our night of close cuddling. She kicks at me, hitting me somewhere in the shin. Ouch. I groan and move to the right, further entangling us in the sheets. She's more tangled up than I am.

"I'd get off if you stop kicking me…"

"GET OFF!"

She lands another kick, which is proving to be an unceremonious wake up. I roll off Fallon but pin her onto the bed with the blankets, wrapping her up in a cocoon of linen bedsheets. Fallon wriggles and grunts as she attempts to break free.

"Stavros! Let me go!"

"I don't think so. I enjoy watching you struggle."

"Don't you have anything better to do?"

"No."

"Ugh! You are insufferable."

It's tempting to keep her trapped and utterly at my mercy. I've just woken up and my morning problem stands at full attention. I'm thankful she hasn't noticed yet because this is the first time since I brought her home that Fallon acts like she isn't scared of me. She wriggles free from the blankets and sits up on her calves, legs splayed. Then she notices. She tosses me a pillow.

"Cover that thing up."

"Some good morning," I grumble.

"I'm not saying good morning to it. I don't want to say good morning to you."

I grin.

"Good morning. Has anyone ever told you that you're beautiful when you're cranky."

She ignores my attempt at flirting.

"Didn't you feel yourself crushing me?"

I shrug and tell her, "I was having an incredible dream about a beautiful woman."

She scowls and snaps back at me, "Keep your perverted dreams to yourself."

"I'd rather not," I tell her, "I'd rather act them out with a flesh and blood woman."

"You'll have to find another girl, then."

"I might. In Ethiopia. But first, I need to get rid of you."

Fallon's expression darkens as I remind her that our time together draws to a close. She's the one who wanted nothing to do with me.

"Come on, beloved. You need a shower."

Fallon squeaks, "Are you saying I smell bad?"

"Not bad. Ripe. It's... difficult."

She lifts her armpit and shoves it in my face.

"Does this turn you on?" She teases, coming just close enough that I can grab her. I hold on to her waist and she squeals as I toss her onto her back and position myself on top of her. I pin her arms over her head so I get a full inhalation of her overnight female musk in my nostrils. My erection strains through the grey sweatpants I wear to bed, and my animal brain has nearly taken full control.

Fallon pants and gazes at me, uncertain of what to expect next.

"You're impossible," I breathe, "What you do to me is impossible."

"Get off me, Stavros," she whispers.

But I've heard Fallon's voice when she's resisting me, and this voice isn't the same.

"I don't want to," I tell her.

"You have to," she insists, calmly.

"I have you here, pinned beneath me right where I can do whatever I want to you. Tease you. Kiss you. Fuck you."

"But you know it isn't right. You said it yourself, you're not a rapist."

My grip around her wrist tightens. My cock stiffens, and I yearn for her wetness wrapped around it. Fallon emits a pained moan as my grasp on her tightens.

"You want it," I growl, leaning in so my eyes lock with hers, "I sense it."

"It doesn't matter what I want," she whispers, "this is wrong. You're wrong."

I lean forward and kiss her. She accepts my kiss, pushing her tongue into my mouth as she closes her eyes. I don't want to stop kissing her. I don't want to stop until I've ravished her. But some piece of me makes me pull away. I let go of her wrists.

"I'm sorry."

She shakes her head.

"Don't apologize for kissing me. It's... sweet."

I roll off her and onto my back, shame and embarrassment coursing through me.

"No one on Earth has ever described me as sweet."

She tilts her head to the side so I can gaze into her deep brown eyes again.

"They don't think you're sweet because they've never cuddled next to you."

My cheeks turn red, and I look away from her.

She teases, "Are you blushing!?"

"Pagonis men don't blush."

"You are blushing. Is it because I said you were cuddly?"

"I am not cuddly. Now get out of bed. You need a shower and today, we set sail."

She rolls over and sighs as she hurries toward my en suite bathroom. I consider following her in, but I hear her lock the door. Damn. She isn't taking chances with me. I walk up to the door and press my weight against it. I hear her in the shower. Crying.

Fuck. I bite down on my lower lip. It's my fault for kissing her. For violating her. What did I expect? Did I think I could pin Fallon Iverson to the bed, and she'd let me have her? I dress in white linen for the trip. We're taking two of the luxury yachts, better suited for a trip to Ethiopia. Once we dock in Djibouti, we'll be in SUVs instead of boats with a private military to stand guard at the estate.

I have our duffel bags packed for the trip. It should be smooth sailing unless we encounter Somali pirates, which I thought best not to mention to Fallon. She'll be freaked out enough as it is without me filling her head with notions of terrifying Somali pirates intent on robbery and rape in equal measure. She exits the shower with a puffy face that I pretend not to notice. She's wearing a pink linen gown that cinches at her waist and she has her hair wrapped up in a towel.

"Are you hungry?"

"No."

"You haven't eaten in hours."

"I know that."

"At least come and have an espresso in the kitchen."

"I'm not going into your kitchen so your stupid grandmother can make me lick coffee up off the floor."

"Yiayia takes time to grow on you."

"She's a bitch."

"I can bring you the coffee and breakfast."

"No. Let's just get out of here."

I don't want to let her go without breakfast, but we'll have a chef on the yacht. At least we won't travel on the same boat as Yiayia, so Fallon will be safe from my grandmother's wicked whims temporarily.

She follows me to the driveway and gets into the front seat of the Jeep. We're the first to leave. Typical. The night before a big trip, Gal always gets drunk and Loukas fights with his children. This will be Antonio's first trip to Africa.

Carlotta's staying behind with Matilda. A horrible idea since they hate each other. But at least Loukas allowed it. Carlotta's too young to witness what we're up to in Ethiopia. Loukas is a nervous father. He keeps trying to make up for how Papa was with us. It isn't working.

When I load the duffel bags, a man's voice explodes across the parking lot.

"MURDERER. YOU'RE A FUCKING MURDERER."

TWENTY-THREE
SUPER YACHT

t's Mister Demopoulos. He's waving a large kitchen knife. I hallucinate a bit of blood on the tip of it. My blood. He's here for revenge.

My grandmother has his son's Greek National ID card and everyone in Thessaloniki knows the boy went missing and I was the last one to see him alive. Sandros' father lunges for me when my brother's voice comes from the balcony hanging above the driveway.

"Come closer to my brother and I will end you."

Loukas points an automatic rifle at the baker. It's the kind of toy too nice for him to wave around like this. Show off.

"Back away slowly."

The baker drops the knife and raises his hands in defeat.

"YOU KILLED MY SON!" The baker yells, "YOU KILLED MY SON, YOU MONSTER!"

I make eye contact with the baker. If I'd killed his son like he thinks, I'm uncertain I could meet his gaze with the same intensity as if I'd murdered his teenage son in cold blood and tossed his body into the Aegean Sea.

"He was only a boy!"

And thanks to me, he'll live out the rest of his days. Safe. And far away from Thessaloniki. But there's no way I can tell the baker. Not in front of my family. Mercy means weakness in our home. I fall back on my programming. A cocksure grin spreads across my face.

"The sun must be messing with your head, old man. I don't know what you're talking about. Perhaps your son wandered into the sea...and *drowned*."

See Fallon, I am a monster. Taunting a man who believes his son dead.

He falls to his knees, wailing. By then, the noise has attracted more attention from my family members on the estate. I gesture to Loukas so he lowers his weapon and I point Mr. Demopoulos off the property. He runs as Gal stumbles onto his balcony overlooking the driveway.

"What's all that fucking noise?"

"Sandros' family," Loukas barks, "Toss a cigarette, Gal."

Galanos tosses a box of cigarettes across the fifteen foot distance and Loukas deftly catches it. A piercing shriek disturbs the peace again. Cassia. Two cousins grab hold of her. One has her arms and the other her legs.

"LET GO OF ME! YOU'RE MONSTERS. I HATE THIS FUCKING FAMILY. I HATE YOU."

Yiayia trails out of Cassia's room, holding her cane this morning. Whenever she has bad arthritis, she's more of a sadist than usual. Something about achy joints turns Yiayia into a super soldier. She's smoking, but it smells like pot this time, which means her joints must really hurt.

"She's too much trouble. Like that mother of yours. The sooner we can get her married, the better. Once she's no longer a virgin, she'll stop squealing like one."

I get in my Jeep and drive to the dock. Loukas and Gal follow. All the boys on one boat and Helen will go with Papa and Yiayia. We have a chef, a bartender, and maids. Last year, Gal lost his virginity to one maid. They're always beautiful. Always dressed in skimpy outfits. It will be good for Loukas. He's been fuming about Carlotta lately, always worrying about his daughter and what Yiayia has cooked up for her when she turns eighteen. Probably marriage if they're both lucky.

Fallon knows the drill. She quietly follows me onto the boat and when we get to my room, I shut the door.

"Like it?"

"Your family has a boat so big, you can fit an entire king-sized bed in here?"

"It's a €200 million super-yacht from our fleet. We can fit several king-sized beds in here."

"This is… twisted. I would have sold my body for like… one percent of that amount of money. And you just have it."

"Would you do what we do to get €200 million?"

"No."

"Most people wouldn't. They see the money, but they don't see the blood."

Fallon scowls. But she hates everything that comes out of my mouth. She doesn't have to pretend to like me. She just has to *obey*.

Galanos and Loukas arrive shortly after, and we meet them in the superyacht's central chamber. It's some mix of a dance floor and a bar. They're both laughing and in good spirits. Antonio trails behind, carrying their bags in a sullen mood. He drops the bags and groans as two of the maids giggle and grope at his biceps before taking the bags.

"So strong!"

"Come here, handsome. We take your bags upstairs and maybe we could have a drink."

Antonio turns red and follows them. Loukas heads straight for the bar, and Galanos follows with a fresh cigar between his lips.

"After Uncle Tony, I'm taking the blond for a ride on my cock."

Loukas chuckles.

"Enjoy it. When you're my age, all the women you love end up dead or they're ignoring your calls."

"Problems with Matilda again?"

"Ever since I told her about Ethiopia, she won't shut up about how someone is plotting to kill her and how she wants me to stay in Thessaloniki. I left her with Carlotta for the next two weeks. Carlotta can handle herself. I trained her at the range myself. I'm a good fucking father."

Loukas waits for validation before continuing. "Does she really think I would leave my own daughter in danger? Fuck. I am a *great* father."

Loukas' insecurity about his parenting comes out in the strangest ways. We get it. He loves his kids. It doesn't explain why all the women he loves end up dead. Gal laughs.

"I can't believe you get hung up on such sluts. You should be more like Stavros. Buy them for sex. Get rid of them when you're done. It's genius."

Gal makes eye contact with Fallon and licks his lips before lewdly rubbing his cock. I smack the back of his head.

"Watch your mouth."

"Ouch! Don't be such a bitch. She can't be that good of a fuck."

I grab his ears and tug.

"I'll rip your fucking earring off and make you swallow it. Now shut up."

Gal whines as I hit him in the back of the head again. Loukas leans over and lights our younger brother's cigar. As the eldest, he's used to ignoring the fights that break out amongst the rest of us.

"Three days on this ship. Three brothers. And one beautiful girl. I can imagine worse ways to spend my time."

Loukas takes Fallon's hand and kisses it. She recoils but allows him to touch his lips to her skin. My stomach tightens into a crude knot. I put my arm around Fallon's waist.

"Worry about Matilda. Not seducing beautiful women. I'll show her the ship. I don't want her getting lost."

"Don't worry. I can help her," Gal says, winking and grabbing his dick again, "Suck me good and I'll make you cum, sweetheart."

"Ignore him," I mutter as I drag Fallon away. The yacht is over 350 feet long. When we aren't using it, we rent it out to celebrities and their families. The company takes care of covering our footprints so the money will never trace back to Greece. Once she's out of the room, her shoulders relax and she sighs.

"Thank you. Your brothers manage the impossible feat of somehow being scarier than you are."

"You're welcome."

My fingers curl around her shoulders like she's my proper girlfriend and I'm showing her around the boat. I want to kiss her and then take her upstairs and make love to her. Like a proper girlfriend.

"This buyer of mine… how do you know him?"

"Family."

"So I'll get to see you?"

"I don't know. I'm a busy man."

"You don't seem busy."

"I travel to Africa seven times a year and I'm hardly in Greece. Believe me, I'm busy."

"This is goodbye then."

"Yes. Soon."

I'm not "showing" her any other part of the yacht. Talking to her captivates all my attention and I want to keep doing it. I point out the pool and she nods. She doesn't give a fuck about my 350-foot yacht. She wants to know about me. Or more likely, what will truly happen to her. I haven't told her yet that my cousin is a worse monster than I am. And that I'm hoping she doesn't fall for his charms.

"Enjoy the yacht while you can. If you want to stay away from my brothers, I don't blame you."

"I want… to be alone right now."

I shouldn't have expected a different answer from Fallon. And I don't deserve one.

Letting her go will stop both of us from getting hurt. I'll never forgive myself if I damage her. Another man will be better for her. I can do this. I can treat her like just another object and get rid of her.

She thinks I'm a monster, right? It should be easy for a monster to let her go.

TWENTY-FOUR
FALLON'S NEW OWNER

Geo Doukas struts into the bar with his sister in tow. They both have long brown hair and deep Sicilian tans. They argue with each other constantly in rapid Italian. Fallon holds a champagne glass precariously between her forefinger and thumb. I put my hand on her lower back and draw her forward, "Your new owner, beloved."

She doesn't want to move, but my firm grasp of her waist propels her forward. She's smart enough to fear Geo despite his broad ivory smile. Fallon doesn't meet his gaze. Geo can't tear his eyes off her once he's close enough. He dispenses with the niceties and wrests his arm away from Marina's. Marina wraps her frail arms around me and kisses me on both cheeks. My cousin gets skinnier each time I see her.

"Ethiopia is never the same without you."

I miss the sea. We do great business in Ethiopia, but there's no country on earth as beautiful as Greece.

"It's good to be back."

"You look good. Sun. A beautiful woman."

"She's not mine. She's for your brother."

Marina swats me playfully and then grins.

"Whatever my brother has, I share."

"I hope that doesn't apply to women."

She pulls a cigarette out of her purse and lights up.

"Don't worry about me and Geo. I think he likes her."

Geo already has his hand on the small of Fallon's waist. He whispers something in her ear while pointing at me, and Fallon laughs. My cheeks redden and Marina links arms with me.

"Leave him with the girl. I want to see little Galanos and have a drink with my cousin, Stavros. Have his pubic hairs come in yet?"

"He's much bigger than the last time you saw him."

"Does he have a girlfriend? He has so many followers. People are always asking me if I'm close with my famous little cousin."

"He spends too much time on his phone," I grumble.

If Gal did some work around here, I wouldn't have to sit around cleaning up everyone's messes and making the voices that torment me worse. Marina sits at the bar and orders a cold lager.

My grandmother and Ofek discuss business at another table with Papa. Yiayia pretends she's only observing the meeting. She says nothing and allows Papa to conduct the business dealings. Once they hammer out the financial details, Loukas and I will take Ofek out drinking to seal the deal.

This meeting isn't only about guns and money. Cassia's locked in the villa now with four armed guards watching the door. Helen stayed at the villa to make sure the men don't seize the opportunity to have their way with my eighteen-year-old sister. They're here to protect her virginity. The product.

Working in our business eats at you. You get paranoid. You assume the worst of everyone. Marina prattles on about her luxury bags and the supermodels she hung out with on an actor's yacht last spring. As Marina prattles on about the actor's strange sexual proclivities (armpit fetish) and the horrific end to her partying (waking up in Lithuania with only a pearl thong on), my mind wanders to more important things.

Geo has his hand on Fallon's thigh. I can see the bite marks from the bar, but Fallon seems entranced by him. My throat tightens. He leans forward and kisses her cheek. Fallon giggles. She wants him. How could I have been so stupid to think Geo would smack her around and mistreat her on their first meeting? Marina touches my forearm, snapping me out of my fantasy.

"Where did you find Geo's girl?"

She taps her cigarette in the ashtray and stares at me. Marina has always been one of those people who stares at people like they're on display.

"Bought her."

"And you want to sell her to my brother? You know what we do to fresh meat in Sicily?"

"I have an idea."

"She looks top class for a whore."

I bite my lip to stop myself from defending Fallon Iverson. She's no longer mine to defend. Yiayia rises from their table. They've completed the deal. Papa shakes Ofek's hand. The fat old Israeli man shakes it while letting out a disturbingly wet cough that probably coated my father and grandmother's face with a thin sheen of his spit. Disgusting. This is the man we have to entertain tonight. Worse than that, he's the man Cassia will marry.

Papa approaches me and Marina at the bar. She kisses her uncle on the cheek and sensing my father has Pagonis family business to discuss, Marina sidles away to Geo and Fallon. Marina doesn't care about business. She only cares about her credit cards, shopping and hanging out with other models. She's a horrible role model for her siblings and an even worse one for her cousins.

"Cass spent the entire morning crying. Go up there and shake some sense into her. Ofek is giving us a £50,000,000 deposit in notes. This guy needs fucking everything. We need the girl compliant. Ofek is a family man. He likes family, yes? He'll be good to her. Your sister needs to understand that."

"She understands. I'll bring her out tonight."

"Are you sure she won't try to run?"

"Where will she go? We're in the Ethiopian countryside, and there are rebel forces patrolling these woods. We'll take her to the bar, she'll get to know that man. She'll feel better about it."

My father grunts and coughs halfway through the grunt like a boar. The cigar hanging between his lips is dangerously wet from his lips. It's difficult to believe there was any point where women voluntarily hung onto my father.

But hey, I can't blame him. I don't believe the shit I'm selling either. When Cass meets Ofek, she'll want to run for the hills even more than before. He's like her father in the most horrible way. He's fat, greedy, and smells like cheap Balkan off-brand colognes.

Cass should have run earlier if she wanted to run. She knows she has to do this. We all have our duty. I carry mine out and I don't just have to lie there to do it.

I can't care about my sister tonight when I have bigger problems. Giving up Fallon. Geo struts over to me while his sister talks to Fallon.

"Is she a biter?" Geo asks.

"I wouldn't know. If you don't rape them, maybe they won't bite you."

Geo laughs.

"Why take all the fun out of women? How much do you want for her? She seems bonded to you."

"She isn't. I'll take €10,000. And count your blessings because I spent triple that."

"She a virgin?"

"I doubt it."

"She won't be after tonight."

"Have your fun with her."

"Do you think she can handle multiple men?"

I flash Geo a cocky grin. He's a little shit and we only pretend to like each other because we both hate everyone else in the family. For different reasons.

"I haven't decided if I'll sell her to you yet. Show me the money."

"It's in my bedroom."

"Bring me cash at our place in an hour. I'm taking her back to... freshen her up."

Geo laughs and kisses his ring for good luck before saying, "Don't leave your cum leaking out of her. I want her cleaned up for me."

My cousin kisses my cheek and disappears to mingle with my father and grandmother. Fallon glances over at me with a look on her face that says, "Help me."

Maybe I imagine the look, but I go over there and excuse her from her conversation with Marina. I lead her back to my bedroom at our Ethiopian villa. I leave the door open a crack behind us. Fallon paces the room, her hands clenched in fists, and then she blurts out, "I don't want to leave here with Geo."

"You were getting along well."

"Did you see the bite marks on his hand? How many women has he hurt before?"

"You don't have a choice anymore," I growl, desperate to push her away.

Damn it, woman. Why won't you let me push you away?

Fallon rushes over to me and grabs my shirt. "What do you want from me, Stavros? I want to stay here. I want to stay... with you," she says.

She's lying to appease me. Right? That has to be it. My breath catches.

"Let go of me," I snarl.

TWENTY-FIVE
ONLY ELEVEN

"You don't want to stay with me. Geo is a good man. You'll get used to him," I continue. She releases my shirt, but she doesn't continue her short-lived obedience streak.

"He's not a good man. I've seen you shirtless, Stavros. You have tattoos on your forearm. Geo has the same type of tattoos. It's a kill count. He has triple the kill count that you have."

"What does it matter how much you've killed? I've killed people too. Geo wants you and you don't want to be around me."

"I've changed my mind."

"Do you know how buying and selling works? I've already agreed to get rid of you. I don't want you around."

"Liar."

"Pack everything. I'll bring your bag over to his hotel."

"No."

She stomps her foot. I want to spank her. And kiss her. But I have to take responsibility here. She'd rather not stay with me, so why not have the worst possible man?

"Don't make this difficult, Fallon."

"You don't have to go through with this. I get it, you want to prove a point. You're an egomaniac and no one ever says no to you."

She unties the string on her wrap dress and it falls to the ground.

"Prove that you don't want me."

"Get your dress back on," I snarl in one breath while my foot shuts the door with the other. She unhooks her bra, and it falls to the ground.

"No."

Her breasts swing into view and make me instantly hard. Fallon hooks her thumbs into the waist of her underwear.

"Stop it. Now."

She has her underwear off and she flicks it around her forefinger.

"Fuck me, Stavros."

"Don't play games with me."

"I want you."

It's my turn to use her own accusation against her.

"Liar."

Fallon shrugs and approaches me, touching my chest as she runs her fingers along the buttons on my shirt.

"It doesn't matter if I'm a liar. You want me."

Her hand traces the outline of my cock through my trousers. I let her touch me without breaking eye contact. I can't let her win. Fallon can't know how easily she controls me. I bite down on my lower lip and shrug.

"I can fuck you and sell you to him on the same day. Tonight, you're leaving my bed."

"Even if I agree to share it with you?"

"That will only make it easier. You're a woman, Fallon. You're made for conquering and fucking... but not much else."

She chuckles and runs her finger over my lips.

"I've been at your side for enough time to know you don't believe that. What are you waiting for, Stavros Pagonis? Claim your property the way you always wanted."

"You loathe me."

"Maybe. But it doesn't matter. We can loathe each other. That'll make this hotter, right?"

I grab her waist and press her body against mine.

"I have to warn you about fucking me," I say to her between kisses, "It will change you. Normal men won't feel the same."

"Is that a threat?"

"A promise, beloved."

I dip her back and kiss her on the lips. I enjoy her weight and her powerlessness as I kiss her. Her body crumbles against mine. She belongs to me. After tonight, she'll belong to me forever. Once I fuck Fallon Iverson, I can't let her go. But I won't tell her that.

Fallon's hands rush to my face, and she kisses me back. If I didn't know better, I'd say she enjoys kissing me. I press her body against mine as her fingers work my shirt open one button at a time. I need her naked beneath me. She has my shirt open and her fingers touch my chest lightly.

"Just to confirm... I hate you. I don't want to become your cousin's sex slave. But I still very much hate you."

"Remember that you hate me when I make you cum..."

I hoist her body onto the bed and fall on top her. I can't hold myself back now. She's given me permission to succumb to my animal instincts. It's the right time. We have hours together. Hours for me to make love to her. I don't want to rush this. Her hands rush to my hair and she giggles as my beard prickles her neck. I kiss my way down to her breasts and she moans as my tongue darts around her engorged nipple.

Her nipples are so dark and beautiful. I want them between my lips. I want to suck her tits until she cums... hard. Fallon moans as I run my tongue over her breasts. She wriggles out of my grasp as I suck her tits, but I grab onto her waist more firmly and hold her still. She's mine. She'll submit to me and accept wherever my tongue wanders.

I kiss my way down her stomach and spread her legs apart lewdly. I need to access every part of Fallon from her damp outer lips to the slippery center at the apex of her thighs. My first move is parting her lower lips with my finger. She moans as I tease her entrance and then move my wet thumb to her clit. She wants me. Her body responds to me with urgent need. As I rub her clit to arousal, my tongue trails behind and Fallon moans as I slide the pink muscle between her walnut-colored lips.

She moans as I spread her lower lips apart with mine and taste her fully with an eager and willing tongue. Pleasing and teasing Fallon until her legs shake was never part of the plan. I wanted to make her cum, but I never expect her to respond like this. Like she has waited for my tongue. I kiss her thighs desperately whenever I rise for breath and then I rub my tongue along her spread lower lips like her pussy is a plate I'm licking clean. The wetter Fallon gets, the more I suck and lick her tender pussy. She cums hard. Her body writhes in my grasp and I pin her down to the bed. She doesn't get to move until I'm finished with her. I drink every drop of clear juice from her cunt before my tongue returns to her clit.

She trembles and squeezes her thighs around my head as she begs me to stop.

"How many times did I make you cum?"

"Stop," she gasps, "I can't..."

I run my tongue over her clit one last time. She cries out and I kiss my way up her stomach and force her lips open with mine. I want her to taste herself and enjoy the flavor of her own cunt. Fallon lies pinned beneath my weight. My cock strains through my trousers, desperate for the soaking cunt I've just eaten out to the peak of desire.

"I can't stop myself anymore."

She says nothing. Her fingers slide down my obliques until she finds the button on my trousers and peels them over my ass. Her hands grab my ass cheeks and she groans.

"Fuck. You could bounce a quarter off that ass."

"Lusting after the man who bought you? Have I fucked you up that bad already?"

"Your body has nothing to do with your attitude. You might be hot, but you're still a murderer."

"Does that turn you on?"

"Shut up," she whispers, "Just shut up."

I grin and wait to see what those pretty little hands do for me next. She touches my cock through my briefs and my body tenses above her. Tease. Fallon is such a tease. And I love it. I'll love fucking her more.

"How big is that thing, anyway?"

"Big enough to be the reason most women dump me."

She giggles and mutters something about me being an egotistical bastard. She peels my underwear off and my cock unravels. That's the best way to describe it. It's nearly impossible to fit my full hard cock in my trousers. I've ripped more than a few pairs of pants from sprouting a boner at the worst time.

"What the fuck is that," says Fallon.

"I think you know what it is."

"It did not look that big in those boxers."

Why does she sound like she's accusing me of something?

I murmur in between heavy breaths, "Open your legs, beloved."

She tries to squeeze her legs shut, forgetting that I've nestled my enormous torso between her legs, and I don't plan on letting her go until I've fucked her.

"No way. I cannot fit your monster cock inside me."

"The men before you were small," I murmur as I kiss her cheek, softening her up for the big dick experience, "I will fix it."

"Stavros. I am not having sex with a dick that's at least thirteen inches long."

"I'm not that big," I tease her. "Only about eleven inches. Last I measured."

I hold her still against me. No running away, Fallon. You're mine... all mine.

TWENTY-SIX
I FINALLY CLAIM HER

She presses her palms against my chest and my abdominal muscles instantly distract her. Her push turns into a caress. My hardness stiffens and my heart races. What I feel for her is beyond desire. I crave her.

I lean over to kiss her, and she grunts as she struggles to push me off again. I retreat for a moment, then Fallon pulls my face close again. My heart races.

She relents and I kiss her until I want more than kissing from her. I press my hand up against her cunt and she gasps out loud. Grabbing her solidifies my control. Her desperate submissive gasp pleases me more than her squirming. I wriggle my fingers around the outside of her panties.

Her lower lips make a squishing sound as they slip past each other. I slip a finger beneath the fabric of her underwear and resist the urge to bury my finger in her slick cunt.

"You're soaked. My cock won't have any trouble getting between those perfect lips."

"It's eleven inches. That isn't meant for a human woman."

"It will feel good. I promise."

"A promise from you means nothing."

There's a sting in her voice. Fallon will have to try a lot harder to hurt me. My mind is quiet for once and all I think about is her. She has gorgeous skin, soft pouty lips and a body that stops me from thinking with my upstairs-brain.

"Good," I whisper, "That will make hate fucking me better for you."

My body mounts her, flat on her back in ultimate submission to my will. She squirms beneath me, providing one last element of resistance before relenting to the desires she's so desperate to suppress.

I drive the tip between her lips and she gasps as it stretches her. That's what normally happens when I start fucking a woman with a dick this big. She freezes and her eyes widen as she struggles to imagine how her tiny cunt can accept such a massive cock.

There's an old joke in Thessaloniki that the men in our family are all hung like horses because we're crazier than other men — part beast at our core.

I press inside her another inch and Fallon's nails dig into my back. Her face contorts in terror and I can't bear looking in her eyes. Have I just convinced myself that we both want it? I lean forward onto my forearms and kiss her as I keep my cock inside her. Her legs spread lewdly apart as shallow breaths undulate her chest. I run my tongue along her jawline and neck. She whimpers as I slide in another inch.

There's still over 2/3 of my cock left to slide inside her. Once I have a woman, I claim her. It's impossible to go back to a regular man once you've had an eleven inch Greek dick inside you. I nibble on her earlobe and Fallon moans again.

"You belong to me, beloved. I paid for you and now you're mine. I'm never letting you go."

I slide another inch inside her, and she cries out again.

"It's too big, Stavros..."

"Shhh," I whisper, "Patience, beloved. I want you to cum. I need you to cum."

Her arms wrap tighter around me. Closer, her body beckons. Closer.

She relaxes as I kiss her shoulders and her lips, and as I tenderly massage her body with my lips and tongue, she moans in pleasure as I slide another inch inside her. Juices squirt from her aroused cunt. The deeper she takes my cock, the more pleasure Fallon experiences.

She rakes her fingers through my hair and whimpers, "More!"

I bury myself inside her, up to the hilt with a beastly grunt. She cries out as I fill her tightness with my eleven inch monster. Cock makes her more conciliatory. She edges her hips forward, begging me to plunge deeper.

"So... full..."

I slide my hips slowly out of her. She moans in pleasure as I withdraw. That's half the fun of an enormous dick. Fallon receives pleasure both ways as I pump my cock into her deeper. I pin her hands over her head and thrust my hips faster. As I change the pace, her screaming gets louder. And louder.

"Cum for me," I command, "Cum all over my cock..."

She can't help herself. She erupts and climaxes over my eleven inch dick while screaming in pleasure. Juices erupt from her and her palms press against my chest again as the pleasure gets too intense.

"I can't..."

"Feel it," I growl, "Let yourself go."

She falls against the mattress as my hips pummel the slick apex of her thighs. Every deep thrust into Fallon's tight cunt feels like heaven. As hot as it is watching her cum repeatedly, I can't shake my desire to empty my seed between her perfect legs. I want to cum inside her and claim her properly. I want to seed her womb and watch Fallon grow thick with my seed and change because she's bearing my child.

I release her from my grasp and press my lips to her neck. Fallon smells fucking amazing. She drags her nails across my buttocks and my seed rises. I grunt and bury my eleven inches between her legs as she cries out from the pleasure of another climax. My cum erupts from the tip of my stiff member. Fallon gasps and loses control. I'm worse off. I can't stop kissing her after I've cum.

I kiss Fallon like I love her. My body tenses as she touches me and my cock throbs between her legs again. I'm seeing stars. No woman has ever made me cum like that. No woman has ever held my pleasure so tightly in her grasp. I don't want to withdraw. Instincts tell me that seeding her can't happen unless I remain between her legs.

"Fallon..." I grunt and gasp her name in the tone of a desperate prayer. She runs her fingers through my hair and gazes at me curiously. Or perhaps in terror.

"I don't want to move."

My voice emerges husky and low. I'm unraveling before her and I find the vulnerability humiliating. Damn it. What is it about this woman that makes me so willing to debase and humiliate myself like this? Her fingers travel to my stubble and I want her to say something sweet. Something that shows me she feels... anything. Because what I feel for her overwhelms me.

Instead, Fallon murmurs, "Can you take your dick out of me?"

I swallow and nod.

"Now."

I move and roll onto my back. Spent. She dresses immediately. I thought women loved cuddling. I hoped she was one of the ones that did. She sits at the foot of the bed and doesn't look at me.

"Fallon."

She reluctantly glances over her shoulder.

"I didn't expect it to feel good."

"*Good?* You came over ten times."

She gets up and storms into the bathroom, shutting the door and locking it. What the hell have I done now? Women. You don't make them cum, they complain. You give them multiple orgasms, they storm off. This is why I'm single. The incomprehensibility of women never ceases to stun me. I approach the door. I don't even care that I'm naked. If I'm lucky, she'll want to go again.

I rap on the door a few times. She doesn't answer.

"It's me."

"I know it's you," she snaps, "Go away."

"Did I hurt you?"

My heart pounds. I know what I did. Shame courses through me and I don't know why I'm looking to her for an answer I already know. I bite down on my lower lip. Perhaps I can will her to come out of there and talk to me. Maybe I can use my words and make it better. Like that has ever worked for me.

"I know," I murmur to the door.

Fallon doesn't respond. Her hurt tears at my heart. Her sobbing makes it worse. At first she tried to hide it but behind that door, Fallon Iverson sobs like I've never heard a woman sob before. I wet my lips and raise my curled fist to the door to knock on it again. But my hand falls to my side. I shouldn't have fucked her.

Fucking her made things complicated. Fucking her made this more wrong than it was already.

"I couldn't help myself."

My voice comes out in a desperate shudder. I realize how weak I sound. How pathetic. I hear a voice, but it isn't from the other side of the door. It isn't Fallon.

The voice hisses one word into my ear. The word is loud and cruel and rips my heart out.

"Rapist."

That's what it is when you make love to a woman you purchased. Rape. There's no way around it. She told me what I'd do to her, and it's exactly what I did. I'm a monster. That isn't news to me. What's news is that I'm worse than even I thought.

TWENTY-SEVEN

FINDING CASS

leave the room angry. Helen comes storming upstairs with a scowl on her face.

"Bee in your bonnet?"

"Shut up, Stavros," she snarls, "We have a problem."

"What kind of problem?"

"Cassia."

Helen's red and her hair mightily disheveled.

"Those bastards left her alone while she took a piss and she jumped out the fucking window. Papa and Yiayia will be here in 20 minutes and she's on foot. We need to find her. We need to get her back."

"You of all people shouldn't care that she's running away from some marriage she doesn't want."

Helen slaps me. Hard.

"Watch your tongue, Stavros. You might be an entitled male, but I'm still your elder. If Cassia was too stupid to get rid of her virginity that isn't my problem. She agreed to this."

"It's not her fault Yiayia orders all her boyfriends killed."

"You're the one who kills them. And Yiayia will do much worse tonight if Cassia messes around."

"Shouldn't we have second thoughts about making her our sacrificial lamb?" I mutter.

Helen remains unmoved by my potential turn of conscience.

"You idiot, are you listening? Cass came here and now she has to do this. Yiayia will *kill her.* Hurry! And what about that girl of yours? Now that you're finished fucking her at the top of both your lungs, we need her help."

"I can't ask for her help."

"Hurry then! We need to find our idiot sister before Yiayia finds out she tried to run."

"Where are Loukas and Gal?"

"Still drinking with the useless cousins. Are you still selling the girl to him?"

"No."

Helen snorts.

"Figures. That's probably why she spread her legs to get away from him. Every woman can smell how repulsive Geo is a mile away."

"That's not why."

I realize I'm getting into another petty argument with Helen. But she's right. We need to find Cassia. An escape attempt so close to her engagement party won't reflect well on the family. And if our grandmother finds out, Cassia will face a worse fate than marrying an old fat guy. Helen remembers what happens when Yiayia found out she lost her virginity. Helen thinks it was worth it to avoid marriage. I think she blocked the memories out. I wonder how she explains the scars from Papa's belt to men.

I stay out of the deals women in our family make for their freedom. We are mafia families. Crazy motherfuckers. And one of us crazy motherfuckers just hoofed it for the rainforest. I get in my car with a pistol in the front seat and an old Kalashnikov and drive off-road. Where the hell could Cassia have ended up? She's smart enough to know what we'll do first. She's smart enough to know that we'll go off-road.

Whether or not she gets away won't be based on cleverness. It'll be based on whether or not she gets enough of a head start. I drive around the acreage of our property. We own acres of rainforest around the house. Some roads are accessible by Jeep. I drive around for ten minutes and don't find her. But she can hear the Jeep. So I park it and get out of the car with my gun drawn.

Wherever my little sister is, I'll find her. I walk lightly in the woods. Hunting for a Pagonis is no different from hunting anyone else. We might be predators in Africa and Thessaloniki, but that's our biggest weakness. We're not used to being the prey.

I see signs that she's run through a path to the east of the main house. Close to her bedroom window. I abandon hope I'll find her by stalking her. We don't have the time. But I can still hunt her down using one weapon my other siblings don't have. Cass's trust.

"Cass! Come out of where you're hiding! I want to help you."

If she can hear me, she says nothing.

"I won't let them take you. I promise."

Again, nothing.

Damn it. She has to be somewhere nearby. If she can hear me, but doesn't respond, I must not be making her an offer good enough to respond to. Pagonis men and women respond best to one incentive.

"I spared him," I call out, "I won't tell you which one, but I spared one of them. I didn't have to, Cass. But I found the capacity for mercy."

I hear a thud. My sister jumps out of a tree about fifty feet behind me. She's on her knees in a pile of fallen leaves.

"Who did you spare?"

Unfortunately, I'm not here to answer my sister's questions. I catch her before she realizes what's happening and clasp my hand over her mouth.

"What the hell were you thinking?" I snarl. She tries to bite me and I hold her against my body so she can't move and twist her limbs so she knows that if she tries anything, I'll pop her shoulder out of the socket.

"You do not belong to yourself. You belong to this family. And when you have a family of your own, you will become their matriarch. So let the old man fuck you and stop making my life a living hell. Do you know how many of your stupid boyfriends I've had to kill? How many fucking skinny jean wearing Greek assholes I've put in the ground because you want to be a slut? I'm taking you back home and you will do what they ask or I will arrange your rape myself."

She nods and trembles. Her tears slide over my fingers that I still have clamped over her mouth. It hurts me to speak to Cass this way. But if I don't threaten her and keep her under control, our grandmother will make what I've threatened a reality. If I won't help her, she'll get Gal to help her. He's become her new golden boy.

She did exactly what I threatened to Helen. And I don't want it to happen to Cass. Loukas killed Helen's rapists. I don't want to kill more boys. I've killed enough.

"I let you go, you walk to the house without complaint."

She sobs as I uncover her mouth. And because I'm the only one to turn to, my sister shoves her head into my chest.

"I don't want to marry him," she sobs, "I don't want to lose my virginity. Stavros... please don't make me go through with it."

I hold her against my chest. Poor Cassia. I don't envy women. It doesn't matter if they're girls like Fallon or Pagonis daughters. They all have to put up with men. I let her cry on my chest for a few minutes. But we don't have time for tears. I have to make Cassia presentable to the man who will take care of her and our family's business.

"You can't cry."

I try to sound tough. But she's still my little sister, and I want nothing to happen to her. I have to be tough to keep her safe. The only way to survive in our family is to become a monster.

"I want to lose it with a man I love…"

My cheeks darken. I don't want to talk about sex with my little sister. Someone must have given her the talk by now. I hope it wasn't Galanos. Despite my better instincts, I have to help her.

"If the old bastard hurts you, I'll castrate him."

She pulls her head away from my chest and hits me. Hard.

"Liar."

"I will. If you want to."

"You're not better than our family," she snarls, "you're the worst of us."

"I know."

"Don't pretend you want to help me or that you're some friend to women."

"I'm sorry, Cassia."

"If you were so sorry, you'd kill him for me."

"Ask your other brother to do it. Now come."

I grab her by the arm and drag her back to the villa. But it's too late. Cass tries to break away when she realizes who is waiting for her and when she realizes what's coming next.

TWENTY-EIGHT
OFEK'S BRIDE

Ofek chuckles as I drag Cass to the middle of the driveway. Yiayia's so angry, I'm surprised her eyes don't set us both on fire. Helen bounds down the stairs, standing intentionally between Yiayia and Cass.

"It's my fault," Helen quickly tries covering for our younger sister, "She's sorry, Yiayia. She only wanted a break."

"I know what she wanted."

Yiayia's voice is ice. A shiver runs through Cass and she struggles against my grip. If I let her go, Yiayia will do worse than whatever she's concocting as she realizes my sister tried to run away.

"Beautiful girl," Ofek says to my father, who has a cigar between his lips and glances at the scene with disinterest.

Compared to my grandmother, my father has always been a passive man. In family matters, he firmly believes decision-making to be women's work. Men do business. Women do family. My father often lacks the sense to notice when the two intertwine properly. He's lazy because he never knew struggle in his childhood, Yiayia claims. I am wont to assume she's correct about him.

He's spoiled rotten.

Cass grunts and tries to run again. I yank her against my chest and put a hand on Helen's shoulder, shaking my head. The last thing Helen needs after what she's been through is to upset my grandmother. We have millions on the line here. If Cass wanted to run, she should have done it in Greece, not Africa.

Helen backs off. She touches Cass's shoulder. It's half an apology. Tears stream down my younger sister's cheeks. The old Israeli hasn't said a word. I don't notice why she's crying until I see the expression on my grandmother's face. It's too late for tears.

"Cassia Pagonis," I announce to the old man, "She'll make a good wife."

"Can she cook?"

Cass sobs.

"Yes," Yiayia says, "And you can train her. But I hope you don't expect your wife to cook when you have enough money for maids."

Ofek chuckles.

"No. I would not eat cooking from such a skinny thing, but my mother is German, yes? She likes women who can cook."

Yiayia shrugs and lights a cigarette.

"Don't worry about what your mother thinks. What about you? You must have other aims with a girl this young."

Ofek chuckles and then elbows my father.

"Growing up with a mother like this one, heh heh! Lucky man."

Papa nervously puffs his cigar and doesn't answer. Most people who do business with the family hardly seem to notice that my father barely says a word.

"She's fit for bearing a child," Yiayia continues, "But she is a flight risk as you can see. I want you to have the marriage at the villa. Have your rabbi meet us in an hour. We will prepare her for marriage."

Ofek pulls out his phone hurriedly. He doesn't want to miss this chance. The man wheezes as he rattles off instructions on the phone in rapid Hebrew. Ofek is more superstitious than most, and he keeps his rabbi close. When he finishes, he wipes his sweat-covered hands on his pants.

"Perhaps I take the beautiful woman inside for a drink?"

Cassia silently pleads with me for mercy, but she sealed her own fate by her attempted escape.

"She will go with you. Don't be afraid to discipline her if you need."

I grin at Ofek, and he links arms with Cassia, taking her to the kitchen. When I'm alone with my grandmother, she slaps me across the face. Hard. Helen gets between us and my grandmother pushes her out of the way.

"Where did you find the little bitch," Yiayia sneers, "Did you help her?"

I recoil but avoid the urge to rub the spot where she slapped. My grandmother derives pleasure from knowing she caused pain. I can't show her any weakness.

"No. I did not. And I'm not in the mood for you to slap me around, old woman. If you want to sell my sister's maidenhead, keep her under lock and key yourself."

It isn't much, but it's the most anyone in the family stands up to Yiayia. I turn around to walk away from her. I hear Helen scream. Then I hear a thud. The pain comes after. Before I can respond, I slump to the ground. When I wake up, I hear Helen and Loukas' voices in agitated Greek. English is too slow for emotional conversations. And I'm in my bedroom, which means Fallon is nearby and they don't want her to understand what they're saying. I groan and Helen stands over me, her bushy brows blackening her scowl.

"Idiot."

Helen storms out of the room, and Loukas sits on the edge of my bed as I awaken. The back of my head throbs. I hear two of the voices — the ones that play in the background like noise from a television sitting in another room.

"How's your head?"

"How long was I out?"

"Papa helped me carry you up here."

"Fallon…"

"The girl's here."

I can smell Fallon's skin, but I don't see her and I can barely crane my neck to look without searing pain tearing through my neck and skull. The chatter of voices gets louder and I grab the sides of my head. Loukas raises an eyebrow.

"You didn't mention the voices were back."

"They're not."

Fallon's voices emerges from the darkened room.

"He needs rest. I can look after him."

Loukas makes a low grunt and gets off my bed.

"Cassia's wedding is in forty-five minutes. Make sure he's downstairs, slave girl."

Fallon responds, "I'm not a slave girl."

Loukas grunts and storms off.

"Fallon…"

"Forty-five minutes. I'll speak to you then. Rest. It looks like she got you pretty good."

It's not the first time Yiayia has injured my head. One more concussion, the doctors said, and I'd lose my ability to form long-term memories. So I hope she was weaker with this blow. I touch the back of my head and groan, falling onto my back. Fuck. I hate this. I don't want Fallon to see me like this. Weakened.

And I don't want to see her at all.

"She's your victim, isn't she?"

"SHE'S NOT MY VICTIM."

Fallon stands in front of me.

"Who are you talking to?"

"That woman…"

Fuck. Fallon sits on the edge of my bed and says calmly, "Lots of people hear voices, Stavros. You can do something about it."

"Smoking takes the edge off."

"Not smoking. I mean something good for you."

"Cigarette."

"Are you always this petulant?" She grumbles. "You act like a child."

"Cigarette."

She searches my dresser drawer until she finds an unlabeled box of cigarettes and tosses one to me.

"Lighter."

"No. Not until you tell me what the hell happened to you?"

"It doesn't matter."

"It matters to me."

"Stop it, Fallon. You are my property. We have no feelings for each other."

"You are such an asshole," Fallon snaps.

"Yes," I reply. "Now stay away from me."

"I should take your damn cigarette and throw it in the sea."

"Do that and I'll spank you silly."

"I dare you to try," she says. Fuck, my head throbs. I growl in response, which makes her roll her eyes. Hmph.

I get out of bed and storm onto the villa balcony. Our family seems to have a fetish for balconies. Maybe it's just that we enjoy looking down on people. I search my pants for a lighter.

The voice of a beautiful woman whispers, "You can have sex with me. Fuck me and then fuck me up, Stavros."

I knew that woman once. She said she loved me. And then she left. Yiayia told her she was an obese pale cow at dinner once. I grip the railing of the balcony and yell at her.

"I won't!"

Fallon's hand rests on my shoulders, and I flinch.

"Won't do what?" She asks. Fallon's voice is soft and comforting. She isn't like the others. First, Fallon is real. And her skin is smooth and the most beautiful shade of walnut. I could pick up her slight frame and take her to bed now. Each time she touches me, I want to.

But who was this woman, eh? Another voice. Another fucking voice worming its way into my head. My head aches. I light up and after a couple puffs, the voices subside and Fallon wraps her arms around my torso.

"What are you doing?" I growl.

"You look like you need a hug."

She sounds sympathetic and it turns my stomach. She called me a rapist, so to hear this softness in her voice jars me. Maybe it isn't real. Maybe she's a vision too...

I growl at her, "What's wrong with you, eh?"

My heart throbs in a disturbing rhythm with my head. She's so beautiful that she almost makes me feel sane.

I turn around, expecting her to pull away, but Fallon rests her head on my chest. I want to push her away, but I don't. She won't give me an answer either.

"I asked what is wrong with you, woman? Why are you out here hugging the man who bought you and raped you? What the fuck is wrong with you?"

TWENTY-NINE
CASSIA'S WEDDING

Fallon pulls away from me then. I grab her by the wrists so she can't get too far.

"Let go of me, Stavros," she hisses.

"Why should I? I want to make you my fuck pet. You've turned me into a monster already. Let me have you again."

"Stop it!"

She wrenches her arms away from me and pushes me. Hard.

"You didn't rape me, you idiot."

I let the cigarette hang idly in my mouth. Fallon snatches it and tosses it over the balcony.

"I was smoking that."

"I don't care. What gave you the idea that you raped me?"

"You cried afterward."

"Yes, I cried. I fucked a guy who bought me like a piece of meat. And that's not even the worst part. I get it, you're a tortured murderer. That's your whole thing. But it isn't mine. And I don't want to be the woman who... you know what. Never mind."

Fuck. Is there any faster way for a woman to drive a man crazy than to tell him 'never mind' when he's just asked her what's wrong?

"Tell me," I insist.

"No."

My voice grows even more stern. "Fallon..."

"I'm not as scared of you as you seem to think," she protests.

"Hm."

"I'm not," she says. Her body shakes before she speaks. I must still terrify her but it's my fault, not hers.

"If you aren't scared, prove it. Tell me."

"The worst part is, I enjoyed it. The first time I enjoy sex with a man in my entire life and it's... you. You're literally the most evil person I've ever met."

"Some might call me *uninhibited*."

"Standing with your dick out at the beach is uninhibited. I watched you nearly shoot a kid in the head and you didn't even flinch."

"We cannot speak of Sandros," I hiss.

The last thing I want is my grandmother finding out that Sandros survived.

"Whatever," Fallon continues, "The point is... I liked the sex. It freaked me out. That's it. But it doesn't matter because I'm never having sex with you again."

"Why not?"

"Did you miss the part where I said you're literally the most evil person I've ever met?!"

"My grandmother made you lick coffee off the ground."

"She's worse than evil. She's a psychopath."

"Careful. She is still my grandmother. I honor her with all my actions."

"Honor her? She beat you in the back of the head so hard you heard voices. She's fucked up, Stavros. Your entire family is fucked up."

"We are different. We are Greek. Mafia. We do what we must."

"For money. For women. For feeling better than other people. I get that part. What I don't get is how someone with a heart can do any of this."

"This rage may hurt people, but it keeps people safe too."

"Is that what you're doing to Cassia? Keeping her safe by selling her to a fat old Israeli man?"

"How do you know about this?"

"I'm not stupid. I've picked up enough Greek to understand what your siblings were talking about."

"I don't need your advice or psychoanalysis."

She smiles and I do not know what's going on behind her facial expression. What on Earth is this woman thinking, eh?

"What?" I growl.

"The voices. They're quiet."

"You can't know that."

She puts her hands on the side of my face and tiptoes so she can press her forehead to mine. Her lips look soft and inviting. Warmth emanates from Fallon's touch. There's nothing on this earth that would be more magical than her loving me.

I can't stand thinking that she never could because of who I am — a monster.

"I'm a nurse. I know," she says.

I stop holding her hips and step aside her. It's time for us to dress and watch my sister get married. I put Fallon in a blue linen dress and white sandals. I watch as she pins her hair in a high messy bun. She doesn't like when I look at her and she pouts whenever I stare. I don't care. She's mine and I will watch her as carefully as I want.

Despite her scowl, Fallon walks downstairs with me. Helen and Galanos have moved the chairs in the living room for the occasion.

Loukas sits toward the front of the room. Fallon and I occupy the chairs next to him. She sits between us and Loukas puts his hand on her thigh, leaning over and whispering the word "Beautiful" into her ear. I can smell the liquor on his breath from my seat. He hasn't heard from Carlotta and he worries. Loukas drinks too much when he worries.

Papa walks Cass down the aisle. She's visibly upset and red-faced, but she doesn't dare make a sound. If the maiden's tears perturb Ofek's rabbi, he doesn't show it.

The ceremony is quick. Ofek grabs my sister by the ass and pulls her close for a kiss, and she nearly squeals. Once it's finished we all cheer, but the sound is hollow. We'll celebrate when we get the big old fucker's money. Galanos has his phone out by the end and he lifts his shirt to show his abdominal muscles to his millions of followers in the kitchen before Papa can stand and make his speech.

"Ofek. Tonight, your men come to my house and we celebrate the joining of businesses and families."

Ofek pinches Cass's butt and kisses her.

"Before we party, I wish to experience my bride," Ofek chuckles, lewdly gesturing toward his cock.

Yiayia points to an uninhabited guest bedroom. Cassia's sobs get louder as Ofek drags her into the room. We hear her screaming. And then the bed squeaks. She screams louder. She screams in Greek. And then the man finishes, presumably inside her. At least the bastard didn't last long. And now Cass is no longer a virgin. He walks out of the room, leaving her to clean up the mess.

"Brother-in-law!" Ofek yells at Galanos, "A drink for me!"

He stuffs his cock into his pants as he walks toward the kitchen. Fallon's face is ghostly. I lean over and kiss her shoulder and she yanks it away. What have I done now? Cassia's virginity is lost and there's nothing I could have done to stop it. Not without subjecting her to a worse fate. Cass shouldn't have trusted me. Neither should Fallon.

Cass comes out of the room with a torn dress and tears streaming down her face. She runs upstairs and Fallon gets up, chasing after her. Yiayia doesn't glance up from her conversation with Loukas. But I can't leave Fallon alone with my sister and have either of them getting ideas. So I follow them.

THIRTY

YIAYIA'S REASONS

Cass sits on her bed upstairs, sobbing into Fallon's arms. She bears no affinity toward Fallon, but with what my sister has just gone through, she'll cry on any shoulder available to her. I stand in the doorway and neither woman acknowledges my presence. My trigger finger shakes and I can hear the low chatter of hallucinatory voices threatening to distract me from my purpose here.

"Fallon. Come," I command her. Cass needs to handle this on her own.

Fallon wraps her arm around Cassia's shoulder and hisses, "No. You get out of here."

Cassia hugs Fallon back and cries louder. I can't find the right words. I'd hoped we would return before my grandmother did, but I ought to have known it would be too late. But to lose her maidenhood for all to hear her screaming... Cass didn't deserve such a harsh punishment.

"I said leave," Fallon hisses.

Through her sobs, Cassia warbles, "He can stay. I want him to see what he's done to me."

She collapses into Fallon again. Fallon strokes my sister's dark brown curls, unraveling and untangling them with loving fingers. No one in my family has held Cassia like this since she was a young girl. I graduated secondary school the year she was born. I remember holding her and watching her run around the villa. She always wanted to come into her big brother's room and play with my video games. Or my guns, unfortunately. I'd killed a man before she was born, already inducted into what it meant to be a Pagonis before she took her first steps.

"It will get better, Cassia."

My words sound hollow. I can barely form a coherent sentence with the distracting voices. I need liquor. Or another cigarette. More than that, I need Fallon. I watch the two of them holding each other as Fallon comforts my sister in a way that only another woman can. My guilt feels pointless because I couldn't save her. And I can't save everyone.

"After the party tonight, you'll go back to Israel with him. He travels often. He won't expect much from you, especially once you are pregnant."

I say to make her feel better. She'll have plenty of time to herself once he has what he wants and a very comfortable life. Yiayia suffered worse in her marriage and she was much younger than Cass.

"I'm not having a baby for that monster," Cass spits.

Fallon's disapproving glare tells me my advice is unappreciated. I thought it would help her know the monster wouldn't have her often. It's better than what Yiayia went through. I leave after I've spent too long standing there. My grandmother sits alone in the living room downstairs sipping on a fragrant jasmine tea. She pats the seat next to her once she realizes I don't plan on staying. I join her.

"Yiayia."

"She will understand what I've done for her when she's older. When she has children."

"The man raped her."

If Yiayia's bothered by the disgust in my voice, she doesn't show it. She smirks and takes a sip of tea, careful not to slurp. It always surprises people how ladylike my grandmother is given what they hear about her.

"For five minutes. My first night... with your grandfather. It went on and on. Hours. I could not walk for a week. I had a child two years after I began menstruating."

My grandmother has a knack for bringing up the very last subjects in the world I wish to speak about with her.

"You do what's best for this family."

She scoffs. Yiayia hates when we become sycophants to skirt trouble. She'd rather hear our honesty and punish us for it.

"Ofek will hand us tens of millions of dollars tonight and next month, another few million. He's worth nearly one billion dollars, and when Ofek dies, that money will be hers. And her children's. And she will have a husband who doesn't sell her cunt for his own amusement. Ofek might be a pig, but he is not a monster."

"Speak to Cassia. Make her understand you have a reason for what has happened."

"I have nothing to say to that impudent child," Yiayia sneers, "If she were smart, she'd fuck him again, so that she doesn't have to wait for the bastard to die to get his money. Men spend more when they're satisfied."

I think to myself that if Cass were smart, she'd kill him.

"She will get better," I say as much to myself as my grandmother, "She'll get through this."

"That is not my concern. My concern is the family business. Has your father told you about his new toy?"

I wonder if she's talking about a boat or a woman. My father never lacks for either. Even with mama around, he had a proclivity towards whores.

"He hasn't."

"A fifty million dollar boat. How many fucking boats does my son need? And he doesn't work at all toward the business. Yet, he's the best I have. I know you think I am cruel, but I do more for this family than your father does."

"Nobody believes you are cruel, Yiayia. We trust you."

Her hand jumps to my thigh. I'm practiced at receiving assaults from my grandmother, so I don't flinch. Her voice is icy.

"You cannot impregnate that African. We will not have her blood tainting our family line. Do you understand?"

"I understand."

"She is filth and nothing more than a slave. If she's pregnant, I will make you cut the child out of her."

"Understood."

"Good. Have her cunt if you wish, but this is not a woman for you to marry, Stavros. I allow you grace because you do the work no one else will. You're the only one with the stomach for it, my child."

I leave without another word and she lets me go. For all her bluster, I think what she's allowed to happen to Cassia affects the old woman. She sits alone for hours at a time, reminiscing on the past, reviewing the various people who have wronged her until she tires of it. And she's getting tired. One day she'll die and my father will head the family. Perhaps she's right to worry about what will become of us. If our family falls apart and Thessaloniki falls to chaos, she would have lived a life of wickedness and cruelty for naught.

I find Galanos in the kitchen, holding a large bottle of port. Our festivities begin in an hour, but the drinking begins the moment the wine touches the counter. My little brother pours a glass of wine for me.

"Changed your mind about the cunt?" Gal asks after I've had a glass.

"Hm?"

"I still want to try her. She has hips. Womanly hips. I've had enough of thin coke whores."

He puts his hands behind his head and stimulates entering a woman from behind. His madly gyrating hips disturb me more than some of my darker hallucinations.

"Stop fucking them, then. You need to work."

"They won't let me! I asked Papa to send me back to Thessaloniki. There's a job there. He sent Marco."

What job could be suitable for our idiotic second cousin?

"I never heard of a job back home."

"Papa never said not to tell you."

"We finished our business there for the month."

"It's personal. Not business."

"A personal job?"

"An enemy destined for the sea. That's all I know."

"Hm. Next job I have, you're coming with me."

"I still have school. I can't run off with you. Unless…"

"Unless what?"

"Please… let me fuck her."

I slap the back of my brother's head.

"Women don't like desperate. You won't have to force them if you behave like half a likable person."

"I'm a Pagonis. We don't have to be likable."

I mutter bitterly, "Not until our reign of terror ends."

Gal finishes another glass of wine and seamlessly moves into a livestream. His generation is broken at its core. Their obsession with those little devices never ceases to amaze me. I missed that movement entirely, and I have no regrets. I retrieve Fallon and Cassia once the party downstairs enters full swing. Fallon won't speak to me, but she follows obediently.

Cassia's aggressive. She struts over to the food and drink and downs three shots of tequila and smokes a cigarette in the middle of the crowd. The music gets louder. I don't know where Loukas found this DJ, but he plays songs I actually know. *Old music,* Galanos would say. Fallon stands dutifully near me as I survey the crowd. Yiayia's in the living room with the family elders and Ofek.

I can't suppress the powerful urge to dance with Fallon. I tug on her sleeve and lean over.

"Will you dance with me?"

THIRTY-ONE
FALLON'S HIDDEN DESIRES

Fallon hisses that she'd rather die than dance with me, and to prove her point, she finds Cassia dancing alone and joins her. Cassia's too drunk to remember that she thinks she's better than everyone, including Fallon. I spend most of the night watching Fallon. She barely touches any liquor, but I can't say the same for myself.

Otek grabs Cassia near midnight and takes her back to his place. Just like that, Yiayia married her off, and she's the Israeli's problem now. We're flying back to the seaport tomorrow morning and heading back to Greece. Fallon stumbles up the stairs ahead of me. With the door shut behind us and liquor coursing through me, my desire for her mounts. She's a somber drunk, and she stumbles into bed, wriggling beneath the covers, fully clothed.

I strip my shirt and pants off and slither into bed next to her, naked except for my boxers. She turns around and her hands come upon my bare chest. Fallon recoils with one hoarsely whispered word, "No."

"I want your cunt," I slur.

"I said no, Stavros."

"Why shouldn't I take what I want. I... I want you."

"Why?"

"Does it matter? You're a woman. You're beautiful."

"Stop it. You bought me. You paid more money than I owed the federal government in student loans. There has to be a reason I'm here."

"Fate, beloved."

She swats at me.

"You don't believe in fate."

I spread her legs and position my weight on hers. Fallon's breathing slows. I want to kiss her. She's right. I don't believe in fate. A man who kills for a living can't believe in fate. Or chance. She wraps her thighs around me and makes a little noise in the back of her throat that sounds like purring.

"I want you," I repeat gruffly.

"We can't. It's not good for either of us."

Her hand touches my cheek. Her fingers burn me with their touch. I'm guilty. I'm wrong for touching her and touching her. My cock strains against my boxers. I'm inches away from her pleasure centers and my yearning for her only intensifies. I run my lips over her neck and enjoy the way she whimpers. She doesn't know yet if I'll take what I want or if I'll wait for her yielding to me.

"You want me, beloved," I whisper, taking her bottom lip between my teeth and sucking on it.

"I shouldn't."

"One more time," I murmur, kissing her and acting like I'm not pleading for her permission, "I fuck you good one more time and then I never do it again."

"Liar."

Her breath tickles my neck, and I grind my hips forward. She whimpers like she knows how close she came to impaling herself on my stiffness.

"Fine. I'm a liar. And a murderer. And every fucking wicked thing on the planet. Then why do I get you so goddamned wet?"

"I'm not."

Her voice changes pitch. I know she's lying.

"Let me touch your cunt. I'll find out how wet you are."

"Don't you dare," she hisses.

"What will you do to stop me?"

"I could push you off. You aren't even pinning me down."

I grin and kiss her on the lips.

"Is that what you want? You want me to pin you down?"

"You... are the worst thing that's ever happened to me."

"Eh?"

"You were right. When we... had sex. You told me I could never be with a normal man after you and you don't know how right you were, okay? It messed with my head. That's why I was crying."

"So I'm right. You're wet."

"Ugh!"

She pushes me off her. I groan and flop onto my back. I tell myself I'm too drunk to fight back, but for the first time in years, I'm having fun. I enjoy her. Not just wanting her. Not only thinking about her cunt. Fallon's company turns the corners of my lips in a smile. I'm having fun teasing her.

"I tell you something about my feelings for once and you turn into a complete dick."

"Can't stop thinking about my dick, can you?"

I pull her back into my arms and roll on top of her again. Her palms press against my chest, but she isn't pushing seriously.

"Stavros... what you did to me... it wasn't sex. I've had sex. It normally ends after three minutes. The guy has a big smile on his face and I feel like I violated my sense of self worth by allowing him to leave without giving me an orgasm. You wanted me for your own selfish reasons, sure. But you... savored me."

"I'd like to savor you now," I whisper.

"No," she whispers back, "Don't savor me. Pin me down and take what you want from me. Do whatever you want to me."

"You're playing a dangerous game, beloved."

"You're worse than dangerous. But that's what makes it... fun."

I chuckle and rip her dress open, popping one button off as I expose Fallon's chest. Her hard nipples stiffen beneath my tongue as I drag her wrists over her head and pin her to the bed. She's everything I want and more. She's delicious.

"I don't have STDs," I whisper between licking her nipples.

"What?"

"Let me have you. No condom. Tonight."

I suck on her right nipple before she can answer, hoping to sway her by putting her judgment in the same questionable position as my own.

"That's crazy. I could get pregnant."

"You won't."

"Is that a Greek form of birth control I haven't heard of yet?"

"Trust me..."

"I'm trusting biology."

"Don't you want to feel my skin on your skin? Wouldn't that make your twisted submissive fantasies even hotter?"

She sighs.

"Getting into bed with you has to be the worst idea I've had in forever."

"You're not getting into bed with me, beloved. I'm taking you. Now spread your legs. I want to feel your wet little cunt."

She spreads her legs and I hike her dress further up her waist, releasing her wrists from my grasp. Fallon resists the urge to rub her wrists. My hands fondle her as I move them down her torso. When I reach her plain cotton underwear, I resist the urge to rip it from her body. Not until we get to Greece and I can get her a nice pair.

I peel the underwear off her, and it's soaked. Completely. Juices dribble down her thighs and her lips are teased open of their own accord, dripping with Fallon's clear dribbles.

"I knew it."

"Shut up."

I chuckle and kiss the spot of flesh beneath her navel. She whimpers and wriggles as I grasp her hips tighter. Within seconds, I have her cunt teased open with my tongue. Her full lower lips hang apart as I slide my tongue in circles around her smooth entrance. She's velvety soft and dripping like a peach. I run my tongue over the hardened pearl at the apex of her opening and she moans.

I'll have her crumbling in my grasp and begging for more in minutes. Then I'll give her what she wants: a good hard fuck with my big white cock.

Fallon rakes her fingers through my hair and presses my face into her eager crotch. I could bury myself in her scent for eternity. I content myself to lick at her folds, tasting every inch of her and teasing her to a loud moaning crescendo. Fallon explodes with her first orgasm for the night, crying out wantonly. I suck the hardened nub as she moans. This won't be her last climax for the night.

THIRTY-TWO
THEIR MONSTER

We leave Cassia behind in the morning and drive back to the coast. Fallon sleeps most of the way in the backseat. Galanos sits in the front next to me, bitching about his satellite phone signal.

"I got a new AR-15 from Ofek. How the fuck am I supposed to post this to Instagram with no signal. Stupid fucking phone."

"There's more to life than your cell phone, Galanos. How have we raised you?"

"You weren't in Greece most of my childhood, remember? Yiayia was like a mother to me. I think she did an excellent job. I'm rich. I'm beautiful. I have women beating down my door and sliding in my DMs."

I don't even know what "sliding in my DMs means". I growl and wave my brother off.

His being raised by Yiayia explains a lot.

Fallon awakens once we get to the coast. She's exhausted after our long night entangled in the sheets together. Galanos gets out of the Jeep with his hand extended as he films himself giving life advice. I snort as he wisely moves me out of the frame. What the hell does my younger brother know about life advice? He was born and raised in the lap of luxury. Yiayia would say he's the reason we work so hard. So none of our future generations know hardship.

I open the back door and Fallon yawns, sitting up and squinting as the bright sun invades her comfortable resting place.

"Are we there?"

"Yes. I'll get you on the boat."

"I can handle it."

She stretches as her sandals touch the pavement. Fuck. She's beautiful. I watch her approach without taking my eyes off her. She climbs the ramp. For now, she's given up on escape. Getting her out of my cousin's clutches wasn't easy, but he accepted my promise to help him find another girl later.

Yiayia's weak today. Papa and her cane aren't enough to help her walk without getting winded. Loukas offers to carry her and she threatens to put her cigarette out on his arm. Loukas was always the obedient one, so he has fewer burns than the rest of us. But today, he's nervous for the trip over the ocean. Once Papa and Yiayia board the ship, he approaches me with his cell phone out.

"I'll be behind you a day or so. We have a rendezvous with Ofek's cousin. Another five million dollars if he likes our merchandise."

"Merchandise?"

"Forty kilos of cocaine."

"Drugs? We aren't dealing with drugs anymore."

Loukas presses a finger to his lips and winks.

"Not officially. Yiayia wants me to do this so she can send her niece in America some money for a new house. Her husband got raided by the FBI. She needs a place to lie low for a while and cash to get it."

"Be careful. Drugs out here make you a target."

Loukas nods, but he doesn't drift away from me. There's something else going on.

"What else?"

"I haven't heard from Carlotta in three days. It isn't like her."

"She's a teenager. She probably threw a party."

"She's seventeen!"

"I don't need to remind you of what you were like at seventeen?"

Loukas smirks uncomfortably. Since he's become a parent, he's forgotten how crazy we used to get. Cocaine. Girls. Guns. It's a miracle we made it to the other side of thirty-five.

"Carlotta isn't like that. Since boarding school, she hasn't been involved with troubling characters. I've kept her away from our life here. I haven't heard from Matilda either. She said she was scared about something. But when I called back, I didn't hear from her."

"I'll check on them."

"You don't know about this?"

"Are you accusing me of something?"

"I've lost three women. Three of my life's great loves. If you kill this one as well, I will take your bitch and have ten men on her in a night."

"Careful, Loukas."

"I am fair to you, Stavros. Everyone knows you are not right in the head. But I am done losing women. Finished."

"I have killed none of your women. And I would not order them dead."

"You'd give your own sister to a fat Israeli."

"It isn't Cassia's fault she didn't run fast enough."

"I tried to help her," Loukas hisses.

Ah. So he's the brains behind her failed escape attempt. That explains why she didn't get further. Loukas and Cassia working together could have yielded no success. Why didn't the idiot get Helen to help? Or me? I can see why Loukas doesn't trust me.

"I want to help her. But my method of helping her won't get her killed."

"You brought her back. I know you, Stavros. You think if you help this family, they'll set you free. If you want freedom, you have to take it."

"Thank you for the advice, older brother."

"Hm. You need it. Because I promise you, Stavros. One hair harmed on Matilda's head and I'm coming for yours."

"I understand."

Loukas storms off. Why does he assume it's me? If someone plans on hurting Carlotta and Matilda, wouldn't it be someone in Greece? He's not thinking straight. A bold accusation coming from me. I board the ship to find Galanos already at the bar. He's arguing with the man behind the counter, and I don't want to find out what he's arguing about.

"Loukas and the others are taking a detour. Where's Helen?"

"She's downstairs complaining about the condition of her bedroom suite."

"Hm. Okay. I'll get us off the docks. One week on the water. I don't know how you can drink before you get your sea legs."

"Strong stomach."

I leave my brother to his drink and find Fallon sitting on my bed, clothed and staring out the window at the ocean.

"Ready for the trip back?"

She nods. I sit at the foot of the bed and sigh.

"I've decided, Fallon."

"Oh?"

"When we get back to Greece... I will let you go. You have no documentation, but I have a contact who can get you a passport from Poland or Serbia. You won't be able to go back to America. But you can go anywhere else in the world."

She bites her lower lip and gazes up at me.

"Why would you let me go?"

"Because. Everyone around me thinks I'm a monster except you. I owe it to you to prove you right."

"Can I ask for something else?"

"What do you want, beloved?"

"My mom doesn't know I'm alive. I didn't want to tell her because I know she'd try something crazy. Or stupid. But I can't keep this anymore. I want to tell her."

"If you make a phone call, the FBI could trace it abroad. I can't let you do that. It puts everyone I know at risk."

"Then let me email her."

"When we return to Greece."

"Okay. I can wait. You promise, right?"

I nod and gesture for her to sit next to me. Fallon scoots across the bed next to me and sighs.

"I'm lucky. I didn't think I was... but I'm lucky to have met you, Stavros. Few men would let me go after..."

"Sleeping with you?"

"I could have screwed myself out of my freedom."

"You'll have your freedom."

I walk out of the room. Freedom. That's all Fallon wants. I know it's why she slept with me. She wouldn't have slept with me otherwise. She's a smart woman. And I have to let her go. She's the only person who doesn't think I'm a monster. My brothers and sisters all know that I'm the crazy one. The one who hears voices. And if I don't let Fallon go, she'll realize that I'm exactly who they think I am.

Helen leans in the hallway outside my door, examining her cuticles until I emerge from my bedroom.

"Brother. We need to talk."

"About what?"

"I didn't want to ask in front of Loukas."

"Tell me."

"Did you send someone to kill Matilda? Tell me the truth, Stavros. I need to know. Now."

"Why does everyone think I'm the one killing Loukas' women? It has nothing to do with me. He's the one who needs a new bitch each week."

"I am serious."

"So am I. There's no reason to believe Matilda is dead. We made the deal. We did what we came here to do. There's nothing more to it. Maybe people in this family would get into less trouble if they stopped looking for it."

218

THIRTY-THREE
CRAZIER THAN I AM

Helen and Fallon get along too well together. Galanos spends most of the day drunk and the rest of his time away sexually harassing the women on the boat. He has none of the polish required for a Pagonis man. But he's Yiayia's current favorite. None of us bother disturbing her golden boy. Helen and Fallon practice Greek in the yacht's dining room.

Helen laughs at Fallon's pronunciation but assures her she's making excellent progress. Why is she bothering to learn Greek, I wonder? She won't be in Greece for long. I call my contact for the passport. He'll need her photograph and other basic biometric information so he can draw up a passport and forged birth certificate. By our last night on the yacht, Fallon can speak enough Greek to ask for coffee or to have a simple conversation with the maid and chef.

She avoids Galanos. And I avoid her. I haven't tried to sleep with her since Africa. She sleeps next to me, not daring to fall asleep until she hears me snoring, wary that I may want her in the middle of the night. Whatever urges I have to sleep with Fallon again disappear when I think of Loukas' threat. I've churned his words in my head nightly since his accusation.

I have no proof anything has happened to Carlotta or Matilda. Loukas is right to worry. He has a way of losing the women he loves. He believes I'm a killer, but I believe the same about him. He kills them when he tires of them. Those were Yiayia's words about her eldest grandson. She expressed her disdain for him several times. Yiayia lies. Of her many lessons, that has been my grandmother's most important one. She lies.

Papa doesn't. And he's mourned with Loukas for each of his losses. I don't think Papa could order a woman dead. But Yiayia? I remind myself there's no reason for my grandmother to kill off Loukas' lovers. She liked some of them. And there would be no reason for her to kill them.

They're not dead, Stavros. They can't be. My head aches as I try to fall asleep, so I climb out of bed and light a cigarette. There's nowhere to blow the smoke downstairs, but I don't want to go above deck and risk running into Helen or Galanos. Fallon coughs dramatically to let me know that she's both awake and annoyed with my poor cigarette etiquette. I grunt an apology and she sits up, her hair cascading down her shoulders. My cock stiffens. Great. The last thing I need to worry about right now is stifling my urges with Fallon.

Avoiding my lust was easier when she was asleep.

"Aren't you going to sleep? You've barely slept in days. That can't be good for your... you know. The voices."

"I can't sleep. Now quiet. I need to think."

"Don't give me that tough bullshit. What's going on?"

"Beloved, my problems are not yours to worry about."

"I get it. You're 'the bad guy'. You're sitting here plotting your next kill or whatever."

"Quite the contrary."

I set the cigarette in the ashtray and gesture to my lap. Fallon rolls her eyes but crawls slowly to the foot of the bed. She's breathtaking.

"I'm not sitting on your lap. I can see that thing straining through your pants over here."

"Fine," I grunt, wishing she'd sit on my lap. Or other parts of me.

"Family problems."

"Isn't it always?"

"Talk it through. Come on. I'm here and... I won't be for long. Trust me, I won't tell anyone your secrets."

"Secrets?"

"You killed Loukas' new girlfriend. My Greek is getting better you know."

"I didn't."

"I believe you."

I raise an eyebrow.

"Why?"

"You may be many things, Stavros Pagonis, but you aren't a liar."

"Hm."

"Do you think she's dead? They don't have any proof she is."

"We'll find out. But Loukas... He makes threats. He's angry. And if she's dead, he won't believe I wasn't the one to kill her. It's a setup. I arrive in Greece first. I'm the one to blame."

"No one could blame you for killing someone if she died three days ago or whatever."

"You don't understand, Fallon. He's threatened you."

"That's why you're setting me free."

"Yes."

"Oh."

Her expression changes. Damn it. I try, but I don't think I'll ever understand women properly. Especially not Fallon.

"What is it now?"

"I thought... I thought you wanted to get rid of me. After last time..."

"Damn it, Fallon. I don't understand. First you want your freedom. Then you want to stay. Now, I'm giving you your freedom. Real freedom."

"Freedom?! Freedom would be sending me back to America with

the documents your idiot friend burned. What you want to do is abandon me."

"Abandon you? My brother will kill you. You stupid woman, don't you understand that everyone in my life is a darker monster than I am. I want you. I want you in my bed. In my home. But I cannot keep you here if your fate is floating face up in the Aegean Sea."

"You wouldn't let anyone hurt me."

"It would not always be my choice."

"Then teach me how to defend myself."

"I could hold a gun before I could hold a pencil. The same goes for anyone in my family. If they want you dead, they'll kill you."

"Give me a choice, at least. You don't get me because you want to make all the decisions. Let me choose when to leave. Give me everything I need. But let me choose. I'll leave when I'm ready. Not when you're afraid."

"Hm. Why would you want to stay at all?"

She takes a pillow and throws it at me. Hard.

"Ouch! What the hell is that for?"

"It was a pillow. It didn't hurt."

"Why did you throw it?!"

"You really don't get why I want to stay here?"

"No. I don't. Maybe you're crazier than I am."

"Maybe. Maybe I realized that... you saved my life. And you've looked after me. And even if you are insane... you've treated me better than any guy I ever dated. Seriously."

"They must have been bastards."

"Oh yeah. They were."

"Tell me about them."

"No. No way. I'm not doing the 'ex talk' with you."

"Why not? I bought you... I ought to know your purchase history."

She tosses the pillow back. Harder. Then she follows, launching her body into my lap and punching me. It hurts, but in the playful way. I pick her up and she squeals as I throw her onto the bed.

"Ex talk. Or sex. You choose."

"You are bad."

"I'm your worst fucking nightmare, beloved."

She grins and waits expectantly for me to join her in bed. I roll on top of her and put my hands on her hips, curving my fingers so I'm poised to tickle her. Fallon catches her breath from laughter and relents, "Fine. I'll tell you. But I don't want to hear about the slew of models and hookers you've slept with. Okay?"

"Hm. Deal. But there have been no models or hookers in a long time."

"Watch it, Stavros..."

"Talk, beloved. Tell me anything to take my mind off my problems."

THIRTY-FOUR
GREEK MEN LOVE C

She squirms beneath my grasp. The last thing Fallon wants right now is to talk about her past. I don't blame her. I have a past that I don't want to talk about either. She sighs.

"There's not much to explain. One awful boyfriend after another."

"Have you ever been in love?"

She pushes against my chest. Hard.

"In love? Don't be gross."

"What's gross about it?"

"Love. Hearing that word from your mouth sounds like a fucked up joke."

"I don't get the joke."

I push hair out of her face, and she squirms again. I'm not allowing Fallon Iverson to wriggle away from me like this, skirting past the real issues between us without ever getting to the truth. Dishonesty kills relationships. It's been the one thing that has killed all of mine. Dishonesty. And hiding.

"You have obviously never loved anyone."

The words shouldn't sting the way they do. She notices my

expression fall, which gets me angrier. I slide my body off hers and roll onto my back. She sighs and responds, "Don't get all melodramatic."

"I am not melodramatic."

"Have you, then? Loved anyone?"

My chest flutters with strange internal throbbing. What kind of question is that?

"I don't know."

"If you loved anyone, you'd know."

"We aren't talking about me. We're talking about you."

"I've been in love. It never worked out."

"He couldn't make you cum. Big surprise."

"Love isn't only about orgasms," she protests.

Hm. She's ten years younger than me so she doesn't realize it yet but love is mostly about orgasms. If you love someone, you care enough to make them cum. You want to please them. When you're in love, you yearn for their pleasure.

"What else is it about, eh? Feelings?"

"Feelings isn't a dirty word."

"Neither is cumming. And you, Fallon Iverson, need to worry a lot less about love and a lot more about cumming."

Fallon hates when I'm crass, and she makes another half-hearted attempt to push me off her again. I grab her arms and pin them over her head.

"I hate you."

But she doesn't mean it. She can't. You don't squeal like that when someone you hate kisses your neck. Unless you do. Unless that's what makes it exciting. If she has to hate me to enjoy herself, I don't care. All I want is to make her cum. Making her cum is the one thing I can give her after all I've taken away. I growl as I force her legs open and she squeezes her resistant thighs around my torso.

"You'll take my cock without complaint," I growl and she nods, offering no resistance against the hands pinning her to the bed.

She hates how much she enjoys her captor pinning her to the bed and having his way with her. Fallon has never had a proper way to escape my clutches. I've always given her a half-choice. I kiss her chest, baring her nipples and running my tongue along them as I move my way down her stomach with kisses. Each kiss pleads for forgiveness I don't deserve from Fallon Iverson, and she knows it. As she wriggles beneath me, her stomach undulates, pushing upward to meet my lips. She's gained weight since I bought her. Greek food has that effect, especially on a girl who pushed everything Khalid fed her aside. She's smart. I enjoy that about her. Not as much as I enjoy her curves filling out.

My tongue juts into her navel because I need to taste every inch of her, leaving no crevice untouched by my tongue. I leave her hands over her head and grab her waist, kissing her stomach and working my way down further. Fallon allows me to slide her underwear over her hips and I spread her legs, revealing the delectable treasure between them.

She cries out as my tongue slides between her lower lips. It shouldn't be possible for a woman to taste this good, but Fallon Iverson tastes beyond incredible. She's soaking wet by the time my tongue slides between her legs and all I want is more of her. My tongue finds her clit and I rub around it in circles until she cries out. Her thighs move against their will, clamping my face between her legs as my long hair falls over my nose. I don't need to breathe in anything but her perfect cunt, anyway.

I run my tongue over her dark lower lips and then return to her pink center, licking her until she climaxes. Watching Fallon climax is always an incredible treat. She tastes like brown sugar and warm honey. She's sticky and sweet with clear juices dripping from her entrance as her screams of pleasure get louder. Eating her feels so good I forget the reason I'm between her legs — the reason I need her this ready.

I eat her to three more climaxes before she pushes a gentle palm against my forehead. She doesn't want me to stop. She's pushing me away because she wants more than my tongue. She needs to feel my eleven inch Greek cock buried between her legs, stretching her tight flesh to capacity around my rigid pole.

I let her push me off and roll onto my back, licking my lips without hiding my satisfaction. Fallon props herself up on her elbows and raises a judgmental eyebrow.

"Can men fake it?"

"Fake what?"

I run my tongue over my lips again in case I missed any drop of her juices. I find some on my upper lip and a rush surges through me as I tongue a burst of her flavor into my mouth.

"There's no way you love eating me out this much."

I laugh. Hard. Eating Fallon out is a much better use of my time than sitting around listening to the voices in my head playing out my terrible life sentence.

"Believe me, beloved, I have no reason to hide my feelings for you... or your cunt."

My heart pounds in my chest. I have no reason to hide my feelings for you. Why would I say those words? What is it about Fallon that brings me so dangerously close to admitting emotion? I remind myself I don't have feelings. I'm the monster she thinks.

"I have never met a guy who likes it."

"Have you dated Greek men before?"

"No."

"Now you know. Greek men love cunt."

She pouts and pushes me, but I'm not near her, so I interpret the gesture as playful. She wants me closer.

"I still hate that you use the word cunt," she protests.

"I don't care," I growl.

She pushes again. Teasing me. Taunting me to play fight back. If I play her game, we both know how this will end.

"All fours, beloved. Let me see my treat."

She folds her arms and shakes her head.

"No way. I'm not letting you get in my head like this."

Fallon squeals as I drag her into the position I want.

"Stavros!"

I push her against the bed and press my body on hers. Not quite on all fours. She's pressed against the mattress with her chin digging into my pillow. I use one hand to push her lower back into the bed and the other to spread her legs. She's dripping.

"When I ask for your cunt, I expect you to give it."

She squirms as I run a finger between her dripping lower lips.

"Admit you want me, beloved," I growl.

"Fine! I admit it."

"Say it."

"I want you."

I release my grip on her lower back. She gives up on her protest and sinks her hips into the mattress. I work my hardness from my trousers and press the tip against her entrance. She's soaked. I don't want to go easy on her. The tip presses between her slick lips and she moans.

"Hurt?"

"No," she whispers, "Harder..."

I slide the rest of my cock between her legs in one swift motion, claiming every inch of her as mine. She will always be mine.

THIRTY-FIVE
GHOST FROM MY PAST

fuck her until I'm tired. She begs me to stop so we can both get some rest. She says she doesn't want my dick to break. Hmph.

Over twenty orgasms and we've both lost count. What's the sense in counting? I don't want to let her go once I'm finished. I keep her body pressed against mine and curl around her, throwing one arm over her to keep her pinned to my bed.

I wake up in the middle of the night. I can't sleep with the boat tossing and turning. I need a drink. Plus, I have a visitor.

The nightmare wakes me. It's her. I killed this woman so long ago that I have forgotten her name but in my head, it's *Ana-Maria*. I was a teenager, and she was too. Yiayia loathed my attraction to her. She wanted it gone. She wanted the girl gone.

"She's a filthy fishmonger's daughter. She's only taking notice of you for your money," my grandmother spat.

I know it now for a lie but I was younger then. Foolish. Eager to impress. Give a young man a gun, stacks of hundred pound notes slung together with thick rubber bands and promise him the world, he'll do whatever you ask. Yiayia convinced me she was spying on the family and reporting to the Sicilians.

"If you don't kill her, your body will be the one floating in the Aegean."

She planned it. Gave me the pistol. Told me how to do it. She sits on the foot of my bed now, a hallucination, but so vivid I can't stop my hand shaking. She's covered in weeds and her lips are blue. The vision's eyes bulge out of its head and her voice rasps like a cartoon villain. That's the proper way I know she isn't real. Ana-Maria never sounded like that.

"You'll kill her too," the vision says, "If you don't chase her away, she'll die."

The boat rocks back and forth. I mutter under my breath, "You aren't real. You're dead, Ana. I'm sorry, but I can't take it back."

"I don't mind being dead. I get to return and torture you. Revenge. That's what your sick family is obsessed with. Revenge. It'll catch up to you, eventually."

I get out of bed and leave for the bar. You can't walk away from hallucinations. They follow you, blending into the environment like they're a part of it. I sit at the bar and pretend that I'm not glancing furtively to my left, out of the corner of my eye.

"What can I get for you, Stavros?"

"Whiskey."

"Only whiskey?"

I glance at the vision. She leans over the counter and grabs her breasts lewdly, shaking them at the bartender, oblivious to the crude workings of my imagination.

"No. I want... the strongest you have."

"Absinthe. Galanos made sure I kept the stock up."

"The good kind?"

"Yes."

"Make it a double."

He pours me the drink, and as bartenders do, he makes conversation. That doesn't stop my vision of Ana-Maria. She talks over him as he asks, "Late night? Much business for you to attend to?"

"Insomnia. It's difficult crossing the ocean, even in a luxurious palace like this one."

"Yes, but it is a great place to work."

Ana-Maria leans forward and yells at him, "He's a MURDERER! Don't you know he's a goddamned murderer! A monster!"

I flinch, and the bartender purses his lips. Our conversation's over. This is how the rumors about me spread. Stavros, the crazed butcher of Thessaloniki. The monster who killed the woman he loved. I deserve everything they say about me. I deserve worse. I take the drink and wander onto the deck.

Ana-Maria follows. I can almost feel her warmth next to me. Except she's dead. So if she were next to me at all, her body would be at least 15 years cold.

"You should jump," she whispers, sitting on the railing, "It would save Fallon a lot of trouble."

"Don't mention Fallon," I mutter, aware that I'm talking to myself.

"You love her, don't you?"

"No. She's... an object. A pretty thing I've acquired."

"Liar. You love her. That's the part I enjoy. Because she'll never love you. Never."

"I can make her," I growl, aware of how pathetic I sound — and not just because I'm talking to myself.

"She'll fuck you up. And you'll deserve it."

I hurl my glass into the ocean. Who cares? I'm a madman. You expect crazy people to throw their glasses of absinthe into the ocean. I wish Ana-Maria would jump the ten stories after it. I wish I could. But out there on the flat sea, I see something. A small boat. Then I hear a motor. I squeeze my eyes shut and shake my head, telling myself it's another vision.

But the boat gets closer and I see the person on the dinghy.

"What the hell are you doing here?!"

She's real. She's very real.

"Help me! Please, help me!"

My sister, Cassia. Covered in blood. How the hell did she find us? I tell myself it's another vision and close my eyes, but the Captain rushes out and tosses a rope overboard. We drag Cassia on deck. She's covered in blood and soaked in sea water.

"Where is your husband?"

Cassia doesn't answer. She collapses into me, pressing her head into my chest with the stink of hot blood coming off her clothes. Her dark brown curls are plastered to her neck and she sobs.

"I nearly died."

"What have you done," I whisper.

"Please, don't tell Yiayia."

The Captain yells, "There's someone else down there!"

I throw Cassia off me and rush to the railing. The Captain drags a body from the boat up. I can't tell who it is. Cassia rushes to me again and begs through her tears.

"Please. Don't kill him. I promised him you wouldn't kill him."

"We'll see about that."

The man falls onto his back, coughing as sea water escapes his lungs. I recognize his face.

"Cass. What the hell have you done?"

THIRTY-SIX

QUITE THE LITTLE CRIMINAL

"Help us," Cassia whimpers.

I clamp my hand over her mouth.

"Shhhh..."

I turn my attention to the adult male lying on the deck. Sandros. *Damn those two*. Maybe I should have killed him. It's one thing for him to live, but if he returns and Yiayia finds out...

"Tell me what you did and tell me quietly. The others can't know you're here."

Sandros lets out a startling, dramatic cough. Yiayia always told me no good deed goes unpunished. Mercy is worthless. But I can't deny what I feel. Relief. I pull Cassia against my chest and cradle her head. She hugs me and sobs. Sandros catches his breath and speaks before Cass can form the words.

"I killed him! I love Cassia and we're going to be married and not a fucking Pagonis in the world can stop me."

"I thought you killed him," Cass whimpers, "I thought you fucking killed him, you stupid bastard."

The Captain pulls his gun out and presses it to Sandros' head. For all his tough talk, he still looks like he's about to shit himself when the barrel pushes his wet curls out of the way. Cassia lets out a sob.

"Captain, lower the weapon."

"Mr. Pagonis..."

"Do what I said. Now."

A Pagonis never has to ask twice. That's a lesson from Papa. The Captain lowers the gun. I gesture to the man for his cellphone. He hands it over to me. The weapon follows. He understands that whatever happens here can't leave this ship. He probably thinks I mean to kill them both. It's what Yiayia would want. Betraying the family and lying are death sentences in the mafia. But I've betrayed my family, too. I'm the reason these foolish children have gone and killed our multi-million dollar contract.

"Captain, you go to your office and you keep this boat moving. Nod if you understand."

The man nods and leaves hurriedly, content that I've allowed him his life. Sandros exhales a premature sigh of relief. I wrest Cassia away from me.

"Tell me what you've found yourself involved with, sister."

"Thank you..."

"Don't thank me," I snarl, "I should have never spared the boy. I approach Sandros and drag him to his feet. He's still coughing."

I take my pistol and press it to his chin. By now, we both know I won't shoot him. Threatening to kill a man only works once. You must follow through or the threat becomes worthless.

"Did you fuck my sister? Are you a thief and a liar?"

Cass recklessly grabs the arm I'm holding my weapon in.

"Cass! I'm holding a fucking gun are you crazy!?"

"I won't let you shoot the love of my life!"

"He's the love of your life now, eh? You're a married fucking woman."

A cruel smirk crosses her face.

"Not anymore."

"They'll find out."

"No," Sandros groans, "They won't."

"I'm taking you two up to my room. Helen and Gal can't know you're on this boat. No one can know."

"The Captain knows," Sandros points out, which I hoped he wouldn't. I'm about to take care of the Captain problem.

"Shut the fuck up, smart mouth. Move. Quietly. Gal and Helen are in their rooms for the night. I should have been sleeping. Stupid girl! You could have died out there."

"Don't yell at me!" Cass hisses, "I've been through enough."

One more glare and she grabs Sandros' hand, and they bound downstairs to my room together. Fallon should enjoy this surprise. She seems preoccupied with my moral fiber. Look how far that got me. I have to kill the Captain and then my sister and her boyfriend. At least that's what Yiayia would want.

Tonight, I don't want to do what my grandmother wants. I can't stop thinking about Fallon. I took her out when I was going to kill Sandros. It's like I wanted her to stop me. Like I wasn't meant to kill him. She wanted me to save Cass too, but I couldn't. I was too scared of something like this happening. Cassia going rogue spells trouble for all of us on board this ship. Yiayia won't view this as simple betrayal. *This will cost us millions.*

I've failed Cass enough. I've failed myself. I failed the family. How could I have become so twisted up in my mind? I should have never let Ofek take my sister and rape her. Money isn't important enough. I walk into the Captain's office and he knows what's coming. He's seen too much, and he knows what happens to people who see too much.

"Make it quick," he says, eyeing my gun. But I can't shoot him. Any gunshots have a chance of waking Gal or Helen, and they'll ask why I've fired the shot. I could let him go in the boat and tell him never to return. Look how far that got me the first time. No, this is my penance for allowing Ofek to hurt Cassia. I tell myself the Captain will be my last kill and my heart pounds as I reach into my pocket for the rope.

"I will pray with you," I breathe.

The Captain closes his eyes and mutters in Greek under his breath. The words are beautiful. I recognize it as a psalm, but I don't know which one. Most people stick with the basics. Our Father... I wrap the rope around his neck and squeeze. His eyes bulge and he sputters the rest of the psalm. My rope kills him before the end.

I drop to my knees with shaking hands as his body slumps over in the chair. We have a co-Captain asleep downstairs for the next shift. I have ninety minutes. I need five. The voices are louder than they've ever been. I drag the Captain to the edge of the railing. The voices tell me to jump in after him. But someone has to protect Cass and Sandros. Someone has to look after Fallon.

I return to my room, grateful that I made no commotion to wake Galanos or Helen. Fallon paces with her hands against her forehead and looks at Cassia and Sandros like a stern parent.

"What were you two thinking? This guy is a *gun dealer.* He could have killed you!"

"He tried," Cass says, wide-eyed.

"It wasn't hard to kill him. I think the pork rib wrapped around his heart protected him from bullets. Pig."

Cass rubs Sandros' thigh. The gesture sends me boiling mad, but I contain my rage. Liars. They pulled the wool over all of our eyes.

"I should have killed you," I tell Sandros, shutting the door behind me and locking it. Fallon glances at me over her shoulders, unhappily.

"I am sorry, Mr. Pagonis. I had to lie to you because... I am going to marry Cassia. And she'll have many of my children."

"You two shouldn't have come here! How the hell did you find our boat?"

"Ofek is a bastard. He tracks his guns. He can track the shipments you're carrying."

"We only have five crates on this ship. He has chips in *all of them.* You could have come to the wrong boat."

"I remembered you planned to go straight home while they rendezvous and I stole Ofek's phone," Cassia admits proudly.

My little sister is quite the little criminal. But she's also put herself and her so-called true love in immense danger.

"This is a big deal!" Fallon says, "You killed someone. You're 18! Both of you know better than this. Especially you, Sandros."

"Why especially him?!"

Sandros restrains Cass gently and kisses her cheek.

"We are safe now, my love. I will take care of you."

"How? If any of the others caught you, they would have killed you on the spot. Especially Galanos, who is on this ship."

"Gal's a pussy."

"Don't talk about your brother that way," I chide her, but I have no moral high ground to speak of.

Fallon stands next to me and folds her arms, glancing between the two of them.

"We should do something," she says to me.

"We?"

"You will not kill them or you wouldn't have let me know they were on this ship."

"We can't help them. We have to send them on their way."

"Ofek's ship might be after you," Cass mutters, "I don't know."

Great. Right when I thought it couldn't be worse.

PEOPLE KILLED BY STAVROS PAGONIS

"Before I wake the co-Captain, I need you two to understand that you cannot leave this room until we get to Greece."

"What?!"

"Cassia. If Yiayia finds out what you've done, she will kill you. She will kill Sandros. And she will kill me."

"That's all you care about. Your own life." Cassia says. It's better than being like her — not caring about anything at all.

What she's done is dangerous and now, I'm her fucking accomplice. I have to make sure Fallon doesn't suffer for this.

"What do you think will happen to Fallon if I'm not there to take care of her?"

"No offense, but I don't care. Sorry, Fallon," Cassia says coldly.

"Offense taken," Fallon says.

"Don't disrespect Fallon. If she hadn't told me to, your precious boyfriend would be dead. She's the reason you two are here... making my life hell."

Cassia's gaze softens, and she tilts her head to the side as if to ask Fallon if it's true. Fallon shrugs and then scowls.

"Wait... you said you'd never even kissed a girl."

"I wanted him to spare my life!"

"I kissed you!"

Cassia rises to her feet and lunges at Fallon. I step between them and push Cassia off.

"You're lucky she only kissed him... and you, Sandros, are no angel. Quite the little manipulator. Are you sure that your mother didn't fuck my father? I've heard there are Pagonis bastards all over Thessaloniki."

Sandros turns beet red and Cassia yells at me all over again, which is worth it considering what I've already done on their account.

"Silence. You stay here, and when we get to Greece, I will help you. But Cassia, no one can know. You are too young to know all the ways Yiayia can be cruel, but trust me, you don't want to find out."

I try to leave, but Fallon grabs my arm.

"I'm coming with you."

"Can we trust them alone?"

I growl, seeking advice from Fallon. She's clearly better at this helping other people nonsense than I am. See what happens when you help people? They just come back needing more help. I glare at my sister, who nods emphatically.

Fallon shrugs.

"We're already trusting them to stay hidden."

I don't push back. I want Fallon to follow me because I want her close. Always. But especially now. We close the door behind us and I walk downstairs into the bar area. The bartender, mercifully, didn't add himself to the ever-growing list of "People Killed By Stavros Pagonis". I lean over and ask him for a shot of vodka, which I hurriedly throw back before I walk to the Captain's room.

"Where's the Captain?" Fallon asks.

I glance over at her, pleading with her not to make me tell her. She folds her arms.

"You killed him."

"I don't need you telling me off over killing him."

"Someone has to! I mean, didn't you ever learn right from wrong as a kid?"

"Are you here because you think I'm a psychological puzzle to solve?!"

"No."

"Then why did you follow me?"

She tries to get close and I push her away. That's the worst lesson I learned as a Pagonis. Never let anyone get too close. It works in business but my love life... Well, it could be better.

"Because... I *care*. "

"Care? About the man who *bought* you?"

"Can we not do this now? Tell me what to do," Fallon says.

"I want to talk more about how you care."

"I don't," Fallon says. "Because it's incredibly stupid. Now focus, Stavros. Focus."

I grunt and glance at the radar.

"This will tell us if there are any ships or large objects in the water. It's not exactly specific. Ofek must have been sailing to Greece as well, or tracking our boats beforehand."

"If he's dead, why would anyone chase us down?"

"Cassia. Our family has many enemies, and one of those enemies already kidnapped Helen."

"She told me."

I often forget they spent time together. I scowl at Fallon and warn her.

"Helen can't know about Cassia."

"I won't breathe a word."

We both lose our train of thought as a red orb appears on one end of the radar screen. Shit. We watch for thirty minutes and the object eventually moves offscreen. We're in the clear temporarily at least. Fallon slumps against me and sighs.

"That was a *long* thirty minutes. And they're still upstairs."

"It's almost sunrise. We ought to get some sleep."

"What are you going to say happened to the Captain?"

"I'll wake the co-captain. He'll understand... strange things happen on the open sea."

Fallon waits and watches the radar while I fetch the co-captain. She slips her hand into mine as we walk toward my bedroom again. She asks, "Did you hear voices tonight?"

I only answer because it's Fallon, and because tonight, I feel close to her. I don't feel close to people. It's not who I am. Stavros, the butcher of Thessaloniki, never wavers in his grim sociopathy. At least that's what I imagine people say about me. I haven't the faintest.

"Yes."

Her hand rubs my back and sends a surge of desire through me. She has nice hands. Healing hands. Peace settles in me as she touches me. This woman feels like healing. Like everything.

Did I know the moment I saw her? I don't want this to...

"Stop," she whispers, "You can stop killing any time. There's always a choice. Always a way out."

"I don't want to betray my family."

"You don't have to. There's always a way. Remember that."

I push the door open and a grim scene sears itself onto both our eyeballs. Permanently. The smarmy little shit Sandros lies arse naked on my bed and my sister Cass sits atop him with bared breasts and head tilted back in the throes of pleasure as her dark brown curls cascade down her back. It takes everything in me not to scream. Fallon covers her mouth to stop herself. Cass gasps and leaps off him, which makes the scene worse as the boy's stiffness crudely juts toward the ceiling.

Cass wraps a blanket around herself as Sandros stands up, bumbling around with his cock growing ever softer. They're both barely covered and my face burns with rage.

"I leave you horny idiots alone for five seconds and this is what you do? I ought to toss you over the ship, you fucking little..."

Fallon clamps her hand over my mouth and the gesture surprises me.

"Shut up, Stavros. We don't have time to get mad at them. Cass, you sleep on one side of the bed. Sandros, you sleep on the other."

"But —"

"Don't argue!"

"Ugh," Cass sneers, "You two are like the boring normal parents I never had."

Fallon has a smug smile plastered on her face. I don't know how I'd survive the night without her. It's one thing to kill a man, but an entirely different thing to deal with two horny teenagers desperate to celebrate their great escape. Fallon shuts the lights off and I lock the door. We'll deal with all this in Greece. We can get out of this. I have to believe that.

THIRTY-EIGHT
YOUR PRETTY BLOND HEAD

know something has happened when we arrive at the docks and there's no one to greet us. Five long days of hiding Cassia and her boyfriend at sea have my nerves frazzled. Galanos and Helen suspect something's wrong with me. Fallon has a plan for that too. For someone who hates my world, she has hundreds of suggestions and answers to my problems.

Helen and Galanos leave the boat with the staff. Helen's having nightmares and too wrapped up in her own problems to care about what I'm doing. But she wonders why there's no one here to pick us up. Yiayia expects us to arrive several days before their boat. We should have someone.

Galanos wants to hang back with me and Fallon. He's been "canceled" as he calls it for using a racial slur, and he thinks hanging out with Fallon on his stupid livestream will get him back on top. I usher him off the ship by the collar while he loudly protests.

"I've lost 200,000 followers! I'm the only one of my friends who hasn't hit 10 million yet. This isn't fair!"

"You got yourself into this mess. Leave us out of it."

I release his collar and throw him at Helen, who wraps her arms around her baby brother.

"Stavros is mean, yes. But you are an idiot. Canceled, eh? What are they saying about you? You're the most handsome man in all of Greece."

Helen has Yiayia's tendency to dote. My sister has never pretended to like me much, but Galanos is far worse than I am in every respect. Hm.

"Call me when you get back to the house," I tell Helen.

"Whatever happened to the poor Captain," she muses, "How horrible for him to have taken his own life. I knew him as a jolly man. Perhaps he found something out that made him feel... less jolly."

Her blue eyes bore into me and I have to remind myself that she doesn't know. Helen's testing me, and she's suspicious, but she doesn't know about Cassia and Sandros. Fallon and I were too careful.

My siblings leave and the staff packs up. I'll have to stash my sister and her runaway boyfriend on my smaller boat. If they anchor a mile offshore, I can send supplies until we figure out a plan. I re-enter the bedroom on the super-yacht to hear Fallon and Cassia arguing.

"You're a mean bitch!"

I hear Cass shrieking like a harpy at Fallon. Does my sister have any control over herself? Heat courses through me as I conjure up the necessary insults to put Cass in her place. Apparently, Fallon has this under control.

"I work with the mentally ill. You'll have to do a lot worse than that to ruffle my feathers."

"Is that why you're *in love* with my brother?"

I stop before I get to the door. My heart pounds. I don't know what I want Fallon to say, but I don't expect what comes next. The sound of a slap. Not across the face. I hear Cassia yelp.

I lean in the doorway and arch a curious brow. Cassia gasps and instinctively rushes behind Sandros, escaping from Fallon's grasp.

"Were you *spanking* my adult sister?" I ask, amused. Apparently, Fallon didn't need my help at all. A slap was plenty to silence Cass for the time being at least.

"She wouldn't listen!"

"She's a monster, Stavros!" Cassia moans.

Sandros puffs up his chest.

"What happened?" He asks, as if he would really have the balls to hit Fallon in front of me. Hm.

I'm rubbing my temples instinctively.

"Cassia planned to call a priest with this!" Fallon says, producing a cell phone. A phone that belongs to me. I keep this stored on my yacht for personal reasons and the thought of my younger sister violating my personal space...

My cheeks darken.

"How did you know about my secret phone!?"

"Your *sexting phone*?" Cassia accuses.

"You have a sexting phone!?" Fallon drops the phone, like the nude messages are going to jump out.

"It isn't a sexting phone. Cass, sit down. Sandros, sit next to her."

"I want to hear about this sexting phone." Fallon says. Great, now she's angry with me too and how the hell can I explain this to her. I glare at my sister. She's always getting our asses into trouble.

We should send her to the Amalfi Coast Doukas family. They're much better at handling trouble than the Sicilians and they would know what to do with a creature like my sister.

"Fallon..." I stammer.

Cass and Sandros sit down. Cass juts her tongue out at Fallon, who responds by sticking her tongue out too. I don't bother glaring at either of them. I get the impression that they like each other. I don't know why that makes me happy. I shouldn't care.

"You'll stay on my other boat. Sandros? You take it one mile around the coast."

"By the rocks."

"Behind the large one. Anchor down. I'll come out in a dingy later with Fallon to give you two food and supplies."

"Fine."

"Don't leave the yacht until nightfall. If anyone sees you... give me their name."

A chill runs through the room. They all know what I mean by that, and they're all uncomfortable with the fact that I'm a murderer. Not just a murderer. A macabre butcher who haunts the streets of our city, keeping the fear in our name alive.

"Yes, brother. Thank you."

"Don't thank me. I... I should have never let Ofek take you."

"You didn't want Yiayia to kill me," she says. "I know she would have but I want to have my own life. If that means facing death, so be it."

"I wish you lacked a death wish. I wouldn't have so many problems."

"Not a death wish! Haven't you ever wanted to stop doing everything Yiayia says? She's old. It's time she retire."

"Don't speak about our grandmother that way."

"I don't care. I'm not old school like you. I'm not covered in scars and bruises and wounds from her. She's crazy. And she's old. Our family needs a new leader."

"Papa is our family's leader. He is the man of our house."

Cassia snorts.

"If you believe that, you're as stupid as Helen says."

"Cass, I don't need a lecture from you."

"It should be you, Stavros. You aren't as bad as Helen says. But you are stupid."

I put my arm around Fallon and toss the keys to Sandros.

"Keep her out of trouble," I tell him, "Or next time, I won't miss your pretty blond head."

Fallon follows me off the boat and leans her head on my arm.

"I hope they'll be okay."

"I'll see them tonight." I explain to her. They'll need more than

I've given them to run away. I'll help them one last time and let them escape. Cassia deserves the happiness that I'll never have.

"I'm coming with you."

"Why!?"

"Because. You kill way fewer people when I'm around. I think I'm good for you."

Yes. She's too good for me. And it hurts to know. Without vehicles waiting, we have to walk back to the villa. It isn't far. The staff had their vans waiting, so they drove Helen and Gal back. Before we head down the main street, my phone rings. Not the sexting phone.

"What is it?"

"Get here. Now. I cannot believe you would do this to your own niece," Helen says, her voice vibrating with anger.

"Are you at the villa? Is it Carlotta?"

"I said get here," Helen snaps. Helen hangs up before I can ask questions. Fallon tugs on my sleeve.

"What's wrong?" Fallon asks.

Her sandals slap loudly against the cobblestone, the noise echoing around my head. I grab Fallon's shoulders and turn to her.

"Something's wrong here. You won't be safe at the house. I'll come find you when I'm ready."

"I'll go back to the boat."

"No. And I don't want you with Sandros and Cassia either. Take this."

I hand her my wallet with wads of euros spilling out. I'm horrible with money.

"You're giving me your wallet?"

"Go downtown, ask for Archimedes. He will give you a room for the night without asking any questions. Don't tell him your name. Only show him my ID. Understand?"

"I don't want to go to a hotel!"

"Fallon, this isn't a discussion. I don't want anything to happen to you."

"Since when do you care?"

I run my thumb over her lip. Her gaze meets mine. She knows. She recognizes what I feel, and she gasps, stepping backward. I don't let her get far. My palm presses into her back and I pull her against me, kissing her. Her hands rush to my cheeks and I open her lips with my tongue.

"I care," I whisper when I pull away, "You make me feel like a human instead of a monster. I don't want to lose my humanity."

She presses a hand to my heart.

"You don't have to."

"I want to stop."

"Then stop, Stavros. I give you permission. You don't have to kill another man again."

"Kiss me, beloved."

She tucks hair behind my ears and whispers before she kisses me, "I still hate when you call me that."

"Good."

THIRTY-NINE
DISCIPLINE

Fallon hurries downtown. I don't worry that I've left her alone. Unless I report that she's run, there's no reason for Khalid to have his men track her down this close to our home town.

I trust she'll look after herself. She's survived me this far. I'm worse than anyone else out there.

Helen stands in the driveway in black sandals and her white dress with a cloud of smoke around her head. Two cigarette butts lie on the ground next to her. Gal lies on his back next to a puddle of his own sick as he groans.

"What's wrong?"

"You go in. She's in the kitchen."

"*Who* is in the fucking kitchen!?"

"Go look. I know it was you. Don't play stupid."

I walk into the open kitchen downstairs. The smell hits me before anything. Death. My old friend. Loukas' fiancee slumps over the counter, dead. *Matilda.*

My throat tightens. He was right to worry about her and now he'll think I did it. I could have done it last night. A speedboat off the side of the yacht would have allowed me plenty of time to kill her and return to the ship. The journey would have been treacherous but feasible for me alone.

Matilda's skin has changed color, but she's rigid. And ripe. She's been here at least three days.

"Where's Carlotta?"

"You tell me."

"Do you think I really killed my niece?"

"You sent Cassia to the Israeli. I know why we do what we do… but when are you boys going to realize that you are the ones with all the power. Women are poker chips to you."

She spits on the ground near my feet and storms off to the pool.

"Galanos. Get up. I need help to move the body."

He sits up, a new splattering of freckles already spreading across his cheeks from the sun.

"She stinks."

"She's dead. Sorry she doesn't smell like one of your escorts."

"We should toss her in the sea," Galanos says.

I drag him to his feet and scowl. I don't want to slap him again, but my younger brother could use some discipline.

"Why didn't you clean up your kill?"

"I didn't kill her."

"Helen told Loukas you did." I say to Galanos, studying him for a reaction. He's young, which means he's still stupid enough to allow his emotions to betray him.

"What? When?"

"On the phone. She says you are the only one who kills that way."

"How?"

"Drugs."

Fuck. Helen is partly right. I kill with drugs when it's easy. The voices are quieter when I can watch my victims slip into a deep sleep and convince myself I'm making the end of their life more peaceful.

"We have to move her. We'll lay her in the garage with a white blanket over her to keep the body cool."

"Helen sent the staff to clean the guesthouse. She wants stronger men to bleach the kitchen."

"Fine. Now come. It'll take us both to lift her."

And we may have to do other unsavory things to get her body to look peaceful. Twisting her limbs. Adjusting her stance. Whoever did this didn't care who found her. But Helen was wrong to tell Loukas it was me. I wouldn't kill with my niece around. Carlotta's only a girl.

When she's a woman, Loukas can decide how much of the family business he wants her involved with. Galanos gags when we enter the kitchen, but eventually we muscle the unfortunate woman into the garage.

"Do you think the smell can get into my Mercedes?"

I smack my little brother on the back of the head. He's concerned with all the wrong things and not concerned enough with having respect for the dead. I crouch beside her, glad that a blanket now covers her contorted face. I whisper a prayer. Galanos at least waits until I'm finished to snort.

"You pray over the people you kill?"

"I didn't kill her."

"But you still pray."

"Yes. Perhaps God will forgive their sins if he cannot forgive mine."

"That would make an excellent caption for the photo I took earlier. My abs are incredible today."

"Quiet, you little narcissist. We need to figure out who did this."

"What I need is to call my fuck buddy. It's been days since I've emptied my cock."

He lewdly grips his crotch and I throw an empty box at him, chasing him off. They all think I killed her, but I thought Loukas was the one dispatching his lovers. He could never handle a breakup well. Before they started dying, even. He loves way too hard and he always loves the wrong girl. A girl destined to break his heart.

He wouldn't have killed her in front of his daughter. Carlotta's the key to all of this. I hear loud Pagonis arguing outside and hurry to find Helen arguing with the prodigal Carlotta.

"I was out!"

"She's been dead for days! How long were you out? Who were you with? Your father didn't give you permission to run off to a party. He's been worried about you."

"I'm seventeen. I can do what the fuck I want."

Carlotta says rudely. Helen arches her eyebrows and searches the room for a wooden spoon which is mercifully out of her reach.

She turns to Carlotta sharply instead, "I am your aunt and you will not talk to me like that."

"I hate this stupid family!"

She tries to storm off, but she's wearing heels that are too high and I'm there to stop her. I grab Carlotta by the shoulders and hold her still.

"Not so fast, young lady. Fishnet tights? Six-inch heels? You're going to explain to uncle Stavros why your stepmother is dead and why you're dressed like a common Thessaloniki whore."

"Uncle Stavros! You can't say I'm dressed like a *whore*. That's so gross."

I push my finger through one hole in her tights and snap it against her leg. She squeals and jumps away.

"Ew! Stop it, creeper."

"Were you letting perverted bartenders feel your body up, eh? Is that what you were doing? What do you think your father will say when we tell him?"

Carlotta turns ghostly.

"He's not here yet, is he? He mentioned he'd be delayed in his fiftieth voice message."

She rolls her eyes dramatically.

"He's not here."

"You can't tell him. Daddy is crazy."

Helen puffs her cigarette.

"And your aunt and uncle are far worse. Now. We need to know everything that happened in the past forty-eight hours."

Carlotta slips out of her heels and settles down to Helen's height. She's still tall. She smells like a night of partying. Loukas might punish her for partying, but it's hard to imagine she could be a bigger party animal than her father.

Carlotta carries her shoes and walks ahead to the patio. I hiss at Helen once my niece is out of earshot.

"Call Loukas and tell him I didn't do this."

"I don't know that yet."

"You don't know what he'll do," I snarl.

"Are you scared, Stavros?"

"This isn't funny, Helen. He could hurt someone I care about."

"Like you've hurt everyone he ever loved. You'd deserve it. Plus, you don't care about anyone but yourself. You're a selfish Pagonis man. And you deserve nothing from me."

Even when we're on the same side, Helen acts like she wants to strangle me to death. Carlotta sits on the patio. A nervous maid comes from the other kitchen with a pot of coffee. She smells like liquor. If she saw the grisly scene in the main kitchen, I can imagine why she'd want to have a few.

One of my ghosts settles on the armchair next to me. My hallucinatory Ana-Maria distracts me. My eyes dart to the side and Carlotta notices, wrinkling her nose until Helen grabs her attention with another aggressive question.

"She'll die," Ana-Maria whispers to me, "Fallon will die and it will be all your fault."

FORTY
LOUKAS' SUSPECTS

Carlotta knows nothing or does a good job acting like it. I send her off to her bedroom to change out of her party clothes and into something decent. The last thing Loukas needs is someone in Thessaloniki spreading rumors about her. Helen paces the kitchen with her third cigarette for the afternoon hefted between her lithe fingers.

"I don't trust her," Helen says.

"She wouldn't kill her own stepmother."

"You tried to kill *your* stepmother," my sister reminds me. I must've been following orders.

I bite my tongue and gesture to Helen for her to pass the cigarette. She reluctantly offers me a puff.

"It's different. I was following orders."

"Maybe Carlotta was following orders," Helen says. "Maybe she's being trained to take your place."

"Yiayia wouldn't go that far."

"She's getting out of control. We need to do something about her."

"What? You would have me harm my grandmother? She's unconventional but... she's the reason we're all here."

Helen kisses her teeth and snatches her cigarette back.

"I know that. But she has no respect for our father. And no respect for us. Unconventional. Humph," Helen says. "I would call it something else."

"She manages the entire family business."

"Loukas should be the one in charge. He's the eldest. Papa can sail away into the sunset and enjoy his golden years," Helen says. Maybe she's right.

They're both in their golden years. Yiayia became a mother young. Before we came along, he'd been her favorite. Our grandmother's favorites are as fickle as her temper.

"Loukas won't do anything to put his children in danger. Or another fiancée."

Helen raises an eyebrow.

"I told him you did it."

"Do you believe that?" I ask her. Just when I think we're getting along.

"I don't know. I want to believe it's you, but... you seemed surprised when you came out. Shaken."

"Hm."

I'm always shaken. If it's not a monster in the waking realm, it's one of my hallucinations. Watching. Judging. Loathing me. Fallon's right. I need to get the voices to stop.

"If Yiayia's responsible for this, she's responsible for the others."

"Well, we finally know Loukas didn't kill this one."

Helen stopped bothering to learn their names. Plus, she has her own problems. I see welts on her wrist and evidence of more torture from her time with Khalid. She's been through hell. She probably wants to escape as much as Cass does. At least now she won't be married off, which suits her nicely.

"That's small comfort, especially since you put a price on my head."

"You want our brother to keep you alive, find out who killed his fiancée."

"We both know Yiayia's involved," I call after Helen as she walks out the side door toward the pool where Galanos loudly answers questions from his fans on his livestream. Is that all it takes to be famous these days? A six-pack and a cocky fucking attitude? Hm. Helen ought to slap him. How would his fans like that?

I didn't give Fallon any way to contact me, and I said goodbye to her too quickly. I investigate the premises and call a few of our usual hired guns in Thessaloniki. None of them will talk.

As night nears, my next best bet is calling Loukas on my way back to Fallon. I don't want her alone for too long. This time, I bring a gun. Helen didn't consider one possibility — someone else entirely killed Matilda. Poor woman. Loukas probably warned her away. He always warns the women away, but there's something he does to them that makes them stay. I can't imagine what he could be, but for a man in his forties, he does nicely. Too bad the women can't say the same.

He has to believe I didn't do this. Loukas picks up after two rings. "Hello?"

"I have your girl. She will be dead in an hour."

"Loukas, it's Stavros."

Like he doesn't know who the fuck I am. But he ought to be a day off Thessaloniki. There's no way he has Fallon.

"I know how you think. You won't bring her to the house because it's too dangerous. I'm one step ahead of you, brother. If you want her back, you'll do exactly as I say..."

I hear Fallon screaming in the background, "DON'T LISTEN TO HIM. STAVROS, YOU NEED TO TALK TO YOUR —"

The phone goes dead. My chest tightens. He has Fallon. He's going to hurt her. And unless I move *now,* there's nothing I'll be able to do to save her. Think Stavros. Think. I hear Ana-Maria's voice saying, "I told you so."

"I don't have time for fucking voices."

I run to the hotel. The door's open. I walk in and find Archimedes slumped over the counter. Two gunshot wounds to the head. He was an associate for ten years. And Loukas killed him in cold blood. For Matilda. A woman I would have never touched.

It's as if someone is playing a cruel joke on us. If he's smart, he wouldn't have kept Fallon in Thessaloniki for long. Loukas would have taken her to the docks. I know because that's what I would have done. *Shit.* I have to hope he doesn't find Sandros and Cass. The last thing I need is more problems.

My face drips in sweat when I arrive at the docks. I hear a cane tapping against the hardwood and Yiayia lurches forward out of the shadows. She waited for me.

"My grandson..."

She comes toward me and wraps her arms around me. It's not the reaction I expected. She puts her hands on my head and pulls me in close. Her lips tremble near my ears and my better judgment lapses. I expect something sweet from Yiayia. Something kind. Or reassuring.

"You lied to me."

"Yiayia?"

She shoves me. Hard. I don't double over, but wisely retreat backward. Yiayia takes the cane and whacks me. Hard. I don't fight back. Not yet. I step back again and she wobbles, using her cane for balance.

"You're alone?" I ask her.

"Yes. I'm alone. Waiting for you to admit what you did."

"I don't know what you're accusing me."

"You killed Ofek. And I know you're hiding Cassia somewhere. When I find out where..."

I take my gun out and point it at her. Her eyes sparkle with surprise and the corners of her lips turn up in a smile.

"This is your solution, Stavros? You'd kill an innocent old woman?"

"You are not *innocent.*"

"Neither are you," Yiayia says, "You will buy women and kill men like any Pagonis. But Ofek? I can't have you costing me money."

"It's loaded. I could shoot you and then all of us will live in peace."

"Is that what you think? Killing me will solve everything?"

Her face hardens.

"You're soft, Stavros. All of you. You enjoy money, but you don't enjoy what you must do to get it. Only sharks make it in this world. I try to make you strong. I try to make you sharks. None of you children were worth the effort it took to suckle you."

"I don't want to shoot you."

"Good. Because you won't. Loukas has your *bitch*."

I can't stop myself. Because I already let Fallon suffer too much at the hands of my family. I hit her in the face with the tail end of the gun. Yiayia doubles over and nearly falls, but I catch her. Grey hair comes undone from her topknot and she clutches her face.

"Yiayia! Are you okay?"

She has to grab onto my chest to stand again. I know that's the only thing preventing her from slapping me back. But she grips my shirt collar to gain her balance again.

"You've had your fun. Take me home. I want to see Matilda's body."

"No. I'm not taking you home."

"Fine. I'll call Helen. Run off to your girl. You'll be too late. Loukas didn't seem in the mood for mercy."

"Do you know who killed Matilda?" I call to her as I untie my speedboat.

FORTY-ONE
BURIAL AT SEA

"t doesn't matter who killed her. She's dead. You hit me again, you'll die too."

"If my brother wants revenge for Matilda, I'm already a dead man."

I step into the boat and start the motor, even if I do not know where I'm headed. I need to get away from my grandmother. I know the way I hit her will leave a bruise. I can't help but think she deserves it. I can't help but wonder why I never stood up to her before. She threatened me, but she couldn't fight back.

She really is getting weaker...

I call Loukas again. He doesn't answer. Damn. Think, Stavros. Where the hell could he possibly take her? The options are as infinite as the Aegean. I need to think strategically. Perhaps I ought to get help. Cass and Sandros weren't on the docks, which means they left before Yiayia could discover them. She thinks she has a clue about what's happening, but I had nothing to do with Ofek's death. I can use her ignorance to my advantage. I turn the dingy toward the area I asked my sister and her lover to anchor down.

Cassia's sneakier than I give her credit for. And Sandros... I'm glad I didn't kill the idiot, because I at least believe he can look after Cassia. I'm still tempted to send her to the Amalfi Coast but for now, Sandros as protection will have to do.

If she's going to be this defiant, she'll need someone to look after her. I only find their boat because I know where to look.

I shut the motor off and paddle to the port side of their boat, where a cocked gun greets my head. Sandros visibly relaxes once he recognizes me.

"Stavros."

"Where's my sister?"

"Downstairs. I heard someone coming, I told her to barricade herself in."

Cass springs out of her barricade, hoisting an AR-15 in an irresponsible stance that would send her flying across the ship if I loaded it.

"I don't keep AR-15 ammo on this boat."

She lowers the gun and shrugs.

"A pirate wouldn't know that."

"Pirates are the least of your concerns. Loukas has Fallon."

I wince as Cass presses the barrel of the gun into the bottom of the ship and leans on it like a cane. She's going to blow her foot off one day if she keeps acting like this around guns. Thankfully, Sandros pulls her off the gun and against his chest.

"What happened?" he asks, "You spared my life. Twice. It's only right that I help you."

I don't deserve his help. But I need it too badly to argue with the young man.

"Loukas thinks I killed Matilda, and he's kidnapped Fallon."

"What do you care?" Cassia answers, "She's only your sex slave."

"She is *not* my sex slave."

"*Sex* slave?" Sandros' ears perk up too eagerly, earning him an aggressive swat from rebellious Cass. Apparently his initiation into sex was seamless and addictive. I violently shove the images of him and Cass out of my head.

Cass snaps at her boyfriend, "Don't get so excited, pervert."

"I didn't kill Matilda," I reassure her.

"What reason does he have to trust that?"

"Jesus Christ, do you *all* think I'm a monster?"

Sandros shakes his head, but Cass picks dirt out of her fingernails, intentionally leaving me without an answer. Fine. Whatever they think of me might be half true, but Fallon sees something different in me. She makes me want to be better. And I have to rescue her.

"Where did he take her?" asks Sandros.

"I don't know. It's Loukas. He must have gone to the sea. We're losing time."

"I know where he took her," Cass says, "He has a secret spot he takes women. Carlotta told me."

"You talk with your niece about where her father takes his lovers?"

"Not his lovers. She thinks he killed her mom there. She has proof."

I grimace. I doubt Carlotta has proof, but it's the best chance we have at a lead.

"Where is it?"

"Five miles up the coast, in a little bay..."

"Smuggler's Cove."

"Yes."

"We'll get there faster if we take this boat."

"Who says we're helping you?"

I think Cass argues for the sake of it sometimes.

"We're helping," Sandros interjects. She's too in love with him to argue. I anchor the dingy and start the engines. Loukas could have done anything to Fallon by now. He could have raped her. Or killed her. I shudder to think at the horrors my brother could inflict on Fallon. He might be the quietest and the eldest, but he's no angel. My conspicuous silence attracts Cassia's attention, and she wraps her arms around me from behind.

"Don't worry, big brother."

She's never this sweet. I wrestle her arms off me and turn to face her, eyeing her suspiciously.

"Have you done something wrong?"

"No."

"You're acting suspiciously sweet."

"I am not! You don't know how to behave when anyone is kind to you. It's a miracle Fallon wants to be around you at all."

"She doesn't."

Cassia laughs.

"You're stupid. Helen's right."

We've already gone over my stupidity. Maybe my sisters are right that I'm an idiot. I mean, there is something wrong with me. I hear voices and that isn't normal. There's certainly a chance I'm as dumb as I am good looking.

"Watch your tongue."

I scold her because I don't want to give Cass any ideas about pulling the wool over my eyes.

"Fallon could have left you long ago. Yes, you say Khalid could bring her back to you, but she knows you'd never do that. She has you wrapped around her finger."

"She doesn't."

"Oh? Then how did she get kidnapped? You let her out of your sight. You trusted her. Pagonis men only trust women they love. It's your greatest weakness."

"And yours."

Cass moves her affections to Sandros, kissing his cheek. He bends his head shyly. I nearly killed him over my sister's honor. He's not eager to have me witness her at her most affectionate.

"Don't worry. I won't kill you for kissing her back."

Sandros turns to Cass and kisses her so deeply that I nearly change my mind about killing him. I pry them apart. Physically. Cass swats me.

"I am a grown woman. I can kiss who I want. And Fallon's a

grown woman, too. If you treat her like a Pagonis pet, she will leave you eventually."

"I don't need romance advice from my kid sister."

"I'm not single. You are. Maybe you do."

Single? I haven't thought of myself as single. Maybe she's right. I doubt Cass is so naïve that she doesn't know I've bedded Fallon. But that doesn't make me not single. It's... complicated. When I find Fallon, I'll make sure it's not so complicated. But finding Fallon won't be the end of my problems. I hit Yiayia.

Cass snaps her fingers in front of my face. I've zoned out again.

"I hit Yiayia. With the butt of my pistol."

"Are you crazy?!"

"Yes. I don't know."

"She will retaliate. If you were going to hit her, you should have killed her."

"That is your grandmother you're talking about."

"She is the one who made the deal with Ofek. I have plans for her."

"Cass... You aren't to come back to Thessaloniki. If I knew you were coming on some revenge mission, I wouldn't have brought you back."

"Too late."

Sandros points at the radar.

"I think I have his boat. It's on the edge of our radar."

"Which means he'll recognize us. How far?"

"A mile."

"I'll swim."

"You'll swim a mile in the dark sea?" Cass grabs my arms, trying to stop me, but she already knows its futile. Once I've made up my mind, nothing can change it.

"I'll bring a knife."

"So you're literally going to bring a knife to a gunfight? Do you want a burial at sea or cremation?"

FORTY-TWO
A KNIFE TO A GUNFIGHT

jump into the frigid Aegean waters without a second thought. Jumping into cold water always feels so deliciously miserable. Your heart thuds in your chest, the shock surging throughout your body as the cold envelops every inch of your skin. I gasp for air as my arms jut out of the water and I begin my swim. One mile in the freezing night waters. Cass is right to wonder if I've lost my mind.

But I'd do it for Fallon. My knife sits high on my hips in a holster, cinched tightly to my body. The first five minutes of swimming is the worst. I move fast through the water, my hands cutting through waves like a smooth blade slicing through flesh. Breathing is the least of my concerns. If I stop moving for longer than three minutes, it'll be enough for me to develop hypothermia.

Swimming a mile in the ocean isn't an unfamiliar practice for Pagonis boys. It's why my father loves the ocean so much. He was younger then and more agile. Wealth has spoiled my father and fattened him up. Yiayia's right about that much at least. Nearing the cove, I stop swimming and tread water as I assess the scene. There are lights in the distance. I blink salt water out of my eyes so I can see better.

Two boats. I tell myself that it's a hallucination. But one boat speeds toward me. I flash my light repeatedly, lifting my hands over my head. Don't run me over, you stupid fuck. I assume Loukas is in one boat and he's left Fallon in the other. She might be able to swim, but she'd have to be a fish to swim back to shore. That's his plan? Leave her out here to die. Or to keep her prisoner. I'll have the element of surprise to use against Loukas when his speedboat nears. I flash my headlamp and make as little noise as possible. The boat slows down, and a face leans over the edge. Not my brother's face.

"What are you doing here?!" we both yell at once. Fallon nearly tips the boat trying to reach down into the water.

"Careful!"

I steady the boat as she falls down on her butt with a thud and a loud exclamation.

"What are you doing here?"

She asks again as she slowly tips her body over the edge in an attempt to pull me onto the boat. It'll take some effort for her to do this without tipping it.

"Careful," I grunt as I work the rest of my body onto the speedboat and flop down on my back. Our family has *way* too many boats.

"You're cold. What the hell are you doing?!"

"If you would give me a moment, I'd answer."

I sit up and take my shirt off. Fallon drops the headlamp.

"Fallon!"

"Sorry! you can't take your shirt off and expect me not to react."

She fumbles with the lamp and holds it up again, glancing furtively over her shoulders.

"I need to get this boat started before he wakes up."

Fallon starts the boat with shocking ease. I work the rest of my clothing off. She has a dry blanket on the boat. My pants come off and then a gust of wind sends them sailing overboard. Shit. Fallon glances over her shoulder and steers the boat around the cove. There's a sister cove to this one — a tourist trap. We can at least hide on the other side of a much larger vessel until we figure out what to do next, and until I figure out how Fallon escaped.

She steers us to a large catamaran and slows the boat down. By then, I'm completely naked and with the boat still, I can stand up. Which I do, so I can get the blanket underneath my ass before it gets splinters.

"Stavros. Your dick is in my face. Like right in my face."

"Problem?"

"Yes. Enormous problem."

"I agree, it's enormous."

"You are so annoying."

"I was on my way to rescue you."

"Rescue me?" Fallon indignantly folds her arms, "I told you not to come. If I can handle you for all those weeks, I can handle your idiot brother."

"Loukas isn't the idiot. I am."

"Loukas is 100% the idiot. And why are you really here? Who comes to do a rescue with just a knife."

"I swam a mile through freezing water for you!"

"I specifically asked you not to."

"We shouldn't argue, beloved. Not with my dick in your face."

She stands and we both wobble as the boat nearly tips. I grab onto the sides, my dick swaying out in the open like an elephant's trunk.

"Fallon!"

"Sorry!"

"Stand. Still!"

"We're not close to shore anymore. If it tips —"

"We are not tipping this goddamned boat!"

Fallon stabilizes herself and then sits. My dick is in her face again. And she can't stop looking at it.

"I hate you so much," she whispers.

I wrap the blanket around my hulking nude body and sit. I feel better. But my feet are freezing. Fallon glances anxiously out at the horizon.

"Do you think he'll find us here?"

"No. But I can know more if you tell me how you got here."

"It's embarrassing."

"I don't care. I asked you a question, beloved. I expect an answer."

"That chauvinist shit is too old school for me."

"Hm. But that chauvinist dick isn't, eh?"

"Shut up."

"Fine. I'll be silent. Now tell me."

Fallon wraps her sweater tighter around her shoulders. Even for someone not soaked to the bone, it's cold out here. She's too beautiful for words. And intelligent. It hurts how unworthy I am of her... affections? It hurts how I can convince myself she feels affection for me.

"Your brother believed I had feelings for you. I convinced him I didn't."

"You fucked him."

"No! Jesus Christ, Stavros. Calm down. He's grieving. I told him about my ex-boyfriend and what losing him was like and basically... he started crying."

"What? My brother, crying?"

"Even bad guys like you have experienced unrequited love."

"That doesn't explain why he didn't let you go."

"That's because he didn't let me go. I escaped. I drugged him."

She reaches inside her bra and pulls out a tiny baggie of blue pills.

"Where the hell did you get these?"

"I stole them."

I cast her a sideways glance.

"You don't believe me," she says, "But I'm not stupid, Stavros. It helps for people to think I'm stupid. But I've been watching. Everything. I understand your family. And you people... you need to stop fighting and just fucking talk to each other."

"That's your solution? A mafia family should sit down and have a big fucking family meeting?"

"It wouldn't hurt."

I grunt and lament privately that I have nothing to smoke.

"We should paddle this boat to shore. I don't want to stay out here."

"Hearing voices?"

"Huh?"

She pinches me to bring me back into reality. I love seeing her face. Always.

"No. I'm not. No voices for a while," I mutter.

Fallon steps over the emergency paddle over to my seat and sidles next to me. She kisses my cheek and whispers, "Good."

Her kiss gets me warmer than the blanket.

"What was that for?"

"For your rescue attempt."

"What do I get for succeeding?"

"A little more than a kiss," she whispers, her hand parting the blanket and resting on my thigh. There's no touching Fallon without guilt, even now, as fire burns between us.

"We can't do it here," I whisper, "In the middle of the ocean surrounded by fancy tourists on yachts?"

"Slow down, mister. A little more than a kiss doesn't mean we're having sex."

She giggles as her hand reaches further. I gasp as her fingers clasp around my cock, getting me instantly hard.

FORTY-THREE
NAKED IN THESSALONIKI

We arrive on shore, and I insist on returning to the villa. I don't want to wear my wet shirt or wetter boxers to get three miles home. So I walk with a blanket around my shoulders and otherwise stark naked. Fallon follows a few feet behind me.

"This is mortifying!"

"I'm a Pagonis, we can move liberally through the city."

"You're not even wearing shoes, Stavros. Gross."

"You didn't think it was so gross when you were staring at my cock."

A couple walking past us on an early morning walk glower at us, and Fallon squeals an apology in Greek and hastens to keep up with me. She has been listening well. Her Greek sounds better than most of the foreign language students who visit Thessaloniki on semesters abroad. I pull her under the blanket with me, sticking her body against mine.

"Stavros! I don't want anyone to associate me with a free-dicked crazy person running down the streets!"

A woman exclaims to her husband how big my dick is, and Fallon shrinks under the blanket and attempts to hide her face. No police officer or concerned citizen bothers stopping me, and I shed the blanket once I walk through the villa gates. It's early in the morning. By now, Sandros and Cassia would have stopped their search. Once I'm clothed and warm, I'll sail out there to let them know I found her. Fallon, I'm sure, won't want to get left behind. Now that we're in the villa, she glues herself to my side.

"Good morning! Is my brother Loukas here!"

Carlotta comes in from the patio reeking of a strong strain of marijuana. At least she's dressed more conservatively than the night before.

"Another party?"

"Uncle Stavros! Your cock is out!"

"Don't look! Get me a towel!"

I grab a plate and cover my genitals. Shit. I'd forgotten I was naked. Fallon helps Carlotta cover her eyes and leads her out of the kitchen. With Carlotta gone, she glares at me.

"You're making a point, aren't you? That you aren't afraid of your brother?"

"I'm not going on the run. Loukas isn't the butcher in this family. I am."

"So what are you going to do?"

"He will come here, and I will kill him for destroying your honor."

"Don't you think you're overreacting? He didn't *destroy my honor.*"

"That's your opinion. My opinion is he fucked with me by touching you."

"Loukas is hurting right now. He doesn't need violence. He needs a *hug.*"

Fallon's dangerously optimistic. Is this the type of insanity that causes her to see the good in me? The only "hug" my brother needs is my hands "hugging" his stubborn neck. If he won't believe that I didn't kill Matilda, what choice do I have? I won't allow him to lay a hand on Fallon.

"He touched you. I will not allow another man to touch you."

"That's what this is about, isn't it? You think you own me?"

"I own you. You belong to me."

She slaps me. Hard. I drop the plate, which thankfully doesn't break.

"What was that for?"

"You don't own me."

"I ought to beat you for slapping me."

"Beat me? I don't care how old school you are, I'm not letting you *beat* me."

"You've got quite a mouth on you now. When did I stop scaring you, eh? I can start again any time."

"Don't give me that crazy Greek man bullshit."

"What are we even fighting about woman?!"

"Your brother. Needs. Affection. He lost someone he cares about. He's lashing out!"

"He is forty years old. He isn't lashing out. He's a bastard. And I won't have my woman defending him."

I lunge for Fallon and grab her forearm. She screams and tries to get away from me but I pin her against the wall, pressing her forearm over her head. Her shallow breathing moves the loose fabric around her chest. I want to cut her dress open with my knife and take her right here. If she doesn't believe she's mine, I'll prove it.

"Hit me and I'll walk away from you. I don't care if Khalid takes me back."

"I'm not going to hit you beloved," I whisper.

I lean forward and kiss her. Hard. She relents, as she always does. Her lips part gently, allowing my tongue in her mouth. I push my tongue in deeper and her tongue jostles against mine, nearly tangling with it. She tastes like the sea. And she smells like woman. My woman. I hike her dress up and she grabs my face to get my attention.

"We can't. Your niece could walk in."

She's right. I let her dress fall and release my grip on her forearm. Carlotta strides in with a towel, covering her eyes as she throws it over to me. I wrap it around my hips and Carlotta breathes a sigh of relief.

"Thank goodness! Where is papa?"

"You tell me."

"He called and said Yiayia was in trouble and that you *abused* her."

"Do you think its possible for anyone to abuse Yiayia?"

Carlotta shrugs.

"I only repeat what they say. We are always fighting in this family. At Tisha's house, they like each other."

"Who the hell is Tisha?"

"She's my friend from university. She's coming to stay with us this summer again. She left last week."

"Tisha's family probably doesn't control several multimillion dollar companies while keeping law and order in one of Greece's biggest cities."

"We don't even keep law and order in our own home," Carlotta says with disinterest. She grabs an apple from the bowl on the table and hurries off. Smart, because I was just about to question her regarding the stench of marijuana on her clothes.

"She has a point," Fallon says once my niece is definitively gone.

"There you are again, defending my family."

"Not all of them. But Loukas... he's not as bad as you think. He wasn't going to hurt me. Probably."

"Not everything can be solved with talking."

"I agree."

She approaches me again and grabs my dick through the towel.

"Talking definitely doesn't solve everything." She runs her tongue over her lower lip. "But it solves some things."

It's so painful to stay away from her.

PURCHASED FOR SUBMISSION

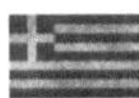

FORTY-FOUR
THE POOL

"You. Bedroom. Now."

She lets go of my dick now that she faces the result of her wanton teasing.

"Now? Your brother could get here at any minute. Enraged."

"One last fuck before I die can't hurt."

I grab her hips and Fallon resists. She always resists at first. It takes more than my yearning to unravel her. My lips caress her neck and she wriggles against me again.

"Stop. Carlotta could come back in here."

"You wouldn't want my niece to catch you with my tongue in your cunt, would you?"

I suck her neck and Fallon lets out an involuntary moan. I have her right where I want her, wriggling and torn between following her sensibilities and following her instincts. As a killer, I've always preferred instinct to common sense. And my instincts drive me to lift Fallon onto the counter and force her legs apart so I can stand between them. Her thighs squeeze my hips and I run my hands along her walnut curves. Those thighs belong to me. Fallon Iverson belongs to me. She rakes her fingers through my hair and pulls my head close but denies herself satisfaction by only allowing her lips to peck at mine.

I spread her lips with mine, and my tongue enters her mouth. She leans away from me, nearly falling over. But I catch her, pushing forward so the tent in my towel threatens to escape.

"Not here," she gasps, "please..."

This time, I relent, despite my urge to bury my hardness between her legs on the counter. I lift her and she wraps her legs around my torso, her forearms resting on my shoulders. She's lighter than I expect. I'm careful not to mistake her size for her fragility.

"The pool," I whisper, "I want to kiss you in the pool."

I bring her to the edge of the pool, standing at the deep end when Fallon grasps my shoulders and her eyes bug out of her head.

"You aren't seriously going to jump in the pool holding me."

"Scared?"

"Yes!"

"Why?"

"Hello!? I nearly drowned. It's the deep end. I don't want to mess up my hair."

"Your hair is fine. And I won't let you drown. Don't you trust me?"

She bites down on her lower lip, her hair coming undone and cascading down her shoulders.

"I don't know."

"Trust me, Fallon Iverson. I won't let anything bad happen to you."

"That's the deal then? I belong to you and you protect me?"

"On the count of three..."

"Stavros... wait!"

I jump into the water. The count of three was only to throw her off. Fallon shrieks as I sink into the deep end holding her. Instincts cause her to wriggle around, nearly out of my grasp where her terri-fied thrashing might properly drown her. I cling to her and lift her head above the surface, wiping her soaked hair out of her face as she gasps.

"ARE YOU CRAZY?!"

"I've got you."

I tread water as she berates me a little more, and I hold her steady above the water so she can breathe and understand that I don't want to hurt her. I never wanted to *hurt* her. I might be cruel, but she's right — I won't allow anything bad to happen to her. Fallon's dress falls off her shoulders as her arms wrap tighter around my neck. She presses her forehead to mine, still gasping for breath. She doesn't forget to be furious. She slaps me.

"You scared me!"

"I've got you."

"You'd better."

"I've got you. I promise."

"I don't get you."

"What don't you get?"

"If I didn't know better... I'd say... you *like* me."

"More than like, beloved."

She rubs water out of her eyes and unwraps her legs' tight grip on my torso. She trusts me to hold her above water. And I won't let her go. Just as I promised.

"Why?"

"There's no reason for love, beloved. If I love you for your looks, what happens when we are old and neither of us beautiful? If I love you for you mind, what happens when your memory goes? If I love you for what you can do for me, what happens when you are sick and I must take care of you? Loving you doesn't make sense. It's a puzzle I want to figure out."

"Is that why you won't let me go?"

"Is that what you want?"

She nods. And it stings. Because I don't want to let her go. She presses her hands to my chest.

"I can't be your property, Stavros."

I want to ask her "why not" even if it's a stupid question.

"I know. But... I love you."

I press my forehead to hers and hear the voices in my head again. Fallon will leave. Everyone leaves. And when she leaves, I won't be able to protect her. She'll fall into danger and it will be my fault. The voices scream at me until her hand touches my lips and reminds me of what's real.

"I'll stay tonight. One more night."

"I don't want you to share my bed out of pity."

She averts her gaze. She feels guilty, but not guilty enough to stay.

"It won't be out of pity. It'll be... goodbye."

"Isn't loving you enough for you to stay?" I murmur.

Her voice stiffens.

"No, Stavros. I want to leave. I've always wanted to escape."

My chest shudders and her palms dart away from my chest as if my emotional response will make her feel too guilty. She has to pretend I'm a monster for this to be easy. And for once, I don't want to make it easy for Fallon to presume I'm a monster. It doesn't matter. She knows who I really am. She knows I spared a young man. She knows I abandoned my family code to help Cassia. She knows I risked drowning to save her. Even a powerful swimmer could die in the Aegean sea. Fallon knows how the guilt of murder eats away at me. I'm not a monster, but I'm not enough, either. I could never be enough for her.

My grasp on her tightens with one arm and I peel away her dress, watching it float away across the pool. She only wears a bra and thick cotton underwear and her nipples jut out through the bra.

"If tonight is my last night with you, I want all of you."

"My last night," she whispers, "So anything goes. Anything you want, I'm yours."

My cock is hard, and my towel has already floated to join her clothing. I don't care that I'm naked and any of my family members could find us here. My only thoughts are about Fallon Iverson and how badly I want to keep her. I could lock her up. I could force her. I could break her. But I won't. Because she's found my one weakness and exploited it. Love.

I love Fallon too much to keep her prisoner.

"What about emailing your mother? Where will you go?"

"You can help me with that before. And I don't know. Maybe Tálín. Maybe Copenhagen. Somewhere nice."

I want her to stay in Greece, not find some tall Nordic bastard to take my place in her bed. My rage and my erection both refuse to yield to my better senses. I swim to the shallow end of the pool and sit Fallon on the edge. I grab my towel and wrap it around my waist before jumping out of the pool and sitting next to her.

I do what I have to so I make this easier on myself. My heart pounds and I try to ignore the pain. I love her. I confessed I love her and she still insists on leaving.

"When I set you free, I don't want you coming back. Ever."

She pulls her body away from me.

"I understand."

FORTY-FIVE
ELEVEN INCHES OF REASONS

shut the door to my bedroom. Her silhouette is nearly hourglass with the delightful imperfections of a real woman. Imperfections that make her... beautiful. Natural. Sensual. I drop my soaked towel to the ground and it lands with a wet thwack as my hardness springs to attention.

"You aren't shy, are you?"

"I have eleven inches of reasons not to be shy."

She unhooks her bra, and it falls away from her breasts. They swing into view, hanging low and feminine. A natural beauty with a body that nearly makes me finish where I stand. I could empty my balls without touching her. She's that fucking sexy.

"How do you want me?"

She drops to her knees.

"On my knees?"

She slips her underwear off and shuffles around on her knees before arching her back and bending over.

"On all fours?"

"I want you in bed," I breathe, "But I'm taking all of you. Mouth. Cunt... And everywhere else."

She moves to sit on the edge of my bed, naked.

"I'm yours, Stavros. Get your money's worth."

Her soft and arousing voice draws me closer. She lies on the bed so her mouth sits at the perfect angle to take my cock. Her lips stretch around it and she moans as I slide all eleven inches into her mouth. Fallon works my cock with her tongue and lips until I'm soaked and eager veins bulge around the sides of my enormous organ. I need it inside her. It takes all my power not to have her ass first. If she wants to leave, I won't let her without a hard anal fucking. A gift for her to remember me... but with eleven inches... there's no chance she'll forget.

I want to burn myself on Fallon so every man afterward can smell my musk on her neck and feel her cunt is used to a much larger cock than theirs. I push her back onto the bed and spread her legs wide. She gasps as I press the bulging knob of my hardness against her entrance. I chuckle. Oh no, Fallon. She isn't getting my enormous cock all at once. There's plenty of teasing for me to have before I impale her entrance. I run my tongue over her neck and kiss her. She kisses back. Don't leave, I want to beg. But I won't let Fallon know how much she's weakened me. Not after she's chosen to leave.

"After all this, you still loathe me," I murmur, "But I'm the best sex you'll ever have. When you're fucking your next Serb or German, remember that it will never be the same."

I drive my tongue into her mouth and wrap my hand around her neck without squeezing. She gazes up at me as I hold her neck. I don't squeeze, but we both know I could. Her chest heaves and her ankles wrap around my torso as she takes what little control she has left around me.

"You wouldn't," she whispers.

"I could," I tell her, "Because that way no other man will have you."

"Trust me, I could use a long break from men."

I chuckle and press my thumb into my neck. Only my thumb. She can still breathe. And even if she's scared, a part of her trusts me or she would put up much more of a fight.

"You don't need a break from me," I murmur, kissing her collarbone, "You need cock. You need your cunt used daily."

"I *hate* your foul mouth."

"You hate many things about me. That doesn't stop you from spreading your legs."

I don't give her a chance to respond. My tongue flicks across her nipple and she cries out. Her pussy grows slicker and the knob of my cock sitting between her outer lips burns with anticipation. Every part of my brain tells me to slide the entire thing inside her and claim her. If I cum inside her, that would make keeping her easier. That's why we do it, isn't it? Men cum inside of women because we enjoy the power of knowing we could tame them with our seed and turn maidens into mothers. My lips find hers again and her nails dig into my buttocks. I still have my hands around her neck.

This is how tonight will be. Rough. Arousing. Dark. Sensual. Everything we've wanted from each other. I press my forefinger against the other side of her neck. Her breathing remains steady.

"I'm not scared of you, Stavros," she whispers, "I know you. You think scaring me off will make it easier. But I'm not scared. When I look at your darkness, I don't want to run away."

"You're running away tomorrow. So don't lie to me or I'll choke you for real."

"I'm not running away," she says, "You can't expect me to be your sex slave forever."

"That's it, then? You won't be my slave. Even if I love you."

"It doesn't matter if you love me."

I shove my cock inside her. It's a hard, angry thrust. I let go of her neck as she screams. She wasn't expecting eleven inches of Greek dick between her legs.

"Nothing I say matters," I growl.

She grabs my back and struggles against the pain between her legs. I move my hips back and thrust again. Fallon cries out and digs her nails into my back. Hard.

"Bastard," She snarls in my ear.

"Your cunt will always belong to me. It doesn't matter how far you run."

I thrust again, and she cries out in pleasure. I expect her to protest but she grabs a handful of my hair and presses my face to hers.

"Harder," she pleads, "Fuck me."

My hips move out slowly, and I slam into her again. We both cry out. My thrusts are slow but each deeper than the last. I'm entering the depths of Fallon's cunt and stretching her so that each stroke pushes her close to an intense climax, made more intense by the insane way we're grabbing onto each other and the refusal to let each other go.

"I want to keep you," I snarl, thrusting into her even harder.

"You can't..."

"Why not?" I whisper in her ear, nibbling her earlobes as my hips move between her legs, "Your cunt likes me..."

She whimpers and moans again as I keep fucking her. She doesn't have any suitable answers for me. Fallon knows I'm trouble and I know she's right. So this is all we get. One night. And then an eternity alone. Because I'll never meet another woman like her. A woman who can tame me and Loukas both. A woman who can take my cock while moaning and begging for more.

"I can't..." she moans.

FORTY-SIX
GOODBYE, FALLON

I hold her body against mine, her pointed nipples grazing my chest as I bury my cock between her legs again. My hips move slowly between her legs, withdrawing my cock and then groaning as I drive between her legs again. Her body responds in perfect sync with mine.

I move from furious thrusting to slowly pumping my hips between her legs. Fallon wants me harder but I can't push myself over the edge this quickly. If this is my last night with Fallon, it's one I need her to remember. I want to hold tonight in my head and remember how every inch of her tasted as I made love to her.

I push her hair out of her face and kiss her lips, cheek, then neck. She moans and bucks against me as my lips fasten against her neck. I suck hard and plunge my dick deeper. She moans and I keep her pinned beneath my torso.

"Remember who you belong to, Fallon."

"No one," she gasps, "no one."

I pull out of her and flip her onto her stomach. Wrong answer. She's pushing me over the edge and saying what will anger me, thinking I'll give her my cock any harder and faster. Wouldn't that make it easier? If I came quickly?

I have no intention of making leaving me easy for Fallon Iverson. Once she's on her belly, I slide my cock between her legs and she bucks once I bury my shaft in her to the hilt. My enormous cock stretches her wide, but her thighs squeezed together tighten her entrance. I nearly empty myself between her curvy walnut thighs. As she moans, I wrap her hair around my wrist and tilt her neck back, leaning forward as I slide my hips out and then push into her, forcing another moan out of Fallon's lips.

"Wrong answer, beloved."

"You," she whimpers, "I belong to you."

"Correct, beloved. Your cunt will always belong to me."

I force myself into her deeper and let go of her hair, causing her to fall forward as I plunge into her from behind. Her cunt can't control itself. She's sopping wet and each thrust gets Fallon's tight pussy even tighter and hotter.

As much as she belongs to me, I belong to her. I cover her with my body, pressing my torso into her back as I move my hips slowly. She moans as my hot breath tickles her ear and I suck on her earlobes and neck as I take her from behind. From this position, it doesn't take long for her to cum.

Fallon grips the sheets and struggles to wriggle free from my grasp as she cums. I hold my cock between her legs until she gives up struggling. When she holds still, I brush her hair off her face.

"Shhh. You came so hard, beloved. Would you like another orgasm?"

"Y-yes..."

I kiss her cheek.

"Good. I love you, so I'm going to make you cum. I will not finish with you tonight until you're tired from orgasms."

"Stavros..."

"Shh," I whisper, "It isn't a debate, Fallon. I love you. I want to be a better man for you..."

She pushes me off. Successfully. I land on my side and nearly off the bed.

"Stop it."

"What?"

"You're taking your dirty talk too far, Stavros."

I push her back down and resume my position on top of her, but I keep her facing me.

"What have I done wrong?"

"You can't have feelings for me. I let it go once but…"

"Why not?"

"Because that makes leaving ten times more difficult."

"Then stay."

"I can't stay."

She struggles to push me off but this time, Fallon won't catch me unaware. I grab her wrists. She struggles and kicks my back but I only grip them tighter and then pin them above her head. She struggles again. My cock rests against her entrance and I'm tempted to slide in, but I kiss her instead.

A kiss calms her down.

"I hate you," Fallon says.

"I know. But you can stay. Always."

I kiss her again and then slide into her. She moans and arches her back so her breasts spill off her chest. I grab one of her nipples between my lips and suck hard as I move between her legs.

One thrust between her legs and she climaxes. I fuck her slowly until she cums several times and then I pull out of her and spread her thighs apart.

"You're going to eat me out after your dick's been down there?"

"Cunt is cunt. And yours is fucking delicious."

My voice comes out raspy and animalistic. I push her thighs open and spread her lower lips with my tongue. Fallon screams and I rub her clit with my tongue. The engorged nub is already soaked with her juices and I can't get enough of the honey nectar that flows freely from Fallon's cunt.

My lips and tongue control her climaxes within minutes of pleasing her. She cums as I rub my tongue under the nub and then flick over it a few times. Broad strokes rile her up close to the edge and direct contact pushes her over. Fallon drips with cum and my spit soaks every inch of her ass, pussy and thighs. Fuck...

Fallon's perfect ass. It's the only hole on her body that I haven't entered. Eleven inches in Fallon's flawless puckered hole would be... *unforgettable.*

Now that the thought enters my mind, I can't get rid of it. I pull away from her cunt and kneel between her legs, weighing my options. She glances up at me, expecting my cock between her legs again.

"I want your ass."

"Um... for what?"

"What do you think? I want to fuck your ass."

Her lids fly open and she stares with a gazelle's confusion that a lion has selected them as prey.

"That's how you ask?"

"You wanted a letter requesting entry?"

"No. But who says 'I want your ass' like that's expected."

"It's expected for a woman I purchased to submit to me."

She scowls and folds her arms over her chest as if me catching sight of her bare nipples would stimulate me to rape her ass instead of politely asking for permission to enter the forbidden hole.

"I promise, it will feel good."

"I've seen your eleven inch Greek dick and I have strong doubts it'll feel good eleven inches up my butt."

"I will make you cum. I'll go slow. Other men won't be able to tell."

"I'm not worried about other men looking up my ass!"

"Not looking then, feeling."

She throws a pillow at me. I laugh and toss it to the ground. Every one of the muscles on my chest flexes as I throw it and a droplet of saliva falls out of Fallon's mouth. She literally drools over my body. If I didn't think she'd slap me, I would wipe the evidence off her lower lip.

"Butt sex. That's what you want on our last night together."

"You call it butt sex… I call it… an unforgettable night."

"Eleven inches in the ass will hurt. Don't lie to me."

"It won't if I do my job right."

"And what job might that be?"

"I start with my tongue. I lick your ass and cunt until you're soaking wet. I plunge my tongue in your little hole to get you ready…"

Her hands jump to her mouth.

"Stavros…"

I ignore her reaction. I don't care if it's surprise or disgust.

"Once your ass is ready, I will use my finger to stretch you. While I stretch your ass, I'll eat your pussy until you cum. By the time you're ready for my cock, you'll be floating. And cumming."

She's quiet for a moment and I think she's finally going to turn me down. I've finally found the request that will turn Fallon away from me.

"It doesn't sound painful."

"I will care for you. Like a lover."

"No need to lay it on thick."

Her head flops back into the pillow. Permission to continue. I kiss my way down her stomach and force her thighs apart.

"It's really happening," she squeals.

"Shh," I whisper, "Don't distract me from your tiny chocolate treasure."

"There is *no* chocolate down there!

I chuckle.

"I meant the color."

"Oh. Right. Is it the same color?"

"You've never looked at your own butt hole in the mirror?"

"Why would I look at my butthole in the mirror!?"

I silence her with a tentative lick. She squeals and I flatten my tongue, licking the warm area around her tender ass. Fallon moans and my tongue travels from her ass back to her clit. I lick her like that a few more times until she bucks and moans, close to an intense climax.

I promised she would like it, didn't I?

My tongue reaches her ass again and Fallon cries out with pleasure. I use my fingers to rub her soft clit to a climax and then I bury my tongue in her ass as she cums. When I pull away from her, she looks bewildered.

"People *do this?!* Why have I never heard of this?"

"Men in America don't lick their women's butt?"

"When you say it like that, you make it sound weird."

"It isn't weird. It's etiquette."

"Eating ass is Greek etiquette?" She says, sounding doubtful. I love the way she wriggles in my grasp.

I shrug.

"Well, we don't eat ass at the dinner table."

"I didn't think you *meant* at the dinner table."

"Good. I will put a finger in now," I murmur, kissing the top of her plump butt cheek. I've waited far too long for this.

"Why am I only noticing how big your fingers look now!?"

"I will go easy on you."

"You never do..." Fallon says.

"Trust, beloved. It won't kill you," I promise her. My cock feels like it's about to burst. I can't wait to claim her tight back door. Even tasting her ass is a fucking luxury.

I think I hear her whisper, "it might."

But I hear voices, so my opinion on the matter shouldn't be trusted. My tongue spreads her lower lips again and dives between her cheeks until I find that forbidden hole and ensure my tongue soaks it well. My thumb teases her entrance and Fallon breathes deeply, like she's about to take a difficult final exam.

My finger penetrates her gently. She squeaks and then my tongue finds her clit and she forgets my finger slowly massaging her back door open as my tongue brings her to the brink of an intense climax.

As Fallon moans, I slide my finger in deeper. I got her wet enough so that my finger enters her insanely tight ass easily. But fuck, is it tight. I'll enjoy having her perfect asshole wrapped around my cock. I'll bury my cum so deep in her ass that it'll drip out of her when the next man eats her cunt.

If I allow her to have another man...

Tonight could change her mind. That's what I really want: Fallon to change her mind and stay with me. With one finger in her ass and my lips wrapped around her clit, I make her cum again before I slide a second finger in her ass.

She cries out as the second finger moves alongside the first. At first I think she's crying out in pain but she cums again with only two flicks of my flattened tongue around her clit. She enjoys this. Fallon loves when I eat her pussy with two fingers buried in her ass.

With her nice and ready, I move away from her and put her on all fours. Before I slide my cock into her backdoor, I press my tongue to her ass again, licking her pussy and sucking on her tight butt hole until Fallon climaxes. Then I press the mushroom head of my enormous dick against her backdoor.

She's too soaked in her own cum and luxuriating in her own pleasure to feel the initial pain as my rounded head slides into her ass. She moans in pleasure as a few inches slide into her backdoor. Fallon cums as I bury the last few inches of my cock inside her. With my cock buried deep in her ass, I grip her waist with one hand and massage her clit with the other.

My hips slowly withdraw and I plunge into her ass again. Fallon cries out my name... I have to take her harder. I plunge into her faster and deeper. She cries out one more word...

"Yes."

I can't help myself. I fuck Fallon's ass until we're both soaked with sweat and cum. When I can't hold back, I grab her hips and bury myself inside her as I fill her ass with my cum. As my enormous eleven inch cock throbs between her legs, Fallon climaxes again.

I withdraw and she collapses onto her stomach. I press my weight into her and pin her down as she gasps. Her heaving chest gets me hot. And hard again.

"We aren't finished, beloved. I have your body for the night and I intend to make use of it."

Fallon whispers, "bring it on."

We make love until the sunrises. She wobbles to her dress on the other side of the room in the morning. Khalid gave me the instructions I'd need to free her. He promised he'd never touch her again if I paid an additional £15,000 fee, an exorbitant sum I quietly agreed to pay because it's Fallon. And despite her doubts, I love her. I'm capable of loving her.

She has her clothes on when I approach her with my phone.

"I have to swipe it over the chip. Where did they put it?"

She lifts her hair, revealing the nape of her neck. My hand wobbles as I hold the phone up.

"I don't want to do this," I snarl.

"Stavros, we made a deal."

"I don't care about the deal. I want you."

"Is that what you think love is? Keeping me as your property?"

"No."

She bites on her lower lip.

"This isn't easy for me, either. I have to start over. I have to find a way to contact my family."

"Let me help you."

She shakes her head.

"That wouldn't be fair to you."

"So this is it. The end of us," I ask her. I hate this. I hate it so fucking much, but I can't stop her from leaving. I can't be the beast she thinks I am.

"Yes."

I press my phone to the nape of her neck. The chip flashes a small orange light a few times and then appears to go dead. Fallon has her freedom. I pull away from her and she drops her hair, allowing it to cascade over the thin, nearly invisible scar marking her passage through the underground human trafficking world in Europe.

She turns to me and exhales with relief.

"Thank you, Stavros."

"Don't thank me. I only did it because I'm weak."

"Loving someone isn't weak."

"Falling for you made me weak. So tell me, Fallon. Is this what you planned? You win my affections to gain your freedom?"

"I didn't plan any of this."

"You didn't have to pretend you wanted to help me with my demons."

"I didn't pretend."

"Then what was it? Because the only reason I would have allowed myself to fall for you is if I thought..."

I want to punch a wall. I want to hurt myself.

"Thought what?"

Fallon's whispers infuriate me.

"I thought you cared for me. I became a better person because you cared for me. I wouldn't stop fighting my demons if it meant waking up next to you. I thought you felt the same way."

"Stavros..."

"No. I'm leaving."

"Back across the Aegean," she whispers.

"Have a good life, beloved."

I clasp my hands over her waist one last time. I don't want to leave her. Leaving her feels wrong.

"Thank you, Stavros..."

I kiss her forehead because I can't bear to kiss her lips. If I kiss her lips, I can't control what I do next. Something stupid. Something terrible.

A kiss on the forehead. And that's the end of us. I've finally done the impossible. I've let Fallon go. And I regret it. I regret not being a monster because at least then I would have what I wanted.

What's the point in being good? Maybe if she stayed with me, I'd learn. But right now, it hurts so much that it doesn't seem worth it.

I miss being the cruel bastard I was before I met her. I love Fallon, but fuck, I hate how she's changed me. This would have been easy before, but now, it's ripping out my heart to watch her go.

FORTY-SEVEN
NO REGRETS

’m not ready to take the boat home. Loukas must still be searching Thessaloniki for me, and I have to check on Sandros and Cass.

I hope they aren't in trouble. My weeks with Fallon are over. How could I have allowed myself to fall for her so quickly?

Love at first sight...

I call Cass once my boat is on the open water. She thankfully answers the phone. Now that Fallon's no longer with me, there's nothing to stop me wringing Sandros' neck if he continues fucking my sister before asking for her hand in marriage — officially.

I understand they're on the run but when a man wants a woman, he should lock her down.

Like I should have done with Fallon.

If he wants to have her, he'll have to protect her. I scoff at my arrogance for even having the thought. Fallon would have argued with me. She would have pointed out that I did a horrible job of protecting Cassia.

I allowed Ofek to rape her. I left her to kill him when, as her brother, I should have killed anyone who threatened my sister.

I've been distracted. Since Fallon walked into my life, all I thought about was touching her. Kissing her. Keeping her. Maybe if I killed Ofek she would have stayed. I would have shown her how protective I could get.

Then again, Fallon didn't approve of killing either. She was better than the voices in my head. She never wanted to hurt me. Fallon never wanted to hurt anyone. She even won Loukas over without putting a gun to his head.

And I let her go...

When my boat gets to Cassia's and Sandros, I announce myself. Loudly. The last thing I need is to catch an eyeful of his pale Greek ass humping the air. The thought causes me to shudder. Instead, Cass sits on the deck crying and there's no Sandros. At least not visible to me. I jump over from my boat to theirs.

"You didn't push him overboard, did you?"

"No! He's sleeping."

"Why are you crying out here?"

"Because... I told him the truth. I don't think he'll forgive me..."

"What truth?"

"Ofek was too drunk to... get... he mostly rubbed my thigh and he never... I didn't want Sandros to think I was a virgin when we did it. But I confessed, and he's angry."

She jumps off the deck and wraps her arms around me. I'm relieved. Maybe it's the reward I get for letting Fallon go. My sister may be traumatized, but at least a man didn't rape her. She could escape with that much. I'm too relieved at first to realize that bringing her to my chest only made her cry harder. She thinks I'll be angry.

"If Ofek didn't rape you, why did you kill him?"

"Because he would have eventually, stupid."

"Right."

"I didn't want to marry him and someone should have listened to me. You should have."

"I know. I'm sorry."

Cass gazes at me contemptuously.

"I will forgive you. One day. But can you please talk to Sandros for me?"

I touch my holster and Cass's eyes bug out.

"Simple," I continue, as if I don't see her freaking out, "I'll point this at his head and tell him to forgive my sister or I blow his fucking brains out."

"Stavros, no! That isn't funny!"

I'm red with laughter as Cass pushes me.

"I will talk to him, stupid. You stay here. And don't shoot anyone," she says.

I lean against the railing and allow the wind to whip back my hair. They've made it out here so far, but we will have to pick a new spot for them to continue lying low. Better yet, maybe I'll sail them back to Africa. They'll be safer there. And I can send Cass enough money to keep her out of trouble. Sandros may have to leave her to work but she can have friends, go to nightclubs and stay out of trouble.

Who am I kidding? A Pagonis could never stay out of trouble for long.

As Cass and Sandros argue louder below deck, my phone rings. A call from my father.

"Papa?"

"What have you done to my mother, idiot!"

"Whatever has happened to Yiayia, she deserved."

My family can't rattle me. When they could kidnap and threaten Fallon, the rest of my family had significant leverage over me. That leverage is gone. Safe across the sea where not even Loukas can find her. I won't make the same mistake twice.

"You don't understand what you've done? She's at the house and she's *armed and dangerous!*"

"She's dangerous when she isn't armed."

"I have a fucking fishing weekend planned with Adrian and

Marco! I don't have time to chase after men who owe me money and my own fucking mother!"

"Papa, have you been drinking?"

He hates when I ask that because he's usually been drinking and hates that I can tell. He prides himself on his nonexistent ability to hold his liquor.

"Come back to the house and *kill whoever she is angry with!*"

"I will not do that. If you have a problem, figure it out. I have enough trouble."

I doubt my father has his story straight. Yiayia might be... difficult. But she doesn't do her own dirty work. Cass and Sandros emerge once I'm off the phone. There's nothing Papa could say or do that would make me kill again. The only thing left I have from Fallon is that last shred of humanity she saw in me. Or at least she pretended to see so she could get her way.

Sandros has his arm around my sister's waist. I loathe them for what they have because I never stood a chance at having it with the woman I truly loved and cared about. Having a shred of humanity didn't stop me from being too monstrous for her to love.

"You two can't stay here long. It isn't safe."

"We have been safe."

"For now. There's trouble at home."

"There's always trouble at home. We should go back home and face it."

"*I* will face whatever we need to face back home. *You* will get out of here somewhere safe. I've made the mistake of putting you in danger before. Yiayia is worse than ever since I hit her."

"You *hit* Yiayia."

"Yes."

"Good," Cass hisses, "Now man up and twist the knife."

"You shouldn't speak that way."

"Don't be stupid, Stavros. Even Fallon saw how Yiayia controls you. But you're bigger than her. And stronger than her. Maybe in some families, there are elders worthy of respect, but the elders in our family treat us like shit. We need a new generation of Pagonis'."

"We can't all sit around and post on our phones like Galanos."

"He earns €50,000 a week!"

"From his cell phone? Are all of his ten million fucking followers or whatever it is sick in the head?"

"Not everything is about guns or drugs. We don't have to be monsters anymore."

"Nothing I could do would change the fact that I'm a monster."

"Fallon didn't think so."

"You don't know what Fallon thought."

"I do."

Cass reaches into her cardigan pocket for a folded paper with black ink bleeding through.

"She told me to give this to you if you showed up here without her."

"When did she tell you that?"

Cass shrugs.

"I didn't read it."

I stuff the letter into my pocket. I don't want to read it. I don't need any reminders of Fallon Iverson.

"Aren't you going to read it?" Sandros asks, "It's clear you were... you know..."

Cass elbows him hard, and he thankfully trails off.

"I won't be reading it. In fact, I should throw it into the sea."

"You can't do that," Cassia protests, with the simpering voice of a hopeless romantic.

"Why not? She wanted me to let her go. If she had something to say, she could have said it when I said goodbye."

"You are *stupid!*"

"I know you think so, but I'm a grown man. I cannot always follow the whims and fancies of my heart. You two can stay until tomorrow. But then I'm coming back and I'm taking you to Africa."

I hastily climb over onto my boat.

"Stavros! I'm not going to Africa until I find out what is in that letter!"

"No one will find out," I snap at Cass as I start my boat, "Because I'm going to burn it!"

I veer the boat around and speed away. I cannot allow myself to *feel* anything about Fallon Iverson. Especially not regret. Or longing. Or love.

FORTY-EIGHT
THE FATE OF THE LETTER

Once I'm out of their line of sight, I stop the boat and open the paper. Fallon's handwriting is tiny. And nurses have handwriting as bad as doctors do. But the letter is real. She touched it. I smell her hair as I open the paper. I imagine her smooth brown skin touching the page. There are a few blots of ink where my fountain pen bled into the page.

Dear Stavros.

I can't bring myself to read past that. I ought to do what I promised Cassia. I ought to toss the letter into the ocean and let her go. What good could come of reading Fallon's words and knowing that even if I wanted to find her again, she'd be long gone. We set it up that way so she'd be safe. If anyone discovers my weakness, she'll remain protected.

My phone buzzes. It's a call from Cass. She probably wants to yell at me about reading the letter again. I ignore her call and start reading. Because Fallon wrote these words. And even if I pretend I can cut her out of my heart, I'll never be able to let go of her. Even if I throw the letter away, I'll remember her touch. Her laugh. The way she showed me how monstrous I'd become.

Dear Stavros,

If you're reading this, Cassia earned every penny I gave her so she would do this. I'm sorry I couldn't say any of this to you in person. I had to know what choice you would make without everything I'm about to say clouding your judgment.

You love me.

I've known for a long time. Do you believe in fate, Stavros? I never did. Before I went to Las Vegas, I hated everything about my job. I wanted to help people with mental illness more than anything. My mom... The reason I haven't pressed more about calling her is because she's schizophrenic.

My aunt looks after her, but it's too painful for us to have a relationship. I studied nursing so I could be a better daughter to her. I studied nursing to help people. But I helped no one. I cried my way through nursing school and the reason I went to Las Vegas was because I got fired that weekend. I couldn't take it. No one cared about these patients. Everyone treated them like monsters, and my bosses hated me for taking their side.

I was a failure. I couldn't help my mom when I was little. I couldn't help anyone with all the B.S. politics in the psych ward. And then I met you...

I thought I could help you. I thought I could fix you. But you made me realize I was thinking about it all wrong. If I loved you, I couldn't try to fix you. I had to give you the space to fix yourself. And maybe I didn't belong in a psych ward. Maybe I can help families.

By the time you get this, I will have asked for the one thing I know you don't want to give up. The one thing you could do that would prove you weren't a monster. And I knew it would hurt to ask you and hurt even more to go through with.

I knew it would hurt because as much as you love me, Stavros, I love you more. I couldn't tell you because I knew you'd never let me go. But it's for the best. I've had a hell of an adventure in Greece. What was the worst week of my life in Khalid's cell became some of the craziest weeks. You brought brightness to my life, Stavros.

When I get to whatever tiny Serbian village I end up in, I'm going to tell them all about the Greek lover I once had. Stavros Pagonis. Maybe they'll know about you. Maybe not. It doesn't matter. I'll tell them about your eyes the color of the Aegean Sea, your immaculate body, tanned by the sun and chiseled by Zeus himself. I'll tell them about the way you kissed me and no man could ever live up to making love with you.

I'll tell them that when I thought life was pointless and mundane, I met a man who showed me excitement, despair, honesty, and beauty.

I love you, Stavros. If it's any consolation, I'll hate myself for never saying it out loud. To you. Maybe when we're both old and grey, I'll have the courage to come back to Thessaloniki. You will have forgotten about me by then, but I'll never forget about you.

I never could.

I will always be yours.

Even if I still hate that you use the word "cunt".

Love,
Fallon I.

I wish I ripped the letter to a million pieces. She makes me want to *feel.* Fallon made me let her go to pass a test. A test I would have been happy to have failed if it meant having her here.

But that was the point, wasn't it? If I'd meant to keep her, I would have done it regardless of her wishes. She had to know the man she loved wasn't damaged. Perhaps I'm damaged, but I still love Fallon. When you love someone, you must let them go.

I glance at my phone. Three more missed calls from Cassia. What the hell...

I call back. Sandros answers.

"Stavros! We need your help! There is a boat after us. We think it's one of Ofek's."

"Stay where you are!"

I know they're going to ignore me before I finish the sentence. Cass never listens but this time, her life is on the line. I failed her once. I won't do it again. I shove two bullets into my pistol.

"We're going back to the villa. Ofek's men have brought an army."

"How do you know it's them?"

"We found one of his men floating. He disobeyed orders, and they shot him. We tried to resuscitate him but he — HANG TO STAR-BOARD, CASSIA YOU'RE GOING TO KILL US!"

"Don't go to the villa!"

Yiayia's there waving a gun. It's the last place Cass and Sandros should be if they want to stay safe.

The phone goes dead. My heart leaps into my throat. I stuff Fallon's letter into my pocket. Fuck. We thought Ofek's men would chase Cassia down, but assumed they'd give up once we returned to Greece. Who could be so motivated by the bastard's death to fight the Pagonis family on their home turf?

Cassia might be right about going to the villa. This could get her killed, but she faces death either way. Better to face her family than strangers.

If Ofek has an army of mercenaries, the villa is our best defense. But a better defense would mean getting there first. Before Yiayia kills half the men on our payroll. I'll think about Fallon's letter later.

Or better yet, I won't. Maybe I let go of her at the right time. I don't see how I can make it through this without killing another person. It's too easy and tempting to pull the trigger. *I love you, Stavros.*

I have to imagine it in her voice. The voice I'll never hear. How could she think I would forget her? I'll never forget the way she stood there. Dignified. Unwilling to let Khalid's den of filthy bastards break her. Setting her free had always been part of the plan. Loving her had been up to chance, or as Fallon might put it, up to fate.

By the time I get to the docks, I'm soaked with water and disoriented. Too disoriented to notice that Loukas' three best shooters surround me and have guns aimed at my head.

FORTY-NINE
THE DUST SETTLES

Papa would call me an idiot for landing so unaware of my surroundings. Fuck. Never let your guard down. Number one rule of being in the fucking mafia.

"Loukas, call them off me. We need to get to the villa."

I gasp at him, desperate for breath. I swam as hard as I could and it's taking it's toll on me. I lean forward, pressing my knuckles into the sand, wet hair sticking to the back of my neck.

My skin burns. Loukas responds unsympathetically.

"Confess what you did to her."

"I didn't kill your fiancée, but for touching Fallon, I might kill your next one."

He snarls at me, "Where is the *slave*?"

"Gone." That's all he needs to know.

He's only calling her a slave to piss me off. In a stand off, the first person who loses is the one who loses their cool.

"Like Matilda," he murmurs, his eyes so pale and glassy they're almost silver. He's been drinking again. Since Africa.

"I didn't hurt Matilda. Neither did I order it."

"Why did Helen say you did?"

"Because it's *Helen*. She always pits us against each other. And she hates me."

"For good reason," Loukas sneers, unable to contain his pure loathing for me.

We get along well when we aren't fighting. Since Carlotta left for boarding school, he's been a wreck. He misses her. And he promised if he lost another girl, he'd send the youngest away.

Loukas doesn't want to lose his children and he blames me for getting between them. *Focus, Stavros. Think. Calm him down. Talk things out the way Fallon suggests.*

"Tell me something honest, Loukas. Is there no chance someone else killed Matilda? Perhaps the killer hurt her for personal reasons."

"What personal reason could anyone have to harm her? Only a sick person would. She was innocent. And I failed her. I fucked up."

"I don't know if you've noticed, but our family is made up of sick people. Yiayia could have ordered her dead. Easily."

"It's not her. She was on the boat with me. I've been watching her."

"Our grandmother has done worse."

"Not to the children. She couldn't watch them losing another parent figure. Matilda and I... we were nearly finished. She didn't deserve to die."

"Yiayia doesn't care. Once we want something, she takes it away. And she has Papa to back her up. There's nothing we can do about that."

"Yes there is. I can kill her attack dog."

He aims a gun at my chest.

"One in the heart," Loukas snarls, "You'd drop to the ground like the dog you are."

"She does this, Loukas. She gets between us."

"It's not fucking Yiayia! You're clouded by your own grudges. She wouldn't..."

"Wouldn't she? She hurt Fallon. She hurt Cass. She'd hurt any of us to keep us obedient."

Loukas considers what I'm saying. I haven't flinched. Liars normally react to having weapons in their faces at this point of the "interrogation". Before Loukas had kids, he did my job. So he knows. No man is as tough on the other end of that gun.

He shoves his hand into his black coat. It's barely chilly but Loukas goes nowhere without the coat, pulled up to his sharp jaw.

"Lower your weapons."

Progress. But Loukas still has his hand on his weapon.

"Carlotta's safe?"

"Yes," I say to him.

Loukas lowers the weapon and juts his chin toward the SUVs. We don't have *time* for this but I need Loukas calm before I press him to leave. He's still unstable.

"And she witnessed nothing?"

"She claims to have spent days at a party."

"You don't believe her?"

"Loukas, your daughter is like we were at her age."

His face goes ghastly pale. I see the youthful Loukas in his purer expressions. He was always the wild one until he became a parent. He stopped laughing and started unraveling. He'd do anything to keep his daughter safe, especially since her mother died.

"If she's anything like us, she's trouble."

"Yes. And perhaps she has a good reason for lying. What if she wasn't at a party?"

"She could have seen who did it."

I purse my lips and nod. I have darker suspicions. All this running around accusing each other has distracted us from the truth.

"I'm sorry for kidnapping Fallon. Where have you stashed her?"

"I meant what I said. She's gone."

Loukas stops me, a firm hand on my shoulder.

"You let her go?"

"Yes."

"That much, eh? I've seen you, Stavros. You never let them go. Even when they're dead."

I look away from him. I hate when my family members bring up my hallucinations. It's an unfortunate reminder of how poorly I hide from them.

"I had to let her go."

"It's back to whispering in your sleep to that ghost of yours, then? Or will you buy another one?"

"There will never be another one."

"We shouldn't waste more time. Now that you're not going to blow my brains out... Ofek's men are coming. They think we have Cassia."

Loukas snickers.

"The little wretch escaped in the end, did she? You might as well tell them she isn't here."

"But she is. And she's on the way."

"Fuck. I'm guessing you have something to do with this. How far?"

"Forty minutes."

"You expect us to raise an army against Ofek's people in forty minutes?"

"Not an army. We can take them."

We don't know how many there are so this could very well be a flat out lie.

"They'll come to the villa. That buys us an extra fifteen minutes."

Loukas spits on the cobblestone and wipes his mouth angrily.

"Fuck, Stavros. You could have told me before I held you up talking about women."

"I'd take talking women over guns any day of the week."

Loukas grins.

"No day is certain. We'll either die in the crossfire or live to fight another day."

"And drink."

"Absinthe."

We break every rule of the road until we get to the villa. There's a fight in the driveway. Papa's car blocks the entrance and Helen points a gun at him.

"Get out of the car, Papa!"

"Helen! What are you doing?" Loukas shouts.

Helen turns her gun on Loukas and screams, "Stand where you are."

Papa points his gun at Helen next. I'm the only one not aiming my weapon and the only one without a gun aimed at my head. So naturally, I point my gun at Papa.

"Papa, put down the gun."

"You don't know what you're getting involved with!" Papa sputters.

"I know you killed Matilda. Stavros' medication. I found it in your half of the villa. I don't want to hurt you, Loukas... But you need to tell me why you would do that to your children? And I want a good explanation."

"I didn't kill her!"

"Papa, lower your weapon. Now," Loukas snarls. He has his hands up and hasn't reached for his gun yet. He's watching Helen closely, estimating how willing she is to shoot him. Considering her red-faced rage, I'd rate her willingness to pull the trigger as higher than normal. I don't have an interest in shooting Papa. And perhaps that is for the best.

I hear the rattle of Yiayia's cane but refuse to take my eyes from my father. Never let your target out of your sight. Yiayia takes advantage of my distracted state.

The cold metal of her small firearm presses deeply into the nape of my neck and Yiayia's withered hand steadies her balance on my forearm. I feel her leaning forward, propping her body up on her cane as she hisses, "It won't hurt. One shot and it will be over, grandson."

"We don't have time for this!" I yell, "We have bigger problems than standing around pointing guns at each other."

"You won't have to worry about this family for long, Stavros," Yiayia snarls.

"Kill me. I don't care."

"And that slave *bitch*?"

I roar at her, "Watch your mouth, Yiayia."

"I am sick of you thinking you can talk to me however you want. I raised you with respect."

"You raised us to be monsters!" Loukas and Helen yell.

Yiayia's hand rustles behind my head and I can tell her finger has moved over the trigger. There's not much except a few pounds of pressure between her rage and the end of my life. I've thought about what standing on this side of the gun would feel like. I've considered death. In my predictions, I'd piss my pants or shit myself. I've seen both happen and didn't think I'd earned enough good karma to escape the fate when it was my turn. But killed by a septuagenarian? Wasn't that a cruel death, even for a trained assassin?

A hallucination appears in the corner of my eye. I twitch but keep my gaze steady. I might have to shoot. Even when the visions start, I can keep a good eye on my target. This time is no different, but the hallucination is Fallon. Brown-skinned. Beautiful. And pleading with me.

"Fix this, Stavros. Without ever pulling the trigger."

Pulling the trigger would end this faster. Killing someone. A few seconds and your problem is over. Now you have an entirely fresh problem, but you can get methodical about dropping a body in the ocean.

No one has time to fire a shot because Cass and Sandros hurtle into the driveway on an apparently commandeered SUV with a sunroof. Loukas and I part from each other as their stolen ride slams into Papa's.

"Yiayia!"

She'd been behind me. Her gun never fires. I don't hear her move. I don't recall when I stop feeling the cold metal on the back of my neck but I tell myself that she had time to get out of the way. Had she? Should I have grabbed my grandmother out of the way?

Just because she was a stone cold sociopath didn't mean she had to die. I stumble forward. The dust took a while to settle. I hear sounds of multiple guns cocking and as I wait for the dust to settle, more spiral into the air. I cough and call my brother's name. And then Cassia's. Then Yiayia. I jog ahead a few steps into the swirling winds of dust and sand, cradling my pistol. *Where the fuck is Galanos?*

It's too late to worry about raising an army or my brother. From the dust, black suits emerge and a trail of SUVs. They can only be Ofek's people, armed to the teeth and ready to slaughter our entire family for Cassia's actions.

FIFTY
MOTHER-OF-PEARL

Sandros stands through the Jeep's sun roof and points an AK-47 at a woman's head. She only came with five suits. I expected an army. But now we have a woman and five suits. No sign of Yiayia. She's not dead, I don't think. There's still dust and I'm coughing as I survey the scene.

My father slumps over the steering wheel, unconscious.

Loukas points his gun at one suit. Before I can get the other one, a bullet whizzes through the air. A suit groans and falls to his knees. The other one searches madly for the source of the bullet, but there's another crack of the gun and he's dead. Sniper rifle. It has to be someone on the top floor of the villa.

Sandros pumps the AK-47 and kills the suit he's pointing at. The woman jumps back. Cassia screams and yanks Sandros back into the Jeep. The woman runs into Loukas, and he grabs her, holding her still as he aims the pistol at another suit.

She grabs his face and then slaps him. Sandros sticks the weapon up through the sunroof and leans over to accept Cassia's next punishment. Another slap followed by a deep kiss. I point my gun at one suit. Loukas kills the other.

"Hurry, Stavros," Loukas snarls, "the bastard has already shit himself."

"Don't kill him!" the woman yells.

"Who the fuck are you? And how dare you?"

"I came to speak to Cassia Pagonis."

"You came to punish her for murdering Ofek."

Helen points a gun at the woman's head and moves in behind Loukas. My family has no trouble putting our problems behind us as long as we have another enemy.

"Stavros, finish it!"

"I won't."

"Fucking hell, you choose now to have a moral crisis?"

"If you want him dead, kill him yourself."

Loukas shoots. The man falls to the ground and a loud girl's voice shrieks. It's Carlotta, suddenly coming up the driveway in a miniskirt that exposes deeply tanned thin legs. Loukas lowers the gun as Carlotta stares at him in horror.

She just witnessed her father kill a man and although all the children suspect what we do for work, we carefully hide the gory truth until they're old enough. Eighteen for most of us. But Loukas never wanted his daughter to know about the family business.

Carlotta screams.

"Where's Yiayia?" I call out.

Carlotta runs from her father. Loukas chases after her, dropping the woman. Helen keeps the gun pointed at the woman's head as Loukas catches his daughter around the waist. Cassia and Sandros get out of the car and approach Helen. Sandros swaggers boldly forward with the AK-47 slung around his body. Carlotta screams as her father grabs hold of her.

"Monster! You psychopathic monster!"

Loukas wrestles Carlotta inside and slams the doors behind him. He has his daughter to look after, for all he cares we could kill each other as long as Carlotta is safe. Galanos whoops from the top floor.

"Two kills!"

Gal's glee is nearly distasteful. He points at the remaining suit and shoots him. Now the woman is the only one left. And she's unshaken. Cassia nods at her.

"What do you want, Francesca? If you hoped to kill me, you won't succeed."

"Ungrateful bitch."

"I lied. I'm sorry. But Ofek didn't deserve his life."

"Neither do any of the men in your family."

"You took something that belonged to me."

Cass pouts and pops her hip out, "I took only what Ofek owed me."

"He had no right to give that to you. I granted him the divorce so he could move in a younger wife. I didn't want you rifling through my possessions and stealing my jewelry."

Cass folds her arms and protests, "I'm not giving it back."

Sandros puts his hand on her shoulder and she sticks out her lower lip.

"I'm not," insists Cass.

"What is this about, Cassia?"

"A necklace," Francesca eagerly supplies, "Ofek gave it to me and... Cass took it when she left. I understand why she killed my ex-husband, but stealing my jewelry from his closet was unacceptable."

"You mobilized your ex-husband's fortune of millions to chase after a teenager who stole from you?"

"It's a one of a kind Van Cleef and Arpels mother-of-pearl neck-lace worth fifty-thousand dollars. Ofek gave it to me when he bought his first hotel in Tel Aviv. Cassia knew what it meant to me."

"You didn't deserve it. I showed you plenty of mercy when I didn't put you in the ground with him."

Cassia's fiery tongue doesn't affect Francesca. She cracks a smile, her greying hair framing her aging but not elderly face.

"I wonder if your grandmother knew giving you to Ofek would be his greatest punishment. He always liked young girls. I couldn't stop him. My husband was a powerful man. But that necklace means more to me than it ever could to you. I will even pay you to get it back. Five thousand dollars."

"It's *mine.*"

"Cass..."

"Don't take her side, Stavros."

I slip my hand into Cassia's pocket, but it's empty. On the other side of her, Sandros lifts the necklace to me.

"Stavros."

I catch the necklace. Cassia pushes him. *Hard.*

"*Stupid!* I didn't want to give it back to her."

"What does it matter? We could end this without anyone getting hurt."

I hand the woman the necklace as Cassia tries to fight Sandros again. The big baker's son grabs onto her and wrestles her wildcat temper into relative submission.

"You should have killed her! Kill her! Don't let her leave!"

Helen lowers her gun.

"No. Stavros is right."

I eye Galanos on the balcony. He's too busy taking a picture of himself with the gun to have it pointed on the woman. He's probably bragging to millions about his two confirmed kills. The only reason Interpol hasn't investigated us is because he never posts proof and everyone assumes he's lying. It's why he's infamous. One reason, at least.

The last thing we need is to pay higher Interpol bribes because my idiot brother gets reckless. Cass spits at Francesca and Helen gestures toward the villa gates.

"Leave. We are sorry about your men."

"Ofek's men. You don't know what I had to do to convince them to come here."

Neither did I wish to know.

"Thank you. I'll remember receiving mercy from a Pagonis. Not many live to make such claims."

"I am sorry for any trouble my sister has caused. It's our fault. We've set a poor example for her."

"Perhaps we don't have to lose the contract between my ex-husband's business and your family."

I reach my hand out to shake hers and Francesca's palm squeezes firmly around mine. She's not as fragile as she looks. I suppose she couldn't be fragile if she were married to a man like Ofek.

"My husband was a complicated man, but I have fond memories of him. That's all I have. Memories."

"I understand. Take care, Francesca."

Francesca turns to Cass and sighs.

"I am happy he did not break your spirit. One day, I hope you can forgive me for allowing him to have you at all. I could have spared you."

Cass spits.

Sandros tightens his grip on her. Francesca crosses the threshold of our villa. She gets behind the wheel of one of her armored cars and we hear two gunshots before we notice who shot Francesca. Yiayia. She hobbles from behind an ornamental agave plant. She'd made it out of the way with time to spare. Francesca slumps over the steering wheel. Dead.

Yiayia drops the gun and clutches her chest.

"My goodness..."

FIFTY-ONE

MY LAST SHRED OF HUMANITY

'm fainting!" Yiayia turns up her play-acting. Like she shot Francesca by accident.

"Help! Stavros… Get me a chair!"

I don't move to help her. Helen rushes to her side and holds her up. This is how I could end this. I rush up to them and press the gun to my grandmother's head.

"You're the reason all of this is happening."

"Stavros, stop it!" Helen screams.

"Move away from her, Helen."

"Stavros, no. Do you hear me? No."

I can hear the tremor in her voice. She's trying to calm a Rottweiler with raised hackles.

"Don't calm me down. I'm calm."

"That's what scares me," Helen snarls, "if you do this, she takes away your last shred of humanity."

"My last shred of humanity is already gone."

Loukas snarls at me as he leaves the villa, "Did you take it with you when you killed Matilda?"

Loukas drags Carlotta outside by her forearm and points the gun at my head. I'm not dumb enough to point my gun away from Yiayia, even for a moment. Helen's right to question my sanity now because the fear in Yiayia's eyes brings me pleasure.

"I told you, I didn't kill Matilda."

"Papa, no! You can't kill your brother."

"You saw him," Loukas snarls at her, "you admitted it. It's time you grow up and learn what happens to people in this family who defy me."

"Papa, *NO!*"

Helen isn't sure which of us to yell at first. But Cassia turns her weapon on Loukas and gives her a new problem. A new problem is always better than an old problem. At least that's the way it goes with killing off my family's enemies. Not so much when we all have guns turned on each other.

"Loukas, get away from him. Stavros spared Sandros. We owe him his life."

Sandros doesn't move away from Cassia because he probably senses the recoil from an AK-47 could blow her halfway across the driveway the way she's standing with her weight all the way on her toes. Big Kalashnikov's were more Galanos' speed.

Naturally, seeing the shooting again, Gal swaggers downstairs with another weapon drawn. He waves it dramatically between Cass and Helen. I hope to God that little idiot doesn't have it loaded.

"I don't know what's going on but I just got a date with a Kardashian and I want you all to stop fighting and tell me I'm a fucking champion."

"It's probably a porn bot," Cass sneers, definitively choosing herself as Galanos' target.

"Alright you little shit, at least I didn't get raped in front of the family."

Yiayia snickers. I let her watch my hand hover over the trigger.

"Careful. I could end this."

My grandmother sneers at me, "Will the nightmares ever stop?

Or will you add me to your harem of ghosts? You don't have the guts to shoot me."

"Don't I? I've dreamed about shooting you for a long time. Noticed that Helen's not just holding you up? She's holding you still for me."

"I don't endorse shooting her," Helen adds, like it changes the fact that she has Yiayia planted in place with little chance at escape. If I kill her, I will be irredeemable. Not even Fallon, a woman drawn to the beauty in the monstrous, could see the good in me if I shoot my grandmother.

"You don't deserve to live," I tell her.

"Neither do you," Loukas says calmly, "And you've involved my daughter in your secrecy."

I address my niece now, calmly, "Carlotta, why are you lying to your father."

Loukas always flies off the handle with her. An utterly useless trait when dealing with teenagers who view emotional outbursts as a contest.

"I'm not lying, Papa! I saw him. Uncle Stavros killed Matilda. He fucked her and then he killed her."

"Carlotta," I repeat, "Why are you lying to your father? I didn't kill Matilda."

"I'm not lying!" she shrills, "I'm not lying about that stupid bitch of a stepmother!"

Loukas releases his daughter's hand. She takes off toward the house but Loukas isn't willing to let me out of his sight and he senses Cassia aiming the weapon behind him.

"What are you getting at, Stavros, calling my daughter a liar? You've upset her."

Yiayia snickers, "Loukas... Carlotta is a girl after her grandmother's heart. I think it's obvious what she's hiding."

Galanos says, "Pretty obvious, brother."

"An idiot could figure it out," Cassia taunts.

Like every Pagonis, she becomes twenty times more insufferable on the correct end of a weapon.

"Everyone can figure out what!?" Loukas snarls.

"She killed her stepmother," Helen says, "Or she knows well who did. She's blaming Stavros because he stopped her from going out dressed like a cheap prostitute."

"Are you calling my daughter a fucking prostitute?!"

"She dresses like one," Galanos says.

"Pervert!"

We're all yelling at each other again when a loud gunshot pierces the air and forcing us all to fall silent. None of us have fired. We all glance over our shoulders and away from our targets just long enough. Loukas throws his gun into the pool and leaps at me, hitting me in the face.

I drop my gun. I didn't kill his woman and I refuse to shoot Loukas. Helen screams but I can't do anything about it with Loukas' fist approaching my face at top speed.

Galanos and Cassia's weapons clatter to the ground. She calls him a pervert, he calls her a slut. Sandros tackles Galanos who is toughest behind a gun or a camera. He's like a peacock came to life in an arrogant blond twit.

Galanos shrieks as Sandros punches him in the face. I can't celebrate for long because I dodge Loukas' first hit. Helen screams again. Then I hear a familiar voice shout, "That's enough old lady. One more fucking step and I'll gladly shoot you in the kneecaps and make you lick the blood off the floor."

A hush falls over the Pagonis family. I wonder where the hell my father is. Loukas drags me to my feet and pushes me forward.

"Liar. You said you got rid of her."

Helen screams again. What the hell happened to her? Yiayia was nearly in the front seat of Cassia's Jeep. But Fallon has a gun to her head and guides her forward. Cassia notices what's wrong with Helen first.

"Helen!"

"She stabbed me. She fucking stabbed me."

"You fucking stabbed your own fucking granddaughter?!" I snarl, reaching for my gun and racing toward Yiayia.

"Stavros, NO!" Fallon screams.

"Get out of here, Fallon. I left you far away from here for a reason."

"Did Cass give you my letter?"

"Not. Now."

"Answer the question."

"Yes," I say to her. She's still beautiful. Why wouldn't she be? I love her. She'll always be perfect.

"So you know."

"Yes," I reply. I know that she loves me and I love her too.

"Okay."

She pulls the gun away from Yiayia's head.

"Smart choice, girl."

"Shut the fuck up," Fallon snaps, "You might think you're still the boss around here but listen up lady, that ends tonight. We're going into the kitchen *right now* and you all are having a family meeting until you fucking figure your shit out. If one person argues with me, I will start shooting. I only barely know how to use this gun so it *will get bloody*. Now MOVE!"

They all walk toward the kitchen without answering her back. Maybe we're tired of fighting, maybe Fallon figured out a way to get into all our heads. But we listen. I follow close to her.

"Why did you come back here? That was stupid. Insanely stupid."

"I didn't come back for you."

"Oh."

She hits my bicep.

"Don't be an idiot. I came back for you. But... it's more complicated than that."

"Wasn't it always with us?"

"Not now, okay? We've got to fix in there before we fix... *this*."

Helen groans as they get her into a chair. Gal and Loukas rush off to get First-Aid. Cass and Sandros help Yiayia sit. Sandros makes her tea. Fallon keeps her gun aimed straight at my grandmother's head.

"Stavros, can you get your dad?"

"My dad?"

Shit. I'd forgotten about him.

"Where is he?"

"He's asleep. I assume he was unconscious at some point but he appears to have lit a cigarette and then fallen asleep after smoking it. I checked on him before I... fired."

"You have some explaining to do."

"Hurry, Stavros."

"Yes, beloved."

She looks away from me when I call her that. Like it hurts too much.

FIFTY-TWO

INTO RETIREMENT

"Helen. Do you need a hospital?"

Loukas complains, "You people are letting this *foreigner* talk to us?"

"I'd let her fuck me too! He he he he!" my dad laughs and then slumps over.

He's put back three shots of whiskey before making it to the kitchen, and he claims his nerves are getting to him from all the shouting. He'd probably rather sit on his boat smoking and drinking. But he's technically responsible for the family business, even if he doesn't act like it.

"You are all some of the most pathological people I've ever met. Galanos, you're narcissistic. I've seriously never for one moment heard you consider another person. Cassia, you're impulsive. I get it. But think first, you'll get into far less trouble. Helen, I don't know why you stick around here. I might be out of line, but it's codependent."

"Parasitic more like," Helen grumbles, leaning over on the counter and clutching the bandage on her stomach, "Painkillers, Carlotta."

Carlotta quietly slides painkillers across the table that look like they shouldn't be in the hands of a teenage girl. Helen downs them without looking at them. Fallon continues her analysis.

"Loukas. Carlotta killed Matilda. I don't know why, but you either need to talk to your daughter or go to the police."

"POLICIA?!" we all yell in protest.

"Fine! No police. Right. I don't live in the real world with you people."

"But you keep coming back," Yiayia snarls, "You'd be better off killing yourself."

"As for you," Fallon snaps, tilting the gun forward and tightening her brow, "It's taking everything in my power not to put two bullets in your head. I wouldn't want your ghost haunting me. You... Yiayia... you are the worst grandmother I've ever met in my life. Seriously. You encourage your grandkids to be sociopathic monsters, you torture them and you don't give a shit about anything except being a huge bitch. You're only leading this family around by the horns because your useless son, no offense Mr. Pagonis, doesn't do his job. Well. You're officially retired. Stavros will be head of the family. Mr. Pagonis retires and you go with him. Get on a boat and *leave.*"

"You can't tell me what to do," Yiayia sneers.

"Yes she can," Loukas says, "Because I agree with her. I have to focus on raising my children. And Carlotta. If she did what you all think she did, I have not been a good father to her. I don't have time to do family business. Stavros has nothing but free time. He can sail back and forth and command the men. I can handle Thessaloniki until we fulfill the contracts."

"And after the contracts?" Helen asks, "What then?"

"Perhaps we transition. Fewer guns. More... real estate."

"Something legitimate," Cass agrees.

"I make €50,000 a week from my social media accounts," Gal chimes in.

We all snicker.

"Gal, you're a *liar*. Seriously," Cass laughs, elbowing her uncle who puts his arm around her shoulder.

"Listen, sorry for calling you a bunch of shitty names. But would you mind flashing your tits to my followers? I think the scandal would make me a mint."

Cass turns red and storms off with Gal and Sandros chasing after her. Fallon gestures to Loukas and me, "Listen, if you two call the doctor for Helen, I can help your dad and grandmother get to the docks. Some guys who worked for you in the village heard the fighting. They helped me get up there and told me where I can find them if you need backup. They didn't want to move without orders."

"How did you get our men to confess they worked for us?" I hiss, leaning into Fallon with fresh suspicion.

"You don't want to know."

I turn red.

"Did you let men who work beneath my command see your..."

"I *said* you don't want to know."

"Are you insane, woman!?"

"Hey! Relax."

Helen sighs and grabs the phone.

"I'll call doc. Loukas, you'd better get them to the docks. Send them with plenty of money and a full crew. I think these two love-birds need time alone."

Carlotta sits at the kitchen counter.

"Can I go with them to retirement?"

Loukas snarls at his daughter, "No. You stay here."

Helen sighs.

"I'll look after her. Stavros, Fallon... the living room might be more private."

Fallon takes my hand and drags me off to the villa's parlor. This is the one we entertain family in. It's decorated with family photos. Many of them have been replaced with Gal's selfies carelessly plastered over our pictures from the Amalfi coast in the 90s. That was a crazy summer. Loukas and I are both squeezing some red-heads arse in the picture. I step in front of it and clear my throat.

"You're back."

"Yes."

"Why?"

"Because... you have a sexting phone. And you never gave me the number."

"Really," I plead with her. "Why did you come back?"

"Because I love you."

"It's not safe near me. You know that. Why would you put yourself in danger like this?"

"Because I love you. And I don't want to leave you, Stavros."

"I bought you. Like a piece of meat. You'll never let go of that."

"But you never treated me like that. You always made me feel... alive. You made me orgasm. You opened up this part of me that felt so feminine and powerful. I made the dumbest mistake of my life and when I ended up in your arms, I thought that was my punishment. But this has always been my escape. My chance. That was what I wanted from my old life. I still want to reach out, but I don't belong there anymore. I belong here. With you."

"Maybe it really was the sexting phone thing."

She swats my chest.

"I'm serious."

"Then stay. I should have never let you out of my sight, anyway."

"That's the lesson you learned?"

"Hm... not really. But I'd go back in time and make ten million mistakes if it meant having more time with you."

"We have right now."

"Yes. Taking over my *insane* family business. How could that go wrong?"

"Speaking of things that went wrong. We need to talk."

"About what?"

"I can't have kids."

"I know."

"Except... I'm pregnant."

"I think I am."

"Are you sure?"

"I had to come back. I had to give you a choice."

She puts my hand on her stomach. I don't feel anything, but I can imagine it. A life growing inside her. I possessed Fallon in every sense of the word and now that she was free, my seed brought her back to me. Fate. Could it have been such a simple excuse? My hand travels slowly up her shirt.

"Pregnant," I whisper, "Oh, fuck."

"Are you happy?"

I grin. Children. I never thought I'd have them. Not because I was particularly cautious aside from regular STD testing. I figured it would happen when the time was right. With the right woman. A little boy for me to play with. Or a girl. Beautiful, like her mother.

"Yes, beloved. I thought my time for fatherhood passed."

"Not as far as I know."

"And there have been no others? Such as the men you flashed your breasts to?"

She pushes my chest playfully.

"You were right about your eleven inch Greek dick. It scrambled my brain."

"Good. I like the sound of that..."

"Are you going to kiss me, or what?"

"Is that what you're waiting for, beloved?"

"It's half of what I'm waiting for."

"Does the other half happen to be eleven inches?"

I kiss her. Because I can't stop myself any longer. And because we can't make love in the living room. If I let her expand on all the filthy things I want to do to her, I might get down to doing them instead of stopping to think for another important moment.

FIFTY-THREE
FIFTEEN COLORS

9 WEEKS LATER

Fallon leans in the doorway in her robe.

"You brought back *fifteen* color choices?"

"I don't want you leaving the house."

"Stavros. When I said I felt like nesting, I meant painting a room in the villa, not buying a brand new beach side cottage."

"My family will only stress the baby out. I won't let her come out like..."

I drop the samples on the bed. Fallon floats across the floor and wraps her arms around me.

"Like you?"

"I haven't heard the voices in a while but... they will come back. I can't avoid them forever."

"I know. But you don't have to worry about our baby. I promise."

"I don't want to fuck this up."

"You won't. Now... six shades of pink?"

"This one is peach. But what if she hates peach? She might prefer... um Carnation Rose?"

"You don't know the difference, do you?"

Fallon elbows me, and I crumble.

"No. The shop lady perhaps was overenthusiastic."

"Does it have anything to do with the giant 'P' on your ring?"

"She would have no reason to fear me."

"People don't know that yet. Give it time."

"Be careful what you wish for, beloved. When you're in labor, I think having the doctors scared out of their minds would help get you priority treatment."

My phone buzzes in my pocket.

"That better not be your sexting phone," Fallon teases.

My cheeks darken. I wish she'd never found out about that stupid thing. I gave it to Galanos as a spare in exchange for him teaching me how to set up one of those pages for pictures. I missed having a childhood like his. He doesn't know how spoiled he is.

"It's Loukas."

Fallon nods and points at the phone, "Answer. I made him promise to get back in time for dinner."

I grab the phone and listen to my brother prattle on.

"Eh? Fine. Yes. I'll send the bouquets."

"What does he want?"

"Matilda's family. He wants to send them flowers. They blame him for her death. He's still guilty. The wake was last night."

"And Carlotta?"

"Back at school with that friend of hers."

"Tisha. She's pretty. Did you see something going on between her and Gal?"

"Isn't she young for Galanos?"

"I don't think Gal cares."

"Fair point. I don't know. The girl was... I don't know. Impish."

"You're such a stick in the mud."

"Hm... I know what I'd like to stick in..."

She presses her lips to mine, stopping my foolish words. I wrap my hands around Fallon's slim waist. She hasn't started gaining much weight yet. But I can't wait to watch her body change as she grows our child. I pull her down onto the bed and she straddles me. Her fingers rake through my chocolate hair and she kisses my forehead.

"I hope she gets your eyes. They're breathtaking."

"Dark hair, blue eyes. It's the Greek playboy look."

"Well, you are *done* being a playboy."

"We can agree on that much at least."

She kisses me again, and my cock stiffens in my trousers. I can't stop my body from responding to hers. I have something *important* to talk to her about but I can smell her essence and I need to get my tongue between her thighs before I allow any other purpose to distract me. I roll Fallon on her back and lift her skirts, urgently pulling her underwear aside for the dripping succulent fruit between her thighs.

"Stavros..."

"I'm tasting you."

She moans as my tongue follows quickly after. I hold her legs open and my tongue easily slides between her lower lips. Fallon moans and allows my tongue to enter her. Once I've worked her up to a fever pitch, my lips and tongue rub around her clit until she explodes from pleasure. I love making her cum. I'll never stop enjoying the way she responds to me. The way her lips part in that round shape and her body tenses and unleashes in an explosion of passionate clawing and grabbing at me. Her fingers tighten around strands of my hair and I push my tongue deeper between her legs.

Once I'm satisfied that she has had enough orgasms to last at least the next hour, I wipe my mouth and reach into my pocket, opening the box.

"Fallon. Will you marry me?"

She shrieks and looks up at me between her legs.

"This is the *worst* view!"

"I'm on my knees. Did I get the wrong ring? I'll kill the bastard who sold it to me..."

Fallon leaps out of bed and then covers my mouth, sitting at the edge of the bed.

"Stavros. I don't want to answer a proposal with my whole pussy out. So I need you to do me a favor. Ask. Again."

"Fine. Fallon Iverson. Will you marry me?"

"This is what you want?"

"Will you answer the question, beloved?"

"Yes. I'll marry you. But… are you sure? This isn't a weird guilt thing, right?"

"Fallon. I love you."

"I love you, too."

"Then marry me, woman. And don't force me to change my mind. I'd marry you off to Loukas. You two are getting along so well."

She pushes me.

"Ew. Don't be gross, Stavros. Your brother needs *help*. He's sad about Matilda."

"He ought to be sad about that sociopathic daughter of his…"

"Like you have any room to talk?"

I lean over and kiss her, slipping the ring on her finger. Fallon's fingers curl around mine. I want to draw her back into bed. Now that my ring sits on her finger, I've claimed her properly. The thought of properly having her — not as a possession, but as my wife, pushes me over the edge. My dick strains through my pants, desperate to slide between Fallon's soaked thighs.

"No. I don't have any room to talk."

"You two have more in common than you think," she says.

It's like Fallon's trying to get under my skin.

"Maybe I'll leave behind diaries. A history of your crazy family."

"*Our* crazy family."

"Right. Our crazy family."

"My grandmother and father are gone. I'll be working more. Will you be okay here with the others while I'm sailing?"

"Promise me every time you leave you'll come back."

"I will."

"Then I'll be fine. Helen and I get along. I can work on Cass. Loukas could use help with his kids. And Gal... I'll keep bear mace in my purse."

"Bear mace. I'm pretty sure he called that the latest kink on his stupid app."

"Your brother needs a parent."

"Good luck with that. Loukas needs to hold him down and tan his hide properly. Maybe with Yiayia gone, he will."

Fallon scowls.

"Stavros. You will not tell Loukas to *beat* your younger brother."

"He deserves it."

"No beatings. Talk to him. Or send him to university."

"I shudder to think of the school that would accept Galanos Pagonis into its ranks."

"I've heard there are boarding colleges in England and Scotland for kids like him. Reform schools."

"He'd burn the school down on the first day. We know because we tried. Trust me, we tried everything with him."

"You might have given up on your family's humanity, but I haven't. If our daughter has to grow up here, I want everyone to at least pretend to be normal."

"Good luck."

I kiss her on the top of her head and then lay her down on the bed.

"Now. Spread your legs, beloved. I'm impatient for you..."

She moans as I slide inside her. The euphoria hits me instantly. Her tightness clamps around my cock and I moan as I drive into her deeper. I fuck her like I'm trying to knock her up again. She cums four times before I spill my seed between her legs. Fallon's legs caress my hips as I slide out of her and kiss her body until she nears another climax. My tongue drives her over the edge again and I kiss her on the lips. Hard.

"Pregnant. I want you pregnant. Always."

Fallon giggles.

"You're crazy."

"I'm just getting started, beloved."

I haven't heard the voices in weeks. I don't think they'll come back for a while. There's only one voice that speaks to me when I close my eyes. Fallon's. Not Fallon's. Our baby girl's. Maybe the baby will be a male. It doesn't matter. I hear that tiny voice when I close my eyes. A reminder that I'm not a monster at all. I'm completely, savagely, passionately human.

FIFTY-FOUR
DID YOU SLEEP WITH...?

6 WEEKS AFTER THE PROPOSAL

"I don't think you should send a drone with a bomb attached to it to your grandmother's yacht."

"You don't understand! When Nikola finds out where I am, he will kill me. He's threatened it several times before."

Fallon listens intently to my sister rambling about her ex, Nikola. Maybe he's a bad guy, maybe he isn't. People in my family have a problem with attracting danger. We are like moths drawn to flames. Our fiery passion in the bedroom only surpassed by our thirst for blood and vengeance.

"Kill him, Stavros. Find him and kill him before he gets here."

"What makes you think I can find him? I'm done killing."

"Nikola is a *psychopath*. He won't kill us. He'll rape us too."

Fallon puts her hand on Helen's forearm.

"Stavros. If the guy is going to rape everyone, I think maybe we should reconsider the killing situation."

"Great. Now my pregnant fiancée wants me to become a murderer."

"You only *become* a murderer when you haven't killed before," Fallon mutters under her breath like I'm not standing inches away from her.

"Nikola will die if he comes onto this property. Otherwise, I have no reason to kill him."

Loukas' voice blares inside from the patio. He sounds drunk.

"IS THAT COCAINE IN YOUR FUCKING SUITCASE?!"

"Why were you looking in my suitcase, dad? I hate you!"

Glass broke. Carlotta throwing another wine glass at her dad. Their relationship had only worsened since Matilda's death.

"I know you hate me because you killed my fucking girlfriend. Do you feel anything about that or can you only feel anything when you're the neighborhood cum dumpster."

"I AM YOUR DAUGHTER YOU FUCKING PIG."

She pushes him. Helen and Fallon rush onto the patio.

"Hey!" Fallon yells, "Can you two knock it off?"

"He's a chauvinist! I hate him! He only wants to keep me here so he can kill me like he killed my mom. I don't feel sorry I killed Matilda."

Carlotta pushes past all of us and storms off. Loukas stumbles and collapses onto one of the chairs. He holds up a tiny white bag. The offending cocaine.

"She's out of control."

"You kept her here for spring break so she could go to counseling. How did that go?"

"I caught her giving the fucking counselor a..." Loukas turns pale and massages his temples, "... with her mouth."

"That's enough!" Fallon shrills, taking Loukas' hand.

"Loukas. You need to send her away," Helen pronounces matter-of-factly, "She's loud. And if she keeps making trouble, Yiayia and Papa may decide to come out of retirement. We don't want that. Right now, they're posting awkward pictures and captions to Facebook that make it seem like they're dating. We don't want them to remember they want to kill us all."

"I'm not sending my daughter away."

"You sent away your other daughter, which was wise. Why can't you send away Carlotta?"

"She killed someone, Helen. It's my fault."

"Yes, and you can pay someone else to fix it."

I lean in the doorway.

"What does Carlotta want?" Fallon asks.

"Who cares?" Helen scoffs.

"She wants to bring her friend here for the summer. *And* she wants me to book her a trip to fucking Dubai so she can bring this over there. Cocaine. To Dubai. She's lost her mind."

"She's acting out. Why not let her friend come here for the summer? Tisha? She seemed like a wonderful influence."

Loukas grows paler, and he leans forward as if he's going to vomit.

"No. I'd rather have her smuggle cocaine to Dubai than have that girl in my house."

Fallon's nose wrinkles.

"Is it a race thing?"

"No. Maybe when I was younger, it would have been but... I've grown up. Tisha is not an excellent influence on Carlotta."

"She's so far off the rails Hitler would probably be an excellent influence..." Helen snipes.

"Helen. Lay off his parenting. We knew Loukas was too much of a man-whore to be a good parent. What did you do, fuck the friend?"

I punch him in the shoulder and Loukas chuckles. But he doesn't say that he didn't fuck the friend which worries me. Loukas? My forty-something year old brother sleeping with a teenager? He acted out plenty in our youth, but he'd never done the younger woman thing. Especially not with someone his daughter's age. I blame his silence on the stress.

"Carlotta is not a bad girl. I need to fix things with her. Get her to stop acting like a prostitute."

"You'll have to earn her trust back, Loukas."

"Trust? Fallon. I know my brother enjoys your beautiful face, but I hardly think trust and love are going to fix things with my daughter. Our problems with each other are old. Too old. And she's right to hate me. I am a horrible father."

I roll my eyes.

"Shut up, Loukas. Grab your daughter by the arm and show her you are the boss."

Fallon folds her arms and glares at me.

"If you think that'll work with our daughter, you have another thing coming."

"Wait, Fallon…"

She pinches my forearm.

"Ow!"

My cry of pain causes her to smirk.

"I'll talk to Carlotta. Stavros, talk some sense into your brother. That eighteen-year-old couldn't be *that* bad."

Fallon leaves the room and I don't leave any pretense to my questioning. Helen follows Fallon so I can speak to my brother alone. And alone, we can speak frankly.

"Loukas. I will not speak about men's business in front of my fiancée, but I'm your brother. We may loathe each other, but it's only because we know each other so well."

"Too well."

"I understand you don't want to hurt Carlotta. That you want to save her in a way you couldn't save any of the others."

"I'm cursed."

"That may be."

"Thanks. Great talk."

"Don't storm off yet. I need to know before you do… Did you sleep with your daughter's best friend?"

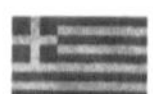

Read Book #2 Next

Purchased For Pregnancy
https://bit.ly/4pregnancy
This is a dark & spicy mafia age gap romance with a pregnancy plot.

Click here to sign up for updates about my future releases.
https://bit.ly/textjamila

ABOUT JAMILA JASPER

The hotter and darker the romance, the better.

That's the Jamila Jasper promise.

If you enjoy sizzling multicultural romance stories that dare to *go there* you'll enjoy any Jamila Jasper title you pick up.

Open-minded readers who appreciate **shamelessly sexy romance novels** featuring black women of all shapes and sizes paired with smokin' hot white men are welcome.

Sign up for her e-mail list here to receive one of these FREE hot stories, exclusive offers and an update of Jamila's publication schedule:
bit.ly/jamilajasperromance

Get text message updates on new books:
https://slkt.io/gxzM

EXTREMELY IMPORTANT LINKS

ALL BOOKS BY JAMILA JASPER
https://linktr.ee/JamilaJasper
SIGN UP FOR EMAIL UPDATES
Bit.ly/jamilajasperromance
SOCIAL MEDIA LINKS
https://www.jamilajasperromance.com/
GET MERCH
https://www.redbubble.com/people/jamilajasper/shop
GET FREEBIE (VIA TEXT)
https://slkt.io/qMk8
READ SERIAL (NEW CHAPTERS WEEKLY)
www.patreon.com/jamilajasper

JAMILA JASPER

Diverse Romance For Black Women

MORE JAMILA JASPER ROMANCE

<u>Pick your poison...</u>

Delicious interracial romance novels for all tastes. Long novels, short stories, audiobooks and more.

Hit the link to experience my full catalog.

FULL CATALOG BY JAMILA JASPER:

https://linktr.ee/JamilaJasper

DARK MAFIA ROMANCE PREVIEW #1

Sample these chapters from my best-selling Amalfi Coast Brotherhood Italian mafia romance series while you wait for my upcoming romance series.

If you enjoy dark & twisted mafia romance stories, you can binge the entire completed series on your eReader.

Enjoy the free chapters.

Click here to sign up for text messages about my new release: bit.ly/textjamila

A BWWM DARK MAFIA ROMANCE

FORCED TO
Surrogate

JAMILA JASPER

DESCRIPTION

The last thing Jodi remembered was a shot of tequila.
Next thing she knows,
Italian sociopath Van Doukas has her chained in his basement...
And he's claiming she agreed to become the mother of his child.

There's a detailed contract and everything... with her signature.
Jodi will do whatever it takes to get away from him...
But she doesn't count on the 6'7" Italian Stallion being skilled with
his tongue and excellent in bed.

SERIES TITLES

Forced To Surrogate
Forced To Marry
Forced To Submit

CONTENT AWARENESS

dark bwwm mafia romance

This is a mafia romance story with dark themes including potentially triggering content, frank discussions and language surrounding bedroom scenes and race. All characters in this story are 18+. Sensitive readers, be cautioned about some of the material in this dark but extremely hot romance novel. The character in this story is ***forced by circumstance*** into her situation.

Enjoy the steamy romance story...

ONE
PRODUCE A PURE ITALIAN HEIR

VAN DOUKAS

There aren't enough cigarettes in the world for meetings with my father. The boss. Tonight, I meet with him to discuss something 'very important'. He calls everything 'very important', but tonight, I know exactly what he wants from me.

He wants me to kill again, this time for my foolish sister, who can't seem to keep herself out of trouble. Everyone in the family heard about what happened to Ana by now. That idiot Jew was foolish enough to put his hands on her with witnesses and expect nothing to happen? That's not how the Doukas family works, which he'll soon learn.

You mess with the Doukas family, we retaliate. If the Jew had any wits about him, he would disappear from the Amalfi Coast and head for the mountains or Sicily, or somewhere we don't have ears. He could go to Albania like Matteo. Maybe then we wouldn't find him. But fuck, I don't want to carry out another hit. Why can't that lazy fuck Enzo do it? Or better yet, Eddie. I carried out my first hit when I was two years younger than him. We spoil the new generation and wonder why our family falls apart.

None of this would be my responsibility if Matteo would get over himself and come down off his fucking mountain.

I stop my motorcycle and approach my father's front door. The all white old European style mansion sits on an excessive and opulent lot on the coast, right above the cliffs with a long path to the beach, a 'fuck you' to the tax collectors and the government who want to stop us from doing business.

Most of my siblings still live here, but I prefer keeping myself far away from papa and his... associates.

I can hear the party from the entrance. Seriously? On a fucking Tuesday afternoon? I assumed he called this meeting because he was working for once. He's intertwined in a different business based on the noise filtering outside. Please, Lord, let me not walk in on my father having sex with a model... *again.*

I open the front door to our old family home without knocking and immediately regret it when a completely naked foreign woman runs giggling toward the door, too high and drunk to feel self-conscious, exposing her completely nude body to a stranger. At least I didn't find her twisted in bed with papa, although this isn't much better.

"Oh! Good afternoon, sir!" she teases me in crude Italian, spinning around to show off her assets. *Whore. Foreigner. Her tricks possess little interest to me.* My brothers Lorenzo and Matteo would sway more easily.

"Where's my father?"

She giggles and spins around again. Fucking hell, I wish the ground would swallow me up. My father's prostitutes do not interest me.

"Your papa?" she says, standing to face me with her legs slightly apart, daring me to ogle more of her body. I have no interest in whores and I want her to answer my fucking question.

Before I can answer, another one of my father's toys saunters into the foyer, naked. This one is young—she looks eighteen just about—far too young for my father. I grimace and keep my gaze firmly fixed away from the nude females. Just because the men in my family are bastards doesn't mean I have to follow suit.

If we don't conduct ourselves with respect, how can we expect the respect of the Amalfi Coast?

"Yes. My father. Sal," I grunt, failing to hide the irritation in my voice.

The woman ignores my irritated tone with her response.

"Oh, he's in the back with Boyka. I can take you there after we take you to bed upstairs."

How much is he paying these women? We're still struggling to get Jalousie off the ground and he spends all his money on Slavic hookers.

"Not interested. I have a meeting with him."

"Are you sure?"

I don't dignify them with a response. I walk past the girls, keeping my eyes away from their bodies. Where the hell is my father? I pass the long hallway with the family portraits and follow the loud music and the louder giggling from near the pool. The familiar sound of pool jets betrays papa's location.

He's in the fucking hot tub again, I know it. He spends all fucking day in the hot tub, dishing out orders and expecting work to happen without him lifting a fucking finger. It's a fucking miracle anything gets done around here.

My father chuckles loudly, and I brace myself before approaching him. He's the boss and you don't question the boss, even if he's your father and even if he cares more about partying and women than our family — than our future.

When I enter the back patio, the pungent smell of tobacco and marijuana surrounds me. Judging by the bottles of vodka on the ground, the piles of cigarette butts and the other piles of detritus, they've been at this fucking party since last night.

Fuck. I put the cigarette tucked behind my ear into my mouth and approach my father's outdoor speakers, unplugging them and stopping the little dance party happening around his hot tub. Three women, each wearing next to nothing with their tits out belly dance for him while he chuckles loudly, his fat stomach causing waves in the hot tub. When the music stops, they stop too and look up at me indignantly.

They don't have to ask who I am. The ones who don't know Van Doukas can tell that I'm related to Sal. I have my father's eyes, but thankfully, I don't have his overweight body or his bald head. The girls make booing sounds at me, but I brush them off.

"I'm here for our meeting," I say sternly to papa.

He chuckles and nods. "Yes. The meeting. I almost forgot."

Almost? He doesn't look like he's fucking prepared for a meeting.

Papa dismisses the girls, except for one — Boyka. She slides into the hot tub next to him, twirling his thick plumes of chest hair around her fingers and sliding his freshly cut cigar between his lips. Nauseating. Papa coughs after a puff and taps the cigar over the edge of the hot tub.

"You're early."

"I'm twenty minutes late."

"Oh?"

"Papa, you said it was important. Shouldn't we conduct this business alone?"

None of the girls are dumb enough to rat on Salvatore Doukas, but unlike my father, I don't see the sense in taking risks.

Boyka's hand moves down my father's chest and I don't want to imagine what sorry shriveled part of him she touches next. I just want my orders so I can get the fuck out of this bachelor pad.

"I'm getting old, Van," he says. "I'm getting old."

He didn't call me down here to bitch about his old age. I furiously puff on my cigarette, waiting for him to get to the fucking point. Papa grunts as Boyka touches something... sensitive. Cristo...

Watching my father grunt through a hand job might be the only thing worse than watching him stick it to a woman.

"Do you mind postponing your fucking hand job until later?"

Boyka's hand rises guiltily from the water and I choke down bile.

She really was touching the old fuck. I shouldn't swear at him or set him off. Papa might seem old, but he can have me killed. Any of my brothers would do it if he gave the command. Tread carefully, Van.

"Maybe I should leave," Boyka says, giving me a flirty glance as she plays with her tiny pink nipples.

"Yes," I snap. "Please get the fuck out of here."

Papa scowls. "Be respectful, Van. Boyka is a very dear—"

"I said please."

Papa smirks. "Boyka, return in thirty minutes. If we're not done…"

"We'll be done," I interrupt, glowering at my father. I don't have all afternoon for his games when I have the club to attend to.

Boyka reluctantly leaves.

"Are the women in this house allergic to fucking clothes?"

"None of them are allergic to fucking anything."

I'm not doing this with the old man today.

"Why did you call me here?"

I start another cigarette. I keep swearing I won't touch another, then I spend five minutes around papa and change my mind.

He leans back in the hot tub, displacing several pints of water over the edge.

"I'm tired, Van," he groans, leaning back and rubbing his forehead.

"From working?"

My father doesn't pick up on the sarcasm. He hardly leaves his fucking hot tub anymore, and he hasn't done anything even remotely resembling working at either of the nightclubs, restaurants, apartment complexes or construction sites around town.

If it wasn't for me and Enzo, he wouldn't have the fucking time to boink Boyka or whatever the fuck he does with all these young Slavic women.

I still have to tread carefully around him. He's still my father, my boss, and I must obey him.

"Yes," he says, coughing. "From working. I need someone to take my place and lead the family soon. I want to retire, Van. You and I both know I need a break."

He spends every fucking day on vacation while his sons and nephews run his businesses. Vacation? We're the ones who need a fucking vacation.

"Perhaps you should contact Matteo about that."

My older brother spent his entire life preparing to be the boss. It's not my fault he fucked off, leaving his worthless children with us, I might add. I'm already halfway through my fucking cigarette and he hasn't closed in on the point.

Papa scoffs. "Matteo hasn't left Albania in four years. He left his children, his business, his fucking money, and he's not coming back. Give up on him."

"You're the one who trained him for the role. Send Enzo after him. Better yet, send his fucking son."

I don't want to go into the mountains to bring my jackass older brother back and I don't want to have this conversation with my father.

"Why don't you go to Albania?"

"Every time I'm in the same room as Matteo, he tries to kill me," I remind papa. I love Matteo, but he isn't exactly easy to get along with.

I'm surprised a woman tolerated him long enough to allow him to give her Eddie.

"Fair. But I need a replacement, Van. I don't want to be the boss anymore. I can't take the stress much longer."

Stress? What stress? Does my father seriously think sitting in his fucking hot tub banging whores counts as a job?

"Have you considered the role?" He asks before I can spew something disrespectful in my father's direction.

"Why would I want to be the boss of this fucking family? It's filled with degenerates, fuck-ups, people who need more violence to be kept in line. I kill enough as it is. You don't want me to be the boss and nobody in this fucking family wants me as the boss."

"People respect you, Van."

"People fear me. There's a difference."

Papa nods. "Exactly. Personally, I think you would make a good boss."

"I disagree."

But I don't completely. Yes, the job would be horrific and I'd have even more blood on my hands than I do now by the end. I could bring honor back to our family, clean the streets of our scum, stop the Jews from fucking with our shit... but I can't. Not with Matteo gone. Even in the fucking Albanian countryside, he would find out what I did and Matteo would kill me.

"No," Papa replies calmly. "You don't. But I agree with your assessment that you're not quite ready."

"I never said that. I said I didn't want the job."

Nobody smart wants my father's job. He spent twenty years walking around with a target on his back before he built up enough trust, enough loyalty, enough captains in the streets of Italy to ensure his safety. I don't want to lose my freedom.

"You didn't have to say anything. I know my son."

"Hm."

Arguing with my father is entirely senseless.

"You need an heir, Van."

"What?"

"I will give you the leadership of this family without the ritual, without the sacrifice and without the financial investment required. All I want is an heir."

"Why don't I go up to fucking Albania, then? Because I can't produce a child out of thin air."

Papa chuckles. "Don't you have women? If you want a woman... I filled this house with them. I have very young ones too. Eighteen. Nineteen. They make good mothers."

"I am not interested in fucking teenagers."

"Then find a whore like that old Greek Pagonis fuck. I don't care how you get the heir. You can prove how serious you are by giving me a child. I'll be generous. I'll give you a year."

"I don't want this role," I snap. "So the likelihood I'll produce an heir is slim."

Papa laughs, which only infuriates me further. There's nothing funny about bringing a child into the world.

"You can't lie to me, Van. You were always the most ambitious child. Maybe it's because you were smack in the middle and we didn't pay any attention to you. Who fucking knows?"

My father spent little time raising any of us, except for Enzo, and look how that fucking turned out.

"Thank you for the psychoanalysis."

Every time I visit my father, my desire for alcohol increases exponentially, along with my cravings for nicotine. He brings the worst out of everyone, especially me.

"No problem," he says, again ignoring my sarcasm.

"What happens if I don't produce an heir? Eh? You still need someone to take your place."

"I make this offer to Lorenzo if you don't produce what I want."

"What?" I would have at least expected him to mention one of our cousins, one of the very obedient captains from the northern coast, or even fucking Eddie, Matteo's 18-year-old son, would be better than my irresponsible fuck of a brother. That old fuck really knows me well because he just said the only thing that could get me to reconsider his stupid fucking offer.

"You heard me."

"Lorenzo would ruin this family. For fun."

"I know. And it would become your responsibility to save it. You would have to act as the boss to save Lorenzo from himself. You might as well earn the position."

Fuck this old man...

"I don't want a family life, papa. I don't want the fucking wife or the fucking family. I want this life. It's what I'm good at. Business. Killing. More killing. That's who you taught me to be."

I'm not a man who can picture himself kicking around a football with my children or taking them to the beach. I'm not built for seducing women for more than a night and dealing with the danger of introducing them to my life or worse, hiding it the way papa did with our mother.

He can pretend it's not his fault what happened to her, but we all know the truth. No woman deserves our life. I can't afford to react. He loves when he can draw a reaction out of me.

Papa continues, as if my reaction is irrelevant. "Part of this life means having a family. I can't expect my other children to carry on my bloodline."

"Matteo has a son. You have a fucking bloodline. Why don't you make him the fucking boss?"

"Eddie? Eddie will not survive long the way he lives."

"That's a way to talk about your grandson, eh?"

"Have another cigarette, Van."

I'm already on my fucking third. But I'm not in a position to turn down his offer, considering the shit he wants me to deal with right now. An heir? I thought he wanted me to kill someone. Producing an heir in a year... It's just fucking impossible. I stick the cigarette in my mouth and light it.

"You can't let the family fall apart. We aren't the only people who would suffer. What would happen to our people, good Italian people, when the only people around they can get money from are the fucking Jews, who hate our guts?" He says.

I can't let his guilt trip work on me.

"I want an heir."

"Hm."

"Consider what you would sacrifice by turning down my offer, Van. It's not just about the family. It's power. You act like you're a fucking saint, but you are my son. You enjoy power. You're just too much of a stuck up cunt to let yourself enjoy it."

"Thanks papa."

"You're welcome. Now, onto the matter of the Jew."

Fuck. I hoped my father would only piss me off one way today, but if we're discussing the matter of the Jew, I won't leave here tonight without an assignment. Someone else could easily do this job, but he wants me to kill. Because I'm good at it.

"I suppose none of my other brothers have the free time to do this?"

"I don't care. I need you to do it. The cunt offended this family."

"Perhaps we waste too much time retaliating for every offense. Ana told you to drop it."

I'm taking a risk just questioning his order, but he's pissed me off so much that I stopped caring.

"Decision making isn't women's work. It's our work. The man signed his own death warrant. I want it done soon. Call me when you finish the job."

"Hm."

"If you don't like the way I run this family, Van, you know what to do. I want to retire. Make an old man happy."

Drugs and whores are the only things that make my father happy.

"An heir," I scoff. "You want me to have a fucking bastard child to continue your bloodline? A bastard won't have any loyalty to his family. Children have a mother and a father, a mother they spend all their time with. If I fuck some poor woman, you won't have an heir. You'll have a problem on your hands."

"Then get creative. If you need to get the baby and kill the mother, do what you must."

What's happening to this family? When did we lose our way and talking about murdering women for our own ends? Papa... This life changed him. It was slow, but it changed him completely. Too bad there's no getting out.

"Thank you for the advice."

"You're welcome. Now get Boyka back in here and get the fuck out. I need relief."

"Good evening, papa."

I drop my cigarette on the ground without bothering to step on it. Maybe my father's right — it's time for him to retire. But how the fuck will I get an heir? I need help.

There's one person I can call on for assistance in these matters. I don't like involving the Greeks in Italian business, but... they're our cousins. She answers after a few rings and it sounds like she's at a nightclub. She has an inordinate amount of time for parties...

"Ciao?"

I can barely hear her over the sound of the music.

"Miss Pagonis. It's Van."

She giggles. "Duh. What's happening? You finally have work for me?"

"How soon can you come back to Italy?"

Click here to learn more about where to buy the book:

https://www.jamilajasperromance.com/blog/forced-to-surrogate

MAFIA PLAYMATE
PREVIEW #2

https://bit.ly/bostonirishmafia1

BOSTON IRISH MAFIA ROMANCE SERIES

Mafia Playmate

Mafia Property

Mafia Surrogate

Mafia Possession

Mafia Stalker

Click here for the complete collection:

www.jamilajasperromance.com/catalog

CONTENT AWARENESS

Read this passage if you require content warnings for sensitive material. I do not give detailed content warnings that will spoil the plot, but be aware of this note.

This is a mafia romance story with dark themes including potentially triggering content of **all** varieties, violence, frank discussions and language surrounding bedroom scenes and race.
All characters in this story are 18+
Sensitive readers, be cautioned about some of the detailed romantic material in this dark but *extremely hot romance novel.*

DESCRIPTION

A large pink box arrives on Aiden's doorstep with a woman inside.
His mail-order bride arrives in her birthday suit and tied up in knots
with a pretty pink silk ribbon.

Aiden never requested a dark-skinned beauty...
His family would never approve of such an impure connection.

Who is this woman? What does she want?
A note in the box reveals the truth...
**The woman in the box - *Valentina* - is a gift from an anonymous
sender who wants something dark and twisted in return.**

CHAPTER
ONE
AIDEN

You have one job in the Murray family. You grow up, you get your marks, you listen to Pa, you marry a nice Irish girl, preferably a blond or a redhead with lighter features.
You do what Padraig Murray asks.
You pray everyday and you keep your rosary wrapped in your pocket. You stay loyal. You keep our bloodline strong.

Pa demands a meeting with me now that I'm back in the city. He claims it's important, but it can't be that important if he wants to meet me during the Red Sox game. It feels good to be home. There's something special about Boston, but maybe that's just it – paradise is wherever our family is.

After Pa, I'll go home and see Roscoe, my Rottweiler. Then get my shit together and call my younger brother Darragh to check in on his training and find out if Rian's around. Over the weekend, I'll head to Leominster to visit Callum and then Sunday after church, stop by to see Ma and Odhran. I brought a gift home with me for Tegan, Rian's daughter, and I can't wait to see my niece's face light up when I give it to her.

If there's one thing I don't miss about being home, it's a never ending list of shit to do.

I meet my father at our usual casual meeting spot, Mulligan's, a place where we aren't afraid to celebrate Irish pride. A place where you can catch the Red Sox game and no one can catch your conversation. *It's as much home as anywhere else.*

I spot my father hunched over the bar from the street, his face illuminated by a warm orange bulb as he watches the pre-game announcer talk. I prefer football to baseball, but Pa bets on all their games, so he likes to keep his eye on the Red Sox each season.

When Pa calls, you answer, and he's desperate to know about the affair with the Italians – what the fuck happened, have I found the renegade cousins who pissed off the Italians, and whether I've killed them yet. *I haven't.*

It's all bad news and my ass is on the line if I don't find a way to sort out all the shit that happened in Long Island. At least we're guaranteed peace with the vicious Italians. *Those greaseballs aren't any better than the blacks. 'Trust 'em as far as you can throw them', Pa told me. But for now, we have peace and that's what matters. At least to me.*

I enter Mulligan's and the conversations fall to a hush. *Aiden Murray's back.* I clear my throat and the conversations continue. But there are more phones pulled out than before and two guys sitting in the back leave. I don't hate the reputation I have. Most of the bar fights I earned this cutthroat reputation in were Darragh's fault, but that doesn't change what people say about me.

Darragh, my younger brother, can still throw his weight around in the ring, but he got his practice here, in this fucking place. Our last fight here was over a girl. Darragh kicked some Puerto Rican's ass and a few of our boys jumped him outside... I don't know what happened to the guy after.

My father slides a twenty-dollar bill across the bar to the

bartender, Finnegan O'Malley, a one-eared ex-hitman, who in turn fills up two glass pints of amber Sam Adams. Pa's already several drinks ahead of me. *Great. The news can't be that bad then.*

I pull out a bar stool next to my father, who barely acknowledges me, although he must've caught me entering the bar through the reflection on the glass behind the bartender. He shoves one of the pints across the bar towards me. He knows I prefer Guinness, but I don't mind starting with this. I can see my dad's reflection in the glass. He looks older than I remember. He's pushing 70, so I shouldn't be surprised by the large streaks of gray through his slick hair which was once blond, but changed color throughout his life, settling on a dark chocolate brown, like Rian's.

I glance at the television to check the score, but the game hasn't even started yet. I can smell the alcohol coming off of him already.

"You can have a Guinness after you drink this," he says. "I heard you did good work with the Italians."

He sounds raspy, but calm. My tension dissipates. This is just a normal, father-son meeting. Nothing to worry about.

"I didn't find Eoin or Robert. Haven't heard fuck since they all screwed with Vicari," I say as I take a sip of my beer.

"Maybe the Italians killed them," he says. "They're a violent, vicious group of people."

"Yeah."

Like we're ones to talk. Pa's done with his Sam Adams already and waits patiently for me to catch up, as if I could catch up to a man who's been drinking for an hour. At forty, it's not so easy for me to keep up with long nights of drinking. I don't know how he does it.

He waits for me to have a few more sips, his eyes glued to the television. Chris Sale throws the first pitch. It doesn't go so well. My father glances down at his glass and sighs. "It's going to be a long night."

"That bad this season?" I grunt, glancing up at the Detroit batter sliding into second.

I've been too busy to keep up with baseball. My father grunts. Yeah, it has been that bad.

"Any other news?" I ask him, finishing off the Sam Adams. Dad grunts and snaps his fingers for the bartender, Finnegan. The buff, tattooed bartender hustles over as dad orders two Guinnesses without opening his mouth. Bad news if he's drinking Guinness.

"Cops got Rian last week. They're charging him with manslaughter."

Manslaughter?

"What did he do?"

"What the fuck do you think he did?" Dad responds calmly. "He killed somebody, they caught him. That boy's not careful enough and I have to pay to get his ass out of trouble. Maybe some prison time would do him good."

"That's what you said the first three times," I grunt. Sale throws a good pitch and my father's face visibly brightens.

"If it weren't for Tegan, I'd let him spend a few extra years behind bars," Dad confesses. "Your mother won't let me do that to his daughter."

"What's going to happen to her?"

"I don't know," my father says. "No one has seen the kid in a week."

"What?" I growl, sipping at my beer and hoping this is my father's idea of a joke since he sounds dangerously unconcerned.

"What do you mean no one's seen her? Is she with her ma?"

My father shrugs.

Rian's notoriously bad taste in women landed him with a child he should have never brought into the world. She's a sweet girl, but doomed by a mobster father and a whore mother.

Her ma doesn't live in Boston anymore. She wants nothing to do with Rian.

"Where does he say she is?"

"Last time he saw her was the night he got arrested," Pa says before taking a sip of his beer.

"What about the cops? Did they give her to his lawyer or something?"

I don't have a single paternal instinct in my body, but my mind courses with worry over Tegan, despite my father's calmness.

"She'll turn up," he says, pouring more alcohol down his throat.

Fuck, Rian. My brother must be an even worse parent than our father. His daughter's missing and he's behind bars and there's no one else to look for her except...

"I can find out where she is. Once I get Roscoe and take care of–

"It would serve him right if something happened to her," my father says coldly. "Her mother isn't Irish. He keeps fucking up. I'm tired of cleaning up his messes. Now *drink*. This is not why I asked you here."

I bristle at his comment, but it's just Padraig Murray. This is who he's always been and my brother should have had the good sense to keep his dick in his pants. I made it to forty without fathering bastards all over Boston. Rian should have been more careful. I drink a few more sips, but I can't let this go. *Who else will worry about the fucking kid if not me?*

"How the hell did Rian let this happen? Can I talk to him?"

"Best that none of us talk to him. The cops listen to everything. I can get messages into the prison and messages out, but I don't want you talking to him."

"Fine," I grunt, finishing off my first round of Guinness and ordering us another. I try to pay, but my father stops me and then finally answers my other question.

"Your idiot brother trusted a woman," he says. "He wants a mother for that little girl so badly, that he's willing to do anything. He's willing to kill for a woman who doesn't deserve him."

"I didn't know he had a woman," I grumble.

"*Had* is correct," Pa says. "She's dead."

I wish I could tell you a chill ran through me, or I had some other human response to my father's announcement. I don't need a university degree to understand what he's implying. Rian had a woman, she got him locked up, so my father had her killed.

"Will that affect his case?"

"No," Pa says. "It was very clean."

"Who?"

"None of your business, Aiden. You worry about your shit, I'll worry about your brother."

I want to feel sorry for Rian, but he deserves it for crossing our father. This is what happens when he pisses off Padraig Murray. More problems for all of us.

"How much time is he facing?"

"Three years since he's been in jail before. I tried to get that stupid motherfucker to get his life together, but your brother just wants to be a fuck up."

"Who's the lawyer?"

"Someone from Nigel & Bancroft."

At least he isn't cheaping out like he did for Rian's first case. I don't want to push my father's buttons, and despite his outward calm, he must be furious at Rian for drawing more attention to us, but Rian has his uses.

"It's Rian," I remind him. "Crazy fucking Rian. We need him out soon. There are some jobs only Rian has the balls to handle."

Padraig snorts. "He takes after my father. Too proud and too violent for his own good."

We created the monster Rian Murray is. He's our responsibility.

"He needs another woman."

"He needs a woman who isn't a fucking spic," my father spits. "At least the child looks white."

"What about this previous woman? What'd she look like?"

"It doesn't matter," he grunts. "She's dead. Now drink. We have more important things to talk about than your idiot brother and his shitty taste in women."

I drink because Pa commands it. I do everything he commands

and have since I was a child. I have the burns and scars to remind me of what happens when you disobey my father. At first, I hated him for what he did to me, but to keep an organization like ours together, you need to inspire fear.

You have to be cruel to survive – that's just how the world works. I can't let Tegan go. The second I see Darragh, I'll ask about her and track her down.

I drink so I don't lose my temper. He doesn't give a fuck about Tegan. No one does. Maybe he's wrong and one of my sisters took her in. But who would do that? Evie's saddled with her drunkard husband and two unruly kids of her own – Katie and Patrick. Kiara's off at university and Maeve's sixteen, too young to have any involvement.

"I need to tell you something important," my father says somberly, as if there could be something more important than my missing niece right now. I'm burning with desire to leave, but if I get up without my father's dismissal, he'll hurt me. Or someone I care about. Not like there are many of those people yet. It's foolish to get close to people in this life.

"Then tell me."

If he notices my tightening tone, my father doesn't acknowledge it.

"There's a plot against my life. I don't know who. I don't know why but... there's someone out there trying to kill me," my father says, the faded tattoos on his knuckles even more wrinkled than I last remember. He's getting older, but aside from his physical appearance, he shows no signs of slowing down. If anything, he's desperate to prove himself more. If he wasn't ordering more killings than necessary, maybe Rian wouldn't be locked up.

I don't want to dismiss his concerns as paranoid, but he's the leader of our family. There's always a plot against his life. It comes with the territory. My father doesn't have to worry because he has us. *Family.*

"Fuck that," I grunt. "No one would be stupid enough to try to kill you. April 2013, four days after the bombing. An entire decade ago. That's the last time anyone tried."

I was thirty back then, old enough to be the one who ended that war before it started. Back then, we only killed when necessary. I got five tattoos that year, one for each kill. Each a painful release, each representing a necessary act to keep my family safe.

My father smirks and keeps drinking. He shrugs. "That's what I thought. But I'm serious. This time is different. This time the bastards might just get me. I'm getting old, Aiden. Most guys in our line of work don't make it this far."

"What happened?" I grunt, urging my increasingly drunken father to get to the point. His cheeks blaze tomato red with alcohol and his blue eyes swim with tears, again brought on by drinking rather than any emotion. He grunts and knocks his biggest gold ring against the bar's surface contemplatively.

If anyone tried to kill him, surely Darragh would have mentioned it. He's responsible for keeping our father alive.

"I feel it in my bones," Pa replies. "Someone wants to destroy our family."

"Yes," I grumble. "Our cousins. But they're gone and if they were anywhere near this city, we would have heard about it."

"I don't know. Something big is coming for us. I feel it."

"We can make decisions based on feelings now?"

"Cut the shit, kid. You know my instincts are good because you're like me. You can smell shit before it hits the toilet bowl."

"I'm home. If anyone tries to kill you, they'll have to get through me, Darragh, and Callum."

My father smirks. "My boys. I'm proud of all of you. Except Rian. He's a piece of shit."

Ah, Padraig. Honest as fuck, especially when he's drunk.

He might not be proud of Rian, but he still loves my brother enough to spring for decent lawyers and to make sure Tegan goes to the best day school in Boston. Once she's old enough, she'll go to Milton or Dana Hall, or another nice private school where she can meet someone to untarnish her sullied blood, that is as long as I can find her. If Rian's behind bars, she could be anywhere. Hopefully not with her mom's people.

She belongs with us, even if Rian made mistakes. She looks like us and that's good enough to cover up his shameful behavior. I don't know what Rian was thinking with that Puerto Rican chick. Tegan's mother was low class.

Let's hope my brother's behavior doesn't come back to haunt all of us. Let's hope his daughter is safe, sound asleep somewhere and protected.

"Thanks, Pa," I mutter, uncomfortable with even this much emotional closeness between us. I love my father, but trusting him too much is dangerous. Rian found out the hard way that it isn't worth it to defy our family beliefs, and it definitely isn't fucking worth it to screw around with the wrong women.

"And Aiden? I need you to hurry the fuck up and find a wife. I'm getting old and I want to retire, but I need a family man to lead this family. You're the oldest. Why the fuck can't you keep a woman? Do I have to send you back to Galway?"

He wants a real answer.

"Not interested in chasing after girls, dad. All they want to do is take your money and ask where the fuck you're going. I've had enough."

"That old dog won't take care of you when you get old."

"Neither will some Boston snob who could take my ass to the cleaners in a divorce."

He laughs, which is the best reaction I can hope for. He quickly moves along to talking about the game and his plans for the business, and then asks me questions about Long Island. They're a mess out there, but doing better under John Vicari's leadership. We're developing a few buildings together and are prepared to make a lot of money in the real estate game. John does cleaner business than his father. Too bad the old man died of a heart attack... that's the word anyway.

"I need you to find a nice girl," my father reminds me once he's almost blackout drunk. He can barely keep his head up. *Great.* I'm not dragging his ass outta here tonight. If he wants to get so wasted he can't sit up straight, I'll leave him for Finnegan.

"We have this conversation every time we talk."

"This time, I'm serious. I want to retire. I don't want you bringing home no spics either like the Duffy boys."

"Fuck's sake, Pa. You can't talk like that around here anymore."

"I can say whatever the fuck I want. I want Irish children. Irish fucking children and I need you to have a wife so I can retire."

"Retire any old fucking day you want," I growl. "It'll be good for you to stop worrying about who I fuck or marry or the fate of the fucking family."

"The fate of the family matters," he says, taking another sip of his newest glass of beer before rubbing condensation off the sides with his napkin.

"I'm too old to have kids," I growl. "I'm too old to get tied down. You and mom were lucky you even found each other."

That's bullshit and we both know it. They stay together because they're Catholic, because back in the eighties, my dad killed someone for her father and won my mother like a prize. He also put a baby in her quickly and then kept her pregnant. There's nothing romantic about their love story or marriage in the Murray family.

"If you can't find a girl, I'll find one."

"The last girl you found me was a crazy fucking redhead who wanted to bring Roscoe Jr. into the bedroom. No thanks."

My father shrugs. "She was white. Do you know how hard it is to find a white girl around here who hasn't been fucking ruined by some fucking Puerto Rican or black guy?"

"What do you want from me, Pa?"

I know what I want. I want an end to this conversation, and I want my father to give me a fucking break about women and dating. All the Irish and Catholic women in Boston know to stay away from us, and the ones who don't learn their lesson pretty fucking quickly.

"Find a nice white girl with big tits and blond hair and get her pregnant so I know you're fucking serious about family. That's what I want."

"Give me time."

He continues, getting to what I suspect was the original point he wanted to make before the liquor got to him. "And get your ass to the site in Back Bay tomorrow bright and early."

"Why?"

This is the first I'm hearing about something wrong at the Back Bay construction site. I know something's wrong because my father doesn't do anything bright and early unless there's a problem to solve.

"You'll find out tomorrow. You just got back. Go home. Pet the dog. Your mom's tired of walking that big fuck. He nearly knocked her over near Harvard Square."

"How is mom?"

"Pissed off."

"Why?"

"Eh. Upset about another woman. It's nothing."

It's nothing. Dad just got his second mistress pregnant and even if we all know about it, we're all supposed to pretend it's no big deal that our elderly father knocked up a Irish teenager who he supposedly hired to clean the construction company office.

I hate how he treats our mother. What's the point of having a family or a woman if you hurt her? There's no getting through to him, but I have to try for my mother's sake.

"You treat her better, pa. Seriously. She needs you."

He grunts. "Get your ass home kid and get a white girl pregnant."

"Thanks, dad."

"If you can't find one, I'll find a good Irish girl who needs a green card and bring her over to you!"

My father is the last person I want picking my romantic partners. I mutter something to him about cutting back on liquor, then I pat my father on the back and leave the bar. This is the closest we've felt in years, but there's still a wall between us and there always will be. I felt closer to him when I was younger, when it was easier for me to justify the life I led. I know I'm a screw up, I know I don't belong anywhere near a woman or a family or any of the fucking things my father wants from me.

He knows it's wrong to bring a kid into this life, but he did it anyway. He knows that we're villains, but he doesn't care. Fuck, I don't care either, I suppose. I'd just rather not ruin a perfectly good woman.

I drive out of the city listening to rock classics on the radio. Just as I turn down my street – I live at the end of a cul-de-sac – I notice the large box on my front step. There are only five large houses at the end of this cul-de-sac, all of us with wide open well-maintained lawns around traditional New England colonial houses.

The box on my front step is fucking enormous – and I don't remember ordering anything for delivery. My hand moves swiftly to the pistol under my seat. I feel no fear as I reach for the gun and slip a mag out of my pocket. I feel ready.

Leaving the city for any amount of time always carries a risk, especially since I didn't exactly leave the place with a house sitter. The last time my teen brother Odhran house-sat, he trashed the place and had a threesome in my bed. I hop out of my black GMC Sierra with the gun under my coat and approach the box slowly, glancing furtively over my shoulder for anyone who might have eyes on me.

The box has holes in it. It's large. Pink. Wrapped in a bow. I reach for the bottom of the box and try to lift it. *Fuck.* It's heavy. I drop the box and I swear I hear a sound coming from inside it. *Is that possible?* I try to peek through the holes but it's too fucking dark and something's telling me opening this box will be a shitshow. It has to weigh about a hundred pounds. Maybe more. I'm no weakling, but it still takes a measure of back strength to lift a box that fucking heavy.

I open my front door and greet Roscoe Jr., my rottweiler, as he bounds towards the door to greet me. His coat looks shiny, the nub of his docked tail wags back and forth. Pa's choice, not mine. He runs up to the box and sniffs at it a bit.

There's definitely something in there and it gets his attention because Roscoe utters a low bark.

"Roscoe, go lie down."

Once he heads off to his bed, I throw my doors open wider and eye the giant box to decide how to carry the fuckin' thing. I would call Rian if his stupid ass wasn't in jail. I could call Callum, but he's still hung up on some fucking girl and won't answer my calls because I won't sugarcoat my opinion of him. Then there's Darragh... He's probably twice as drunk as Padraig. Not a good option either.

I'll have to carry the box myself. I stretch a little and then grab the edges of the box and grunt as I carry it a few feet inside my doorway. I set the box down more gently. *Is there something alive in there?* If it were an animal, I suspect Roscoe would be barking from his spot in the house, but he's laying down as I commanded, gazing at me curiously and wagging his tail.

He's probably wondering why I'm not taking him for a walk since I'm back. *At least he didn't bite the sitter this time.* I close my front doors and then search for an opening on the giant pink box. Finding none, I start with the ribbon and peel it away. The box comes up to my waist. It's *enormous.*

If it didn't weigh a hundred fucking pounds, I would assume it's a novelty gift or something extra special from one of my brothers. Which of my piece of shit brothers would get me a welcome home gift? It's not like either of them are here with a six pack of Guinness right now...

I peel the top of the box open and there's another box inside it, also pink. I open the second box and stumble backwards as I expose the contents. I don't mean to act like a fucking idiot, but I nearly fall over, because this is the last thing I expected to find on my doorstep. I just got back to Boston... How long has that box been out there?

Holy fuck, why isn't she screaming?

I gain control of myself and approach the box again, heart pounding because my second assumption is that the human female in the box might be dead and that's the reason she hasn't made a sound. The sick thought twists my stomach into an unyielding knot.

I slowly approach the box again, ignoring my heavy breathing, focusing instead on taking in as much information as possible about the situation. I move the flaps of the box open and stare at the woman's face.. Suddenly, her eyes snap open before swiveling around and looking me directly in the eye..

Holy fuck, this woman is alive.

"What the fuck is this?" I grunt to myself. Not to myself. I'm not alone. I dry swallow and run my fingers through my hair. She's black. Someone tied up a black woman in a pink ribbon, wrapped her up like a gift and put her in a box on my doorstep. This has to be a sick joke.

I'm almost too scared to reach into the box and touch her, but I have to touch her to get her out of the fucking box. Whoever this woman is, she ran into the wrong fucking people and ended up in the wrong living room.

I have tattoos and vows of loyalty to prove how I feel about people like her. "Don't worry. I'll get you out of there."

I don't know why I'm bothering with comfort. I reach into the box and grab her at the base of her spine before hoisting her out of the box and gently setting her on the ground. My stomach lurches. This is some sick, twisted shit. Whoever did this to her stripped this woman naked, bared every inch of her dark skin, the color of Arabica coffee, and wrapped her in a pink ribbon, contorting her limbs and running the ribbon over her bare breasts, between her thighs and in loops around her body so she's wrapped up like a chocolate present.

My body has an unconscious, primal reaction. I could unwrap her like the present she's been wrapped up to be, but I need answers quickly.

She has a gag in her mouth, a round white ball that keeps her lips spread open and hooks at the back. Her eyes roam around the room in terror as I reach into my pocket for my knife. I've killed people with this knife and now I'm using it to save someone.

Her skin prickles with goosebumps as I touch her. I apologize, but I need to brace myself against her to get her free. I press the serrated edge to the ribbon and make the first cut.

I cut her legs free. She groans as her legs fall in a curled heap. She cries out and tries to jerk them again, but however long she's been in that position was far too long for her to have full control of her legs and hips.

"Don't move," I remind her. I touch her skin again and my stomach lurches. Fuck, her skin is so dark. I look pale as fuck touching her and even putting my hands on her drives guilt through me. She's black. She's the wrong kind of person. I run my tongue piercing over my lower lip as I focus on all the parts of the ribbon I have to cut free.

When I have her limbs mostly free, she rolls onto her side, groaning in pain as her arms and legs curl in an awkward and splayed mess next to her. Even her wrists bend at an unnatural angle. I know she's alive, but the woman still looks dead.

I swallow slowly. What the absolute fuck is this?

"I'll take the gag out, but you can't spit or bite or do anything of that nature. Do you understand?"

She stares at me, but she can't say anything. I approach her mouth slowly and reach around her to find the clasp of her ball gag. I unhook it and take it out of her mouth. She groans again and winces in visible pain as she attempts to close her jaw. She slowly moves her hand to her face and rubs her cheek, groaning.

I crouch next to her, staring at her in awe, knowing that I shouldn't but am completely incapable of taking my eyes off the naked woman in front of me. If her nudity makes her uncomfortable, that hasn't sunk in yet. My cock stiffens inappropriately in my pants and I clasp my hands in front of my dick, refusing to take my eyes off her.

Her breasts are small, but they protrude forward in tiny, dark orbs with nipples that are even darker than her extremely dark skin. Holy fuck, I didn't know nipples came that dark. My eyes widen inappropriately and I pray she doesn't notice my leering. Who sent this woman to me and what exactly did they send her for?

Christ, Aiden. Get a grip. You're staring at her crotch now and it's obvious.

She's waxed completely and my gaze snaps to the bare, dark brown lips. I wonder what this strange woman conceals between those lower lips and what color her flesh is between those thin, toned legs. I clear my throat.

"Who are you?"

"Read the card with the gift," she manages to say, with a raspy voice and an accent I can't place.

"I asked you a question."

"Read the card with the gift," she repeats.

I raise an eyebrow and walk towards the box. There's a large card at the bottom, about 8 x 10 inches, printed on thick paper. I pull it out of the box and read the note, muttering it out loud to myself. *What the fuck is this?*

Dear Mr. Murray,

We hope you enjoy your object. Your task is simple. Use the object wisely. Have unprotected sex with the object and film a 4K quality video.

Compress the video file and send it to the email address below.

The object may be initially unwilling but both of you will face strong motivation to comply. The object understands that documentation of her existence belongs to us and if she fails to comply enthusiastically, we will destroy her identity.

If we do not receive the video within one week of today's date, you will both lose what's most important to you.

Tegan Murray counts on you to succeed. We have possession of the girl and you would be wise to listen to our orders if you or your family want to see her safe.

Do not call Padraig Murray. Do not call anyone else, or you will both suffer.

It takes less than a second to fire a bullet.

You must comply. When you're finished with said object, it is yours to keep.

Sincerely,

Your Benefactors

OA

"What is this sick shit?" I growl, throwing the card back into the box, causing the woman still kneeling on the ground to flinch. My heart thuds.

These people have Tegan and this woman might know where she is and who they are. I won't be a part of this sick fucking game.

Click here to order Mafia Playmate:
https://bit.ly/bostonirishmafia1

PATREON

13 SEASONS OF SERIAL CHAPTERS

NEW preview chapters published WEEKLY on my Patreon.

Read all 6 seasons of *Unfuckable* (Ben & Libby's story)...

UNFUCKABLE

For a small monthly fee, you get exclusive access to over 375 chapters of my first completed bwwm dark and spicy serial romance, as well as the spin-off serial...

DESPICABLE

The second serial, despicable has 300 chapters available for all Patreon subscribers to access instantly and... we officially have a **third completed spin-off bwwm romance series.**

And yes you get access to all of this at the $5/month tier with more benefits at more pricey tiers.

The third serial is about Clover + Thomas. Thomas has a shocking connection to a character in the second serial and Clover is an all-new African American female lead.

POWERLESS

This series has three *very long* "seasons" of chapters, the length of five full-length novels all-together.

You will probably have over three months of binge-reading before catching up to current content, making this one of the most 'bang for your buck' author Patreon subscriptions out there.

Don't take my word for it.
Check the post history:
www.patreon.com/jamilajasper

PATREON HAS MORE THAN THE ONGOING SERIAL…

INSTANT ACCESS

- NEW merchandise tiers with **t-shirts, totes, mugs,** stickers and MORE!
- **FREE paperback** with all new tiers
- **FREE short story audiobooks** and audiobook samples when they're ready

- #FirstDraftLeaks of Prologues and first chapters **weeks** before I hit publish
- Behind the scenes notes
- Polls and story contribution
- Comments & LIVELY community discussion with likeminded interracial romance readers.

LEARN MORE ABOUT SUPPORTING A DIVERSE ROMANCE AUTHOR

www.patreon.com/jamilajasper

THANK YOU KINDLY

Thank you to all my readers, new and old for your support with this new year.

I look forward to making 2023 an INCREDIBLE year for inter-racial romance novels. I want to thank you all for joining along on the journey.

www.patreon.com/jamilajasper

Thank you to my most supportive readers — my Patreon subscribers!:

Queen Ke
Jamie C
KimW
Warrior_pprincess
SavageSam
Roslyn H.
Katrina
LMSYT
Lainey R.
Naomi
GrumpyMillenial
Jay

Asia A.
Angela D.
Danyelle C.
WakeupMakeup Slay
Jocelyn F.
Nikki O.
Cdublu
Carla
Jonathan
Kelly
Jessica
Jasmine
DARSHELL
Dawn
Tiabuena3
Leigh
Yvonne
Ashlee
Crystal
Marshybabyyy
Shout
Quaniquequia
TK
Kayla
Shronda C.
Ma-Eyongerie
Kayla
Chantell
Kheiara
ophelia
Vickie
Cass
Kamil
Kaela

Love

Miryam

Charlene

Summer

Lola

Eryn

DD Davis

Symone

Deborah

Beatrice

Valescha

Khadija

makhalaab

Kaya

Glitter Garden

SavageSam

sybil arroyo

Ncsportsfan79

Jessica G.

Danielle

Yola

Joslin

Alexciz

Stacia

Ayanna

Asia

Hailey

Kaya

Nikki

Naomi O.

Jessica J

Chakiya

Noelle

kourtnee

Martha

Nikki Valentina

xjkpop

Valeria

BlkBae

SweetS

Msteeq

Rhonda

Darrah

Killa

Shavon

Misty

India

Kassandra

Imani

Nala

Chantell

Benvinda

Roger

Lexi B

Zapphire

Vbrooks

Tasha G

Kiera

Valencia

Stacy

YANITZA

Texansgurl76

Emma

Tinette

Jenny

Mariah

Nale

Tanisha

Trenita

Shelle

dulcemaria413

Shanice

Letarsha

Tania

Neeka

Julia

Linda

Lisa

Jiannie

Jillian

Tameka

Asia

Scarlette

Olwyn

R W

Fayefaefee

Brianna

Tiffany

Katie

Diamond

Kera

Tia

Love Reading

Dominique

Sheria

Jennifer

Georgette

Monique

Wendolyn

King Turtle22

Jessica

Nic M.

JustChill

DJC

Atira

TheeLastHokage

Yvonne

Chrissy

Janelle

Rian

LaRonda

LaRonda

Deanna

dlawson382

Jasmine

Haley

Belinda

Sercee

Yvonne

Jadelock

Farah

Tamiya

Quin

J.Payton

Geek Girl

Ashley

Rubi

Pilar

Sandra

Jurnee

Anni

Shannet

Joneesa

GlitzyHydra

Amanda

Barbara

Brianna

Jamica

Lyons

MARY ANN

Marketia

SarahD

LoverofHawaiiHearts

ceblue

Yolanda

MonaGirl Lewis

Dianna

Mary

amna

Nysha

fayola

Ty

Abria

Shyra

Andi-Mariee

Jamila

Naee's World

KEISHA

Jennett

Fredericka

Candece

Chante

Pholuv

Lydia A

Sabrina

JM

Jackie

Mo

Natrilly83

Ashaunte

Tolu

Margaret

Wendolyn

Lori

Dionne

ZLB

Kristina

Nicol

ELBERT

A. Harris

Jesi

Brenda

Desiree

Angela

Frances

LaShan

Only1ToniD

Debbie T.

Tiffanie

April L

shawnte

Kay

Lisema

Yvonne F

Natasha

Colleen

Julia

Amy

Jacklyn

Shyan R

Kiana B

Pearl

Javonda

Sheron

Maxine
Dash
Alicia
margaret
Love2Read
Juliette
Monica
Sandhya
MaryC
Trinity
Brittany
June
Ashleigh
Nene
Nene
Deborah
Nikki M
Dee
TyKira
Kimmey
Laytoya
Shel W
Arlene
Judith
Mary
Shanida
Rachel
Damzel
Ahnjala
Kenya
momo
BJ
Akeshia
Melissa

Tiffany

sherbear

Nini J

Curtresa

REGGIE A.

Ashley

Mia

Tink138110

Phia

Sharon

Charlotte

Assiatu C

Regina

Romanda

Catherine

Gaynor

BF

Perpetua

Tasha G

Henri Ann

sara

skkent

Rosalyn

Danielle

Deborah J

Kirsten

ANA

Taylor R.

Charlene

Louanna

Michelle

Tamika

Lauren

RoHyde

Natasha
Shekynah
Cassie
AnnaBooms
Keitheena
Nick R
Gennifer M
Rayna
Anton
Jaleda
Kimvodkna
JaTonn
Jazmine
Anoushka
Raynischa
Audrey
Valeria
Courtney
Donna
Patrisha
Jenetha
LaKisha J.
Ayana
Taylor
Christy
Monica
FreyaJo
GRACE
Kisha
Christine
Alexandra
Amber
Natasha
Stephanie

LaKisha

kristylove7

Cynthea

DENICE

Latoya

monifacd .

Doneishia

Mariah

Gerry

Yolanda T

Yolanda P

Susan D

Phyllis H

Alisa K

Daveena K

Desiree S

Kimberly B

Robin B

Gary S

Stephanie MG

Georgette A

Kathy

Marty

JanetDaniels

Megan

Shelle

Delores

Janet

Lydia

Phyllis

Freda

Charlott R

Join the Patreon Community.